Readers love ANDREW GREY

A Serving

"…delightful characters to root for ar[...]you aching for more."

—Love Romances & More

Love Means… No Fear

"I would recommend this story to anyone looking for romance. I also found this series to be a lovely introduction to m/m erotica."

—The Romance Studio

Accompanied by a Waltz

"A story about first love, loss, and the rediscovery of love all wrapped up in its pages."

—Fallen Angel Reviews

A Troubled Range

"…Andrew Grey delivers a solid, sweetly romantic, and delightful story that will leave you clamoring for more after the last page is read."

— Love Romances & More

The Best Revenge

"…one of the most romantic and heartwarming stories I've read."

—Man Oh Man Reviews

http://www.dreamspinnerpress.com

Novels by
ANDREW GREY

Accompanied by a Waltz
Dutch Treat
Seven Days
Work Me Out (anthology)

A Taste of Love
A Serving of Love

THE BOTTLED UP STORIES
Bottled Up
Uncorked
The Best Revenge
An Unexpected Vintage
Legal Artistry

THE RANGE STORIES
A Shared Range
A Troubled Range

THE CHILDREN OF BACCHUS STORIES
Children of Bacchus
Thursday's Child
Child of Joy

THE LOVE MEANS… STORIES
Love Means… No Shame
Love Means… Courage
Love Means… No Boundaries
Love Means… Freedom
Love Means … No Fear

All published by
DREAMSPINNER PRESS

LEGAL ARTISTRY
ANDREW GREY

Dreamspinner Press

Published by
Dreamspinner Press
4760 Preston Road
Suite 244-149
Frisco, TX 75034
http://www.dreamspinnerpress.com/

Legal Artistry

Cover Art by Anne Cain   annecain.art@gmail.com
Cover Design by Mara McKennen

ISBN: 978-1-61372-113-1

Printed in the United States of America
First Edition
September 2011

eBook edition available
eBook ISBN: 978-1-61372-114-8

To Dominic, Jennifer, and Vince.
Your input and support were essential.

PROLOGUE

DIETER hurried up the stairs and down the hall as fast as his legs would carry him, not thinking that of course his grandmother could hear every footstep he made. Slowing down, he stopped in front of the linen closet that was tucked beneath the stairs to the attic. Opening the door, Dieter ducked inside. He closed the door behind him and backed into the deep closet, careful not to knock anything over. He could barely see, as a thin line of light shone from under the door. Closing his eyes tight, he waited a few seconds before opening them again. Now he could see the outline of the shelves against the one wall that held all the linens, neatly sorted and stacked. Careful not to knock anything off, he inched farther into the closet, ducking under the tablecloths and quilts that hung from fat, fancy hangers, to where the ceiling started to meet the floor. Settling on the floor with a stifled giggle, Dieter knew he had found the best hiding spot yet, and he waited for Gramma to find him.

Listening for the sound of Gramma's footsteps kept him entertained for a while, but when he didn't hear anything, Dieter began to inch toward the door and bumped into a box that scooted across the dusty floor. Obviously Gramma hadn't been in here in a long time, because she hated dust of any kind anywhere. Once, he'd heard Gramma say she was looking for dust bunnies under his bed. Dieter had immediately gotten onto his knees to peer under the mattress so he could see the bunnies. Gramma had laughed before running a broom covered with a cloth under the bed to clean. Pushing the door open a little, he suddenly heard feet on the stairs, and he closed the door again, moving to the back of the closet.

"Dieter Johan Krumpf, come out of that closet this instant before you get all my linens dusty." She'd used all three of his names—Dieter knew he was in trouble now.

"Gramma," he said, walking forward before pushing the door open and blinking into the light. "I was hiding and you were supposed to find me."

"I was, was I? How about you help me with the dusting, and then we'll have milk and cookies. Katherine just took some molasses cookies out of the oven."

"I can dust in there," Dieter said, pointing toward the closet. "It's really bad, see?" Dieter turned around and heard his grandma hiss before she started to dust him.

"You're filthy," she said as she cleaned off his pants legs before swatting his butt lightly with the cloth. "There, that's better. Now, go get the dust mop from downstairs, and you can use it to clean the floor."

Dieter looked up at her stern face and didn't move until she broke into a smile. "What is it? Scoot," she said.

"There's a box way in the back," Dieter told her before hurrying back into the closet, ducking under the hanging things. Finding the box, he pushed it like a train across the floor. He would have made train-engine noises, but Gramma liked it quiet, and Dieter didn't want her to be mad. "See?" Dieter said happily as he pushed the box near her feet. He expected her to say something, but she slowly bent down and opened the box before gasping and putting her hand over her mouth.

"I haven't seen these in twenty years," Dieter's grandma said softly, and he straightened up, smiling proudly that he'd found what he imagined was buried treasure.

"What is it?" Dieter asked, peering into the box.

"They're photo albums and pictures from when I was a girl." Dieter watched as his grandma carefully pulled out two thick books with black pages, setting each one on the floor next to the box.

"Can we look at the pich-ers?" Dieter asked.

"Yes, but only after we get our work done," she answered, placing the albums back in the box. Dieter lifted the box off the floor, following his grandma along the hallway and down the stairs. Setting the box on the coffee table in the living room, per her instructions, Dieter hurried to the broom closet to get the dust mop and finish his chores.

Back upstairs, he used the mop to clean the floors of all the closets, and he even pushed it under the bed the way Gramma did, before taking it back downstairs, displaying all the dust for inspection before Gramma took the mop outside to shake it. Dieter sat down at Gramma's round kitchen table. "Auntie Kate, can I have cookies?"

"Of course you can, sweetheart," she answered, handing him a small plate with three small, brown disks covered with white icing. He immediately took a bite and then another.

"Auntie Kate, are you my real aunt?" Dieter asked as she set a glass of milk in front of him.

"Don't talk with your mouth full," she replied, and Dieter took a gulp of milk before swallowing everything.

"No, honey," Gramma answered from behind him. "Katherine isn't related to you by blood, but she loves you like you were her own. We both do."

Dieter sputtered as he was kissed on the cheek by Auntie Kate, but he didn't wipe it off like he normally would. "Then how come she lives here?"

"That's a story I'll tell you when you're old enough to understand." That was Gramma's standard answer whenever she didn't want to explain something. "But Auntie Kate was the housekeeper and saw your Gramps when he was born and your mama when she was born." Gramma had told Dieter once that Auntie Kate was eighty-two, which was really old, even older than Gramma.

"And she saw me when I was borned?"

"I sure did, sweetheart," Auntie Kate said, giving him a hug, rocking him back and forth as she did. "I sure did." Dieter put his arms around her, hugging Aunt Kate back before returning his attention to what was really important—the cookies.

Once the plate was empty and the dishes whisked away, Dieter and Gramma sat on the sofa in the living room with one of the photo albums on their laps. Auntie Kate sat in a nearby chair knitting a pair of mittens that Dieter knew were probably for him for Christmas. But he'd learned already not to ask if things were for him. Gramma said it was selfish. Dieter opened the album, looking at the photographs. "Where's the colors?"

"Pictures were only in black and white then," Gramma said, and Dieter looked at the first picture.

"Who's that?" He reached to touch the picture. But Gramma gently stopped his hand.

"That's my father, your great-grandfather." Gramma pointed to the picture next to it. "And that's your great-grandmother." She turned the page, and Dieter saw pictures of them sitting together on a small sofa in front of a painting. "Is that her?" Dieter pointed to the painting hanging just behind them.

"Yes, it is," Gramma said softly, and Dieter looked at her, wondering what was wrong. He'd only seen her cry once, and that was at his mama and daddy's funeral. Before he could ask any more questions, she turned the page, and Dieter saw more pictures of people. Gramma explained who everyone was, and Dieter listened, committing what Gramma said to memory as best he could. "What happened to them?" he asked, turning back to the first page of the album.

"I'll tell you when you're older," Gramma told him, and he looked into her eyes, about two seconds from asking again, but stopped himself and turned back to the photo album. She turned to the page where they'd left off and began telling stories about what it was like growing up, and Dieter wondered what it would be like to live in these pictures. After a while, Dieter lost interest in the pictures and slid off the sofa.

"Can I go outside?" he asked, looking out the living room windows.

"Yes, you may," Gramma answered, "but stay where we can see you, and don't go near the street."

"I won't," Dieter promised as he pulled open the front hall closet door, pulling his coat off the hook before shrugging it on.

"Come here, sweetheart," Auntie Kate said, and he walked to her. She made sure he was all zipped up before giving him a hug. "Have fun."

Dieter ran through the house and out the back door. Rushing into the garage, he carefully worked his bike out from next to Gramma's car. He had to be careful of the training wheels, but as soon as it was free, he hopped on and rode down the short driveway and onto the sidewalk in front of Gramma's East Side Milwaukee home. Auntie Kate had given him the bike for Christmas. The tag had said it was from Santa, but Dieter knew better. He'd heard Gramma and Auntie Kate fighting over it when they thought he'd gone to bed.

"It's too dangerous for him to have a bike in this neighborhood. What if he gets hurt?" his grandmother had said, as Dieter snuck down the stairs on his butt so he wouldn't make noise.

"What are you gonna do, Gertrude? Wrap him in cotton and wool? He's a little boy, and he needs to act like it," Auntie Kate had said. "So he's getting a bike for Christmas if I have to walk to the store to get it." A door had shut hard, and Dieter had slid back up the stairs, and a month later, he found a bike under the Christmas tree. Regardless if the card said "Santa" on it, he knew his Auntie Kate had given him his most prized possession, and he loved her for it.

Dieter rode on the grass to turn around before pedaling as fast as he could back toward Gramma's. "Hey, baby!" He heard from behind him, and Dieter pedaled faster, but he was stopped anyway. "Nice bike, little baby."

"Leave me alone, Billy," Dieter said indignantly as he tried once again to pedal away.

"I want to ride your bike!" Billy said, and he began to push Dieter toward the grass.

"No. Leave me alone." Then he was falling and Dieter found himself on the grass, and Billy was on his bike riding away. Dieter jumped up and began to chase him, but he was too slow, and his bike got farther away.

"That's enough, Billy!" Dieter heard someone call from up ahead, and Billy stopped. Dieter saw someone approach his bike and saw Billy jump off his bike and run away. As Dieter got closer, he saw Tyler standing next to his bike, smiling at him. "Are you okay?" Tyler asked, and Dieter nodded, smiling as he touched his bike. Tyler turned it around for him and helped Dieter get back on. "You have fun, okay?"

Dieter nodded again. "Thank you, Tyler."

"You're welcome," Tyler told him, and Dieter waved before riding away, back toward Gramma's. Tyler was one of the big kids in the neighborhood. Dieter didn't know how old he was, but Tyler stayed sometimes with Mrs. O'Connor, a friend of his grandmother's, and Tyler was always nice to him. Dieter continued riding up and down the sidewalk, waving to Tyler whenever he passed, and Tyler waved back as he cut stuff away from the bushes in front of Mrs. O'Connor's house, making them round instead of pointy.

Once he got tired, Dieter rode his bike back down the driveway to the garage, carefully putting his bike away, taking care not to scratch Gramma's car. After closing the garage door, he hurried inside and took off his coat. "Don't forget to hang that up," Auntie Kate reminded him.

"I will," Dieter said, walking to the closet and hanging his coat on the hook that was at his level. Closing the door, he walked into the living room. Gramma still sat on the sofa with the photo album on her lap. Dieter scooted up next to her, looking where she was at the picture of her mama and papa. "Do you miss them?" His grandmother nodded. "Like I miss my mama and papa?" Dieter said as he leaned against her side, closing his eyes to try to hold back the tears that came sometimes.

Gramma set the album on the coffee table, and Dieter found himself gathered into her arms and held tight. "I know you miss them," she soothed him. "I miss them too."

Dieter lifted his head off her shoulder, looking at the book. "Was your mama pretty?"

"Yes, she was. Very pretty," Gramma told him.

"So are you, Gramma," Dieter said, hugging her again. "Where is the painting now?"

"It's gone. It's been gone for a long time."

Just like his mama and papa.

*C*HAPTER *1*

DIETER parked his gram's old green Toyota in the only parking space he could find. Getting out of the car and dropping a few quarters in the meter, Dieter hurried down the sidewalk. Thankfully, the meters were free after six, so he only had to pay for a little more than an hour. Approaching the wine store, Dieter pushed open the front door, entering near pandemonium. There were customers everywhere. Dieter saw Sean helping customers, and he hurried to the office, dropping his jacket on the futon before returning to the sales floor. "Young man," an older lady said as she approached him. "I need a case of this," she said, pointing to the wine they'd been featuring, "but everyone's so busy."

"No problem. Let me check in the back to make sure we have an unopened case, and I'll be right back." Dieter walked to the stock area, locating the last full case of the Cabernet she'd requested. Placing it on a cart, he wheeled it up to the register area, setting it out of the way before returning to the customer. "I have your case by the register for you," Dieter told her, and she began handing him loose bottles, which he carried to a table behind the register. Dieter continued to help her until she was ready to check out. He thanked her before moving on to help another customer find a special Chardonnay that wasn't too oaky.

After a good hour or so, the flow of customers diminished, and Dieter was able to catch his breath. "You didn't have to come in," Sean said from behind him. "I understand that you've got a lot to do."

The work and being busy had pushed his grief aside for a while, but now it threatened to come forward again. "I needed to get out of the house and do things that are normal."

Sean nodded slowly. "I'm sorry about your grandmother. She was a special lady," Sean told him seriously.

"I wanted to thank you and Sam for coming to the funeral. It meant a lot. She outlived most of her friends, but it was still sad to see so few people there." His grandmother's funeral had no more than a few dozen attendees. It had been small and solemn, especially for Dieter. Leaning quietly against the counter, Dieter felt the sadness and loneliness of the last week begin to catch up with him.

"Have you decided what you're going to do?"

Dieter shivered slightly. "About some things. Gram left me everything, including the house. I haven't decided if I'm going to sell it or not yet, but the place needs to be cleaned out, and there are things I'm not sure what to do with."

"You know you don't need to make these decisions now," Sean cautioned, and Dieter nodded his head blankly.

"I know, but the entire place reminds me of her, and it needs so much work. I'd like to fix it up, but I don't have the money to do some of the repairs that are needed." Dieter had started making a list, and he'd been a bit overwhelmed by what he'd come up with. "Some of them I can do, but some are going to be really expensive. The attic is full of stuff, and some of it looks really old, but I'm not sure what to do with it."

"What about school? You still have a year left, right?"

"Yeah. I have the money for tuition," Dieter told Sean. "Gram put all the money my parents left when they died in a fund for me. All those years, she never used a cent of it for herself." Dieter reached across the counter and grabbed a napkin, using it to wipe his eyes. "I'm sorry," he added, embarrassed at his display.

"Like I said, your grandmother was quite a lady. You know, when she was in the store once, she told me that her greatest wish was to see you graduate from college. I thought she'd make it, too. She was a force to be reckoned with right up until the end."

Dieter sniffed and wiped his eyes again before stuffing the napkin in his pocket. "She told me that too. Before she died, she made me promise I would finish regardless of what happened to her." She'd had a stroke, and at the end she could barely talk, but she'd made her wishes abundantly clear to Dieter. "At least she went quickly and didn't linger. She always said that was what she wanted." The door to the store opened, and Dieter excused himself before going to greet the customer. He needed something to think about other than Gram's death.

Even keeping himself plenty busy for most of the evening, Dieter still found his mind turning to his loss. Gram had been the only family he'd had left, and now she was gone. Auntie Kate had passed away a few years ago, and Dieter still felt her loss as well. Those two women had raised and cared for him for as long as he could remember. He had vague memories of his mother and father, but as far as Dieter was concerned, Gram and Auntie Kate were his parents.

"Dieter." He jumped when he felt a hand on his shoulder. "You've been filling that same location for ten minutes," Sean told him without heat. "It's slowed down now. Why don't you finish up, and we can talk if you'd like."

Dieter emptied the last bottles from the case into the display before breaking down the box and carrying it to the recycling area. "Giuli's okay out front for a while," Sean said as Dieter walked back by the office. "Come in and sit down." Dieter sat on the futon, and Sean took the desk chair. "I know things can be a bit overwhelming right now, and if I can help, I will. You said there were things in the attic."

"Tons. The thing is that some of it's really old, and I don't know what to do with any of it."

"Well, that's easy. Give Tyler a call and he'll take a look. If there are things you want to sell, he'll give you a fair price," Sean advised, and Dieter wondered why he hadn't thought of that before. "Doesn't he live just down the street from you?"

"Yeah. He lives in the house that used to be his grandmother's. I should have thought of that. I've known him since I was a kid."

"You would have. You're tired and overwhelmed. I want you to go home and get a good night's sleep," Sean admonished lightly. "You'll think better when you're not so wiped out."

Dieter agreed but didn't get up yet. "I was wondering if Bobby and Kenny were coming home from school this summer."

"Kenny's staying at school to take some summer classes, and Bobby's spending part of the summer on an artist's retreat. Regardless, you have a job here if you want it, and I'm planning a number of special events this summer, so we'll be busy."

"Thanks, Sean."

"You're welcome. Now go on home and get some rest," Sean told him with a concerned smile, and Dieter got up, taking his jacket. He hadn't slept well since before Gram's stroke, and he was definitely feeling it.

"I'll see you tomorrow," Dieter said before leaving the office. After hugging Katie, Sean's longtime salesperson and second in command, good-bye, Dieter walked to his car and drove home. He called it home, but to him, the house would always be Gram's. Parking his car, Dieter got out and closed the door, peering up at the dark house he'd lived in for as long as he could remember.

"Dieter!" He looked around and saw Tyler coming down the sidewalk. "I wanted to see how you were doing," Tyler told him as he approached.

"Okay, I guess," he responded with a sigh. "I was going to call you tomorrow. There's a bunch of stuff in the attic, and I don't know what to do with it. Sean said you might be able to look it over and give me an idea what some of it is."

"Do you want to sell, or are you looking for an appraisal?" Tyler asked.

"I want to fix up the house," he said, looking at the front, where some of the paint had worn off.

"I understand," Tyler told him. "I'm booked with appointments for the next two weeks, but I can look in my book in the morning and let you know when I can come by."

"Oh," Dieter said. He knew he should be patient, but if he got some of the money together, he might be able to get some of the projects done during the summer while he wasn't in class.

Tyler must have read the disappointment on his face. "Come on, then. Mark is still working, so I have an hour. Let's go take a look."

"Are you sure?"

"I've known you since you came to live with your grandma. I'll help you any way I can." Dieter's fatigue seemed to slip away as he led Tyler up the walk. "You know, I can still remember you riding your bike with the training wheels up and down the sidewalk."

"Thanks, I think," Dieter replied as he unlocked the door, and he heard Tyler laugh.

"Come on, let's go look for treasure," Tyler told him as he turned on the lights. Dieter led the way up the stairs and then opened the attic door. Gram had always kept the door locked, and it had been the devil for Dieter to find the key.

Dust motes floated in the air as Dieter turned on the light, leading Tyler up the steep, narrow stairway. At the top of the stairs, he got out of the way and let Tyler look. "Jesus, you weren't kidding. It looks like there's eight lifetimes of stuff up here," Tyler told him as he began moving through a narrow winding aisle created by breaks between all the stuff. "Where did this come from? Your grandmother never seemed like the type to collect things like this," Tyler inquired as Dieter watched him peer around a trunk.

"Gram said Gramps kept dragging things home. She made him put anything she didn't like up here. Until she died, I doubt anyone had been up here in years." Dieter walked to where Tyler was kneeling next to a trunk. "Did you find something?"

"I think so, yes," Tyler answered without looking up.

"That's just an old trunk," Dieter said, already moving away.

"No, it's not," Tyler explained as he pulled the trunk into the aisle. "Would you give me a hand?" Dieter helped him lift it. "It seems really heavy. Do you think we can get this down the stairs? I'd like to take a better look at it, and I can barely breathe up here."

Dieter took one side and Tyler took the other. Carefully, they carried the heavy wooden box down the narrow stairs, setting it on the landing. Dieter turned off the light and shut the attic door. "Do you really think this is anything?"

Tyler nodded, smiling broadly. "You see the interlaced iron work on the top? That's all handmade, and look at the lock." Tyler pointed to the front of the trunk and lifted the iron cover.

"There's no hole," Dieter said, confused.

"That's because the lock isn't on the front. That's a trick." Tyler opened a small hidden iron flap on the top. "It's lucky you have the key," Tyler commented as he untied the thong that held the key on and inserted it into the hole. "There's nothing delicate about opening this," Tyler said as he strained to turn the key. At first, Dieter didn't think it would work, but the key turned almost all the way around, and then Tyler lifted the lid on the box.

"It's empty," Dieter commented, really disappointed. He'd hoped there would be something interesting inside.

"Yes, but that doesn't really matter," Tyler explained. "It's the trunk that's important. See the lock?" he said as he lifted the lid. "That is the lock, the whole underside of the lid. It's all hand done and between four and five hundred years old."

Dieter's eyes bugged out of his head. "It's how old?"

"This is a real treasure chest. It's continental, probably Spanish, I'd say, based on the decoration, and it could very well have been used to haul gold from the Americas back to Spain. This is an amazing find and probably worth six to eight thousand dollars. And I saw other things up there that could be interesting as well."

Dieter felt his mouth hang open. At first he thought he'd heard Tyler wrong, but he saw Tyler's smile. "I'm not kidding. I have to tell you that if you want me to buy the piece, I can't give you that because that's what I could sell it for, but if you want to sell it, let me know. But don't make a decision right away. Think it over."

Dieter could barely speak and simply nodded as Tyler helped him move the chest into one of the bedrooms. He led Tyler down the stairs and into the living room, feeling less worried than he had since Gram got sick. "Thank you, Tyler."

"You're welcome," Tyler answered, looking at one of Gram's photo albums on the table.

"Those were Gram's. I was looking at them last night," Dieter explained, picking up the one album to close the cover.

"Do you mind if I look at that?" Tyler asked, and Dieter handed him the album, moving to peer over Tyler's shoulder.

"That's Gram's parents," Dieter said, pointing, "and that's Gram. That was taken in their house before the war." Tyler looked at him and then back at the photograph. "The painting behind them on the wall is Gram's mother."

Tyler stared at the photograph for a while longer before closing the album. "I'd like to ask a favor. I'd like Mark to see this. I promise I'll get it back to you tomorrow. Okay?"

"Is something wrong?"

"No. There are just some pictures that I know Mark would love to see. I'll bring it back."

"Okay, and I'll think about the chest and let you know when I see you," Dieter said as he walked Tyler to the door. After saying good night one more time, he closed and locked the door before walking back into the living room. Dieter sat down in one of the large chairs, the quiet of the house becoming almost oppressive. Over the past week, there were times when he'd wanted nothing more than to sell the house and move someplace that wasn't so full of memories. Everywhere he looked he saw Gram. Her chair was right across the room from where he sat. He hadn't had the heart to sit in it. Gram had taken care of him, and in a way she still was. He knew he couldn't bear to sell the house, but he also knew he had to make it his or he'd never be able to move on. Reaching to the coffee table, Dieter picked up the photo album that Tyler hadn't borrowed and began to thumb through it. He smiled at the pictures of Gram and Gramps. He didn't really remember him, but he could see how happy he'd made Gram. There were even a few pictures of Auntie Kate. The one he liked best was a picture of her holding his mother. Even then she looked old.

Placing the album back on the coffee table, Dieter decided it was time for bed. He'd try to rest. The wine store didn't open till noon, and he could sleep in before going to work. Dieter turned out the lights before walking up the stairs and down the hall to his bedroom, the one that had been his since he'd come to live with Gram. He passed Auntie Kate's room, still made up as though she lived there. He passed Gram's, too, its door closed because he couldn't think about going in there without her, at least not yet.

Dieter went into his room, closing the door behind him. This was the one place in the house where he didn't feel like Gram was going to walk into the room at any minute. Turning on the light, Dieter stripped off his clothes and put on his bathrobe, the one Gram had gotten him last Christmas, before padding to the bathroom to clean up.

Showered and clean, Dieter went back to his room and climbed under the covers, hoping that sleep would come. But all he did was lie there, staring at the ceiling. Gram was gone, Auntie Kate was gone, and so were his parents. Dieter was the last of his family, and he felt very much alone. Rolling onto his side, he closed his eyes and tried to fall asleep.

DIETER woke the way he always did on a Sunday morning, listening for Gram's footsteps, but of course he heard nothing. Sighing softly, he closed his eyes once again and fell back to sleep, waking again with the sun shining through the window. Sean had been right— Dieter felt better after a good sleep. Pushing back the covers, he got dressed and checked the clock before cleaning up and preparing to go to work.

By the time he made it downstairs, it was too late for breakfast, not that he really wanted any. There were certain things he'd always miss, and Gram's breakfast was one of them. Retrieving his jacket from where he'd thrown it over the back of one of the chairs, Dieter left the house, locking the door before strolling down the walk to his car. He felt as though a cloud had parted and everything was going to be okay. Getting into the car, Dieter started the engine and eased out of his parking space and onto the quiet street.

Dieter found a parking spot not far from Sommelier Wines. The store had a small parking lot, but Dieter tried to leave those spaces for customers, especially on weekends when the store was busiest. Walking to the front door, Dieter saw Sean inside working, and he rapped lightly on the door.

"You're looking better," Sean told him as he held the door open. "You must have gotten some sleep."

"I did, and I talked to Tyler about the stuff in Gram's attic. He came over last night and looked around. You won't believe this, but he says that there're some great things up there, and he already found a real treasure chest. It's from the sixteen hundreds or something. You should come see it. The thing's really cool."

"Have you decided what you're going to do with it?"

"Yeah, Gram said the things in the attic were mostly stuff Gramps dragged home, so I'm going to sell what I can so I can fix up the house." Dieter fidgeted a little. "And I think I need to make it look less like Gram's."

"Good," Sean told him as he relocked the door. "If you want to stay in the house, you need to make it your own. Otherwise it's just a memorial to your grandmother, and you'll never be able to move on. But like I said last night, take your time," Sean cautioned. Dieter appreciated Sean's concern. Walking through the store, Dieter put his jacket in the office before getting right to work.

"Dieter, I'm opening the doors," Sean told him, and Dieter finished up his task, taking the empty boxes to the back and making sure there were no obstacles on the sales floor. A few customers trickled in and began to wander through the store. Sean greeted them and offered a tasting while Dieter continued filling shelves. As the store got busier, Dieter stopped filling and went into customer-service mode, helping people with their purchases.

Later in the afternoon, Dieter saw Sean's partner, Sam, walk into the store, looking handsome in his police uniform. At one time, Dieter had had a bit of an infatuation with Sam, but he'd gotten over it. "Hey, Dieter, how are you holding up?" Sam asked after he'd greeted Sean with a quick kiss.

"I'm okay," he answered. It had become his stock answer, but he was starting to feel as though he truly would be. "It's getting easier."

"You know if you need anything or just want to talk, either Sean or I will listen and do whatever we can." Sam looked so serious but caring at the same time.

"Thank you."

Sam squeezed his shoulder before returning to Sean. Dieter saw them talking quietly for a few minutes, and then Sam said good-bye and waved before leaving the store.

During a lull in the afternoon, Sean ordered sandwiches, and they took turns eating before returning to work and helping customers for the rest of the day.

Near closing time, Dieter saw Tyler and his partner, Mark, enter the store, with Mark carrying Gram's photo album like it was a precious relic. Sean greeted them, and they talked for a few minutes before all three of them walked to where Dieter was just finishing with a customer. "Tyler and I have something we'd like to talk to you about," Mark said very seriously. "Would you mind coming to the studio after work? It's important."

Dieter looked to Sean, who looked confused, and then to Tyler, who looked as serious as Mark did. "Okay," Dieter answered slowly, wondering what was wrong. He felt just like he had the day Gram found a certain magazine under his mattress.

"It's not bad," Tyler clarified, "but it is important."

"I'll walk down after the store closes, if that's okay," Dieter answered, becoming curious as to what they wanted to talk about and what Gram's photo album had to do with it. Mark and Tyler seemed pleased, and smiled. Mark continued holding the album, and after they purchased a bottle of wine, Mark and Tyler left, with Mark still carrying Gram's album. It looked sort of like he didn't want to let it go.

For that last half hour, Dieter kept wondering what Mark and Tyler could want with him, and by the time the store closed, Dieter was jumpy, his nerves getting the best of him. "It's okay," Sean told him as he closed the door. "I'll come with you if you want."

"Thanks, Sean, but I'll be fine. I'm just wondering what they could want."

"They didn't tell me," Sean said as he emptied the money from the register, carrying it to the back. "Go on and find out. Sam is taking me to dinner, and he'll be here soon. He and I can drop the deposit on our way." Sean had a rule about two people going to the bank with deposits.

"If you're sure."

"Go on, you look about ready to explode."

"Thanks, Sean," Dieter said as he grabbed his jacket. He heard Sean chuckle from behind him as they walked to the front door and Sean let him out, locking the door once he was outside. Dieter hurried down the sidewalk, walking the short distance to where Tyler had his antique store.

Tyler seemed to be watching for him and opened the door as he approached. Dieter had walked by the store a number of times before, but he'd never been inside. Tyler closed the door behind him. A small dog, curled up in a doggie bed, lifted its head and barked softly. "Jolie, be good," Tyler scolded, and the miniature dachshund got up and padded toward Dieter to investigate him. He let her sniff his hand and gave her a few gentle strokes. Satisfied, she turned and went back to curl up in her bed again.

Tyler led the way through displays of bedrooms and living rooms, the store largely dark, but a number of things still caught Dieter's eye as they made their way toward the back of the store. "Where are we going?"

"Mark has a studio in the back of the store, and he wants to talk to you there," Tyler answered as he led them through a door in the back room. Tyler's partner, Mark, was quite a famous artist. Dieter had seen a few of his pieces when he was at Sean's. Mark had done an amazing portrait of Sean's son, Bobby, that hung in Sean's living room. Tyler opened a large door, and the scent of paint obliterated everything else. Mark sat on a stool behind an easel, brush in hand, his attention so riveted on what he was doing that he didn't even look up when the door opened.

Dieter looked at Tyler, about to ask what was going on, but he stopped when he saw the warm, soft look on Tyler's face. Dieter closed his mouth and stood silently, watching Mark work for a few minutes. "Oh, you're here," Mark said once he lifted his eyes from the canvas. "I get busy and don't hear anything," he explained as he set aside his palette. "Let me clean up a minute, and I'll be right back." Mark picked up his supplies, hurrying out of the studio, and Dieter stepped further into the large area. Paintings and canvases leaned against the far wall. One caught Dieter's eye, and he stepped closer to take a look. Mark rejoined them a few minutes later, and Dieter stepped away from the painting, curiously looking toward Mark.

"Dieter," Mark started to say as he pulled a stool up to a rudimentary table that lined the side wall, "I know we were a bit mysterious when we talked earlier, but I thought this was something we should talk about privately." Tyler pulled up a chair as well, and Mark set Dieter's grandmother's photo album in front of him. "I have a few questions for you that I hope will confirm my suspicions."

"What is this about?" Dieter asked, placing his hand on the album. "And what does this have to do with Gram's pictures?"

"I'll explain everything I suspect, I promise," Mark told him, and Dieter nodded, his eyes focused on Mark.

"Did your grandmother ever tell you the names of her parents?" Mark asked him, and Dieter could tell he was quite excited.

Dieter opened the cover of the photo album, turning to the page that had the picture he wanted. "Gram said their last name was Meinauer. This is Gram's dad, Joseph, and this is her mother, Anna. That's Gram sitting between them."

Mark's excitement seemed to ramp up, and Dieter saw him glance toward Tyler. "Did she ever tell you what happened to them?"

"Gram said her mother died after she'd been sick for a while. After that she said her father wasn't the same. She told me that when she was about twelve, her dad came to her after she had already gone to bed and told her to be very quiet. She said he led her through the house and out the servants' door. They got into a car and made their way through the streets. She told me her father took her out of Austria just ahead of the Germans. Gram told me stories of how they survived in Switzerland during most of the war. She said they were lucky because her father managed to take some of his wealth with him, at least enough that they were able to live during the war. Her father died still in Switzerland after the war, and she came to the US where she met Gramps."

Mark appeared to listen intently. "Do you know who this is in this painting?" Mark pointed to the one hanging on the wall above them in the picture.

"Yes. That's Gram's mother. Gram said she was a real socialite and spent a lot of time with artists and writers. Gram said her mother had commissioned that painting for her father. But it was lost in the war," Dieter explained, remembering how Gram had said that everything from her family was gone except these pictures. "She told me that these photos were in the bags her father packed when they left Vienna. Why?"

Mark seemed to get more excited and pulled out a heavy book from the stack on the table. "Does this look familiar?" Mark turned to a page with a piece of paper in it, letting the book fall open.

"That's...," Dieter stammered as he looked at the full color plate and then back at the photograph in Gram's album. "That's her. That's

Gram's mother." Dieter could hardly believe it. "But Gram said it was gone."

"Maybe gone to her, but the painting survived," Mark explained. "This painting is entitled *Portrait of Anna* and is by a very famous Austrian artist named August Pirktl. I looked through your photo album, and I was able to identify four other paintings by Pirktl in the backgrounds. All of these paintings are in the Belvedere Museum in Vienna." Mark closed the book. "Dieter, you need to know that *Portrait of Anna* is also known as *The Lady in Blue* and is world famous. This painting," he said, pointing to the photograph in Gram's album, "is one of the most important paintings of the early twentieth century and is considered an Austrian national treasure. I had a poster of the painting on my dorm room wall when I was at art school."

"Oh." Dieter didn't know what else to say.

"I did some more research online, and there are a number of sources that say that the painting was confiscated during the war and that it was given by the Nazis to the Belvedere. These other four paintings I was able to identify by Pirktl are also hanging in the Belvedere."

"What are you saying?" Dieter asked, as Mark looked like he was about to bounce off the chair.

"I'm saying that these paintings may not belong to the Belvedere. If the Nazis confiscated them and gave them to the museum, then the museum may not own them."

"Then who does?" Dieter asked.

"You."

CHAPTER 2

GERALD increased his pace, walking faster as he tried not to look like he was hurrying toward the conference room. Nothing betrayed inefficiency and a lack of decorum worse than looking like you were rushing to get somewhere—at least from the viewpoint of Harold Prince, the senior partner in the law firm where Gerald hoped to someday be offered a full partnership. Approaching the conference room, Gerald checked his watch once again and slowed his pace; he had two minutes. Pulling open the glass conference-room door, he walked in and quietly took his seat at the far end of the table where all the junior attorneys sat, proximity to Harold during the daily case briefing being a coveted show of status within the office.

"Good morning," Harold called to the assembled group as soon as he walked into the room, starting the meeting even before he'd taken his seat. "Where do we stand?" As though it were scripted, everyone gave the latest update on their cases in fifty words or less, and unless there were questions, the spotlight moved from attorney to attorney, the more senior attorneys with the most interesting cases going first. Gerald listened to each of the updates, even making a few notes when he had a question he wanted to ask later. As the meeting progressed, the cases got more and more mundane until it was time for the junior associates to give their updates. Even though their cases were often downright boring and every attorney at the table had dealt with dozens of similar cases, the partners gave them their attention and asked questions to help guide and teach. It was one of the things that Gerald liked about the office. Yes, there was a strict hierarchy, but they were still a team, and they acted as such. "Gerald, how is the

Anderson case progressing?" Harold asked. He knew by heart every case that everyone had active.

"Very well. Settlement negotiations should finish today, and it looks as though we're very close."

"Ballpark?" Harold prompted, cocking an eyebrow slightly.

"Half to three-quarters of a million," Gerald answered succinctly, and he saw Harold's lips twist into a smile before he moved on to Mildred, next to him. She was a high-strung woman and the most competitive person Gerald had ever met, himself included. She gave her update, as did the last junior associate, and Gerald smiled, because among the junior associates he was top dog, at least for the day. His case would bring in a sizable fee to the firm, and that made him look good.

"Is there more?" Harold asked looking around the room. "No? Good. I have a case," he said, looking down the table toward the junior associates, and Gerald could feel himself and the others straighten as a bit of excited energy shot through their end of the table. "It involves a certain amount of pro bono work, but it might be interesting," Harold added, and Gerald could almost feel the other two attorneys slump slightly back into their chairs.

"I'll take it," Gerald said, and he saw the more senior attorneys and the partners nodding their heads.

"Excellent. Thank you, Gerald. Come to my office right after the meeting, and I'll explain," Harold told him before standing up and walking toward the door. The meeting was over, and it was time to get to work. Gerald stood up and followed everyone out of the conference room, ignoring the looks from his fellow junior associates. Walking down the hall toward the front, he passed associates' and then the partners' offices before approaching Harold's office. Betty, Harold's assistant, motioned for him to go right in, so he knocked lightly on the door frame before stepping into the plush office that was definitely meant to impress.

"Gerald, please close the door and sit down," Harold told him as he stepped away from the window and walked around the rich mahogany desk to take the seat next to the one Gerald had chosen.

Harold was one of those people who could be tough as nails, but always managed to do things in a way that was constructive. In other words, Harold was old school—demanding, but always a gentleman with everyone. Truth be told, when Gerald had first come to the firm, he had found himself a little enamored of him. Harold was tall and fit, especially for a man in his midfifties, and his graying hair made him look incredibly distinguished, as did his expensively tailored suits, although Gerald figured Harold was equally at home in an old pair of jeans. Not that he'd ever actually seen him outside of the office or an office function. Harold was very private, almost reclusive, when it came to his personal life. At least that was what Gerald had heard around the office.

"The case I spoke about earlier is a bit unusual. The client is a young man—Dieter must be twenty-four or so now. His father and I went to school together, and when he died, I helped Dieter's grandmother with some legal issues regarding the boy's custody. I'm only telling you this so you'll know that I consider your help a personal favor. When Dieter called yesterday, I promised him we would see what he had and do some basic research to see if he had a case. So I'm authorizing up to fifteen pro bono hours for this that the firm will pick up, not you. I have no files or background information. Dieter told me what he's curious about, and his story is intriguing enough that I thought we should look into it."

Gerald was about to ask about the story and had even opened his mouth to speak when he realized Harold was going to continue.

"I'm not going to tell you. I think you should hear this from Dieter himself. He's coming in to the office right after work. He'll be here at five today. I hope that's all right." Gerald nodded his assent. Not that Gerald was about to say anything different. His heart was already pounding in his chest. It looked like he might be getting an interesting case as well as doing a favor for Harold.

"Of course," Gerald answered, and when Harold got up from the chair, Gerald knew that was his dismissal. "Thank you, Harold," Gerald said before leaving the senior partner's plush office and heading to his own, which was down the hall in the back. By most standards, his office was quite nice. The furniture was a rich-looking cherry wood, and his chair new and comfortable. It just paled in comparison to the other offices, but Gerald knew he'd get there someday. Greeting Annette, his admin, and picking up his messages as he passed her desk, he entered his office and got to work. From the stack of messages she'd given him, he was going to have a busy day.

Gerald's morning passed swiftly as he returned phone calls and got ready for his eleven o'clock settlement conference, which went better than he'd hoped. His client and the insurance company had agreed to a figure that was even higher than Gerald had expected, and just after lunch, the insurance company had sent over the papers, and they'd been signed, sealed, and a huge check delivered to his client.

"I heard you settled the Anderson case," Mildred said as she slithered into his office, looking for gossip.

"Yes," Gerald answered, feeling proud of himself.

"I heard Brian had his doubts," she commented, trying to get under Gerald's skin.

"No, I didn't," Brian, Gerald's managing partner, said from outside Gerald's door before joining them, and Gerald saw Brian flash Mildred a look. "I just came in to tell you that you were amazing. I thought you should have stuck with three-quarters, but you saw something that I didn't and pushed for the full million, and they caved."

"They were scared," Gerald explained. "The lead negotiator kept looking at our client, and there was this tiny twitch in his eye that wasn't there before. Something had changed for them, and I'm not sure what it was, but it cost them a quarter million," Gerald explained happily, and he saw Mildred leave his office without another word.

"Well, that was great work, and you made a tidy chunk of change for the firm and really helped the client. Well done!" Brian flashed one of his winning smiles before leaving the office, and Gerald basked in the glow of success for a few minutes until he glanced at the clock and realized he needed to get ready for his next appointment.

By five, Gerald's brain felt like mush, but he had the client he'd agreed to take for Harold, so he rebuttoned the collar he'd loosened an hour ago and walked to the lobby, where he saw a man a few years younger than he was fidgeting in one of the chairs with what looked like a photo album and some papers on his lap. "Are you Dieter?" Gerald asked as he pushed open the door.

The man held his papers and stood up. "Yes."

"I'm Gerald Young." He held out his hand, and Dieter fumbled with what he was carrying before shaking it. "Let's go back to my office where we can talk." Gerald led Dieter back down the hall to his office and offered Dieter a chair before sitting at his desk and getting out a legal pad to take notes. "What is it we can help you with?"

Dieter fumbled with some of the papers he'd brought before placing the photo album on the desk. "These are pictures of my great-grandparents in their home in Vienna, and this"—Dieter pointed to a painting on the wall behind them in the photograph—"is a portrait of her. The thing is that this painting is really famous now, and it's in the Belvedere museum."

Gerald looked intently at the photo as Dieter fidgeted in the chair. "A friend of mine is an artist, and he did some research for me. He found out that this painting, along with the others in the pictures, were taken from Gram's parents' house by the Nazis, and they ended up in the Belvedere. What I want is to get the paintings back."

Gerald stared across his desk at the man sitting across from him. He looked so young and appeared so innocent with his huge blue eyes staring back at Gerald hopefully. Gerald didn't quite know where to start. "Okay," Gerald began, turning the album around so he could see the photographs better.

"Those are my great-grandparents, and that's my grandmother. This photograph was taken in their home in Vienna before the war," Dieter explained to him.

"Okay. There are some things we need to do. I think we need to establish the family lineage, and I need to do some research on the artworks themselves," Gerald explained, and Dieter handed him a number of Internet printouts, which Gerald perused briefly. "It seems to be well-documented that this is indeed a portrait of Anna Meinauer."

"Yes. She's my great-grandmother, and Joseph Meinauer was my great-grandfather. My grandmother's maiden name was Meinauer." Dieter seemed excited, and Gerald found it catching.

"Okay. There are a number of things I need to research, but I think we need to start with proving that if these paintings aren't the property of the Belvedere and belong to your family, then we need to prove that they truly belong to you. The easiest way to do that is to prove that Gertrude Meinauer, your grandmother, is truly their daughter. Do you know your grandmother's birth date?"

"September 27, 1926. She told me she was born in Vienna," Dieter told him before adding, "I have a copy of her marriage license, and I looked for a birth record, but didn't find anything."

"That's not surprising. However, since I know where she was born, I can see if the records still exist. Do you happen to have a copy of your grandmother's will with you?" Dieter shook his head. "Then why don't I make a list of things I'll need you to try to find for me." Gerald began a new sheet of paper and began writing. "If you can find them, I'd like both you and your parents' birth certificates and any records you have, along with the will."

"Does this mean you'll help me?" Dieter looked so earnest, Gerald couldn't have turned him down, especially not when he looked at him so filled with hope like that.

"It means that I'll look into it and see if there's really a case. I can't promise anything, except to do my best. One of the difficult things is that the paintings are in Austria. Even if we can prove that they belong to you, we'd have to file suit in Austria." Gerald could see Dieter's hope slip out of his eyes like water through a sieve. "Let me look into this a little deeper. Would you mind leaving the photo album and the research you did here with me?"

"Yes, but be careful. It's all I have from Gram's family." The care and concern in Dieter's eyes was incredibly sweet, and Gerald found himself drawn to it.

"I'll take very good care of them, I promise," Gerald said as his stomach rumbled. "Excuse me."

"It's okay. I'm hungry too," Dieter said as he got up to leave.

Gerald got a good look at him as he turned to leave, and his breath caught in his chest for just a second. "I was about to get something to eat on my way home. Would you like to join me?" Gerald blinked a few times, not able to believe he'd just invited the adorable man for dinner. He didn't even know if Dieter was gay, and he was a client. "I'd really like to hear any family stories you can tell me," Gerald clarified, to give himself cover.

Dieter turned around, looking confused for a few seconds, but then Gerald saw his smile, big and warm, lighting up his face. "Okay." Dieter looked like he was bursting to tell these stories, like no one had ever asked him before. "Gram told me a lot of stories, mostly because I used to bug her until she did. I don't know how many of them are true. But you never know what could be helpful, right?"

"Exactly," Gerald agreed, making sure his desk was clear and that the material Dieter had given him was all properly stowed in one of his locked drawers. "Do you have any ideas for dinner? There's an Italian place just down the street."

"That would be great," Dieter said, and Gerald turned off his office light before leading the way back to the lobby. They rode the elevator down and then walked the block or so to the restaurant, enjoying the warm summer evening.

"So what do you do?" Gerald asked Dieter, making small talk.

"I'm a computer programmer," Dieter answered without much enthusiasm. "It's not as exciting as I thought it would be, but it's okay."

"Do you mind if I ask when your grandmother died?"

"About three years ago. I found out about the paintings not long after she died, but I had to finish school, and when she died, Gram left me her house, and it needed work, so I sort of let the whole painting thing sit for a while." Dieter sounded as though he had so much energy. Even walking, he practically bounded down the sidewalk rather than walked. "If it would help, I could arrange for you to meet Mark Burke. He's the artist who helped me find a lot of the information I gave you."

"Let me do some research first, and we'll see from there," Gerald cautioned, although he found Dieter's energy and excitement enthralling, and he found himself wanting to help him more and more with each passing minute.

"I really want to help."

Gerald stopped at the front door of the restaurant. "I know you do, but if this case seems viable, it could be years of fighting before anything concrete happens. Are you prepared for that?" Gerald watched Dieter's eyes and knew he hadn't thought of that, or of all the obstacles that were going to be thrown in the way. "Don't worry about it right now," Gerald reassured him as he opened the door to the restaurant.

The hostess greeted them before showing them to an out-of-the-way table. "Why don't you tell me some of the family stories?" Gerald said once they were seated.

Dieter launched into the story of his grandmother and her father's flight out of Austria just ahead of the Nazi occupation. "The only reason I have the photographs at all is because Gram's father was interested in photography, and when he fled, he took some of the pictures he couldn't bear to leave behind. Gram said he always lamented that he had to leave behind the portrait of his wife, and she told me that the woman in blue was the love of her father's life and he was never the same after she died," Dieter told him proudly. "Gram always said I reminded her of him."

The server took their drink orders, and they looked over the menus and ordered once the server returned with their drinks.

"Would you tell me what you know about your great-grandparents?" Gerald asked once the server had left. He was curious about the story, and he realized with a bit of a start that he loved the sound of Dieter's voice. It was almost musical, and the way his eyes lit up when he became excited about something was infectious.

"Well, I can try," Dieter answered, and Gerald saw the way the tip of Dieter's tongue licked his bottom lip. The man was adorable when he was nervous. Gerald blinked a few times and made himself stop those thoughts. He was with a client, and he wasn't here on a date or to seduce the kid; he was here to have dinner and get as much information as he could to help with the potential case. He had to keep his mind on the prize and away from his libido. Gerald waited quietly while Dieter took a sip of water.

"Some of what I know came from Gram, and some from Internet research," Dieter explained. "My great-grandmother, Anna, was some sort of socialite, while my great-grandfather, Joseph, owned factories in and around Vienna. They were very wealthy, and I was even able to find out where they lived and found a picture of the outside of the house on the Internet. It's still there." Dieter became more animated and Gerald smiled at Dieter's happiness. "As I said, Anna was a real socialite, and they were both patrons of the arts. Anna became the center of a group of artists, and through them she met August Pirktl. My artist friend Mark told me that Pirktl was already famous at the time, and it appears that he and Anna became friends and she asked him to paint her portrait for her husband's birthday. At first it seems he refused, but eventually she convinced him, and she sat for him. The result was to be *The Woman in Blue*, which, also according to Mark, was a departure in style for Pirktl and the beginning of a whole new artistic style—in addition to being very beautiful." Dieter paused when the server returned and placed their plates in front of them. They began to eat, and Dieter continued talking between bites.

"Anna gave the painting to Joseph for his birthday, and shortly after, according to Gram's stories, Anna became pregnant and had Gram. She told me that the house was an amazing place to grow up in when her mother was alive. Gram said she remembered a lot of music, dancing, and balls when she was young." Dieter smiled, and Gerald's mind flashed for a second on what Dieter might look like dancing, his lithe little body gyrating to the music.

"Jesus," Gerald said under his breath as he adjusted things under the table. He really needed to get laid if he was fantasizing about his clients. Maybe this dinner invitation hadn't been such a good idea after all.

"All that changed once Anna died. Gram told me once that her father retreated and became very quiet and...." Dieter gazed across the table at him as he thought. "Gloomy was the word I think Gram used once. She said he set up her mother's room like some sort of shrine and moved the painting in there."

"Your grandmother seems to have told you quite a bit," Gerald commented after swallowing a bite of his pesto pasta.

"Only because I asked her," Dieter said. "She never volunteered any information about that time. I think it was too painful for her." Gerald saw some of the fire dim in Dieter's eyes. "I only ever saw Gram cry one time after my parents' funeral, and that was when she was looking at the pictures in her photo album. She didn't know I saw her, because I was supposed to be in bed."

"It sounds like you were a bit of a scamp as a kid," Gerald said, imagining Dieter as a wide-eyed child.

"I don't think I ever was," Dieter countered thoughtfully. "Looking back, I'd say I had a sheltered childhood." A look of pain crossed his face, and Dieter set down his fork. "In a way, I was very lucky. My parents died when I was four, and I came to live with Gram. I know now that I wasn't loved as a child—I was *adored*. Gram and Auntie Kate poured love, attention, and affection on me for as long as I could remember. Once, when she was looking through her photo album, I asked Gram if it was her most precious possession, and she said it wasn't, that I was." Dieter became quiet and seemed to draw inward a little before picking up his fork again. "Where was I?" he asked, taking another bite of his lasagna. "Oh, yeah. Gram said that after her mother died, her father turned her mother's room into a shrine. Gram said that she snuck in there once and her father punished her for it, but the room looked the same. Nothing had changed."

Gerald found himself enthralled with the story and with the storyteller, and he continued eating, watching Dieter as he continued between almost genteel bites of his dinner. "What happened before the war?"

"Gram was ten when her mother died, and I can only imagine that the house was quiet and lonely for her. In what must have been 1938, two years after Anna died, Joseph packed what he could, and according to Gram, she and her father slipped out of Vienna just ahead of the Nazis. Gram said that the day after they passed into Switzerland, the Germans closed the border. They took only what they could carry in one of the cars. Unfortunately, Gram said her father lamented the fact that he couldn't take his wife's portrait until the day he died."

"But why would he leave? He was Austrian and probably would have been safe if he'd have played along the way so many did."

"Gram said he had factories that the Germans would want, and her father was afraid they would hurt them, because her father was no Nazi." Dieter sighed softly. "That's what she told me, but I heard her talking to Auntie Kate once, and Gram said that she always suspected that her father was at least part Jewish. She was never sure and thought that the traditions had possibly been lost with Gram's grandparents."

"That would make a lot of sense and account for his actions, because it wouldn't have mattered if the family was practicing or not—if he had Jewish blood, he would likely have been persecuted." Gerald tried to sound dispassionate, but he was finding it difficult. The story was so moving, and Dieter incredibly engaging. "It sounds like your great-grandfather was a smart cookie."

"I'd like to think so," Dieter said with a smile. "He and Gram made it to Switzerland and spent the war there. He was able to take what portable wealth he could, and Gram said they lived simply. Growing up she'd had servants and governesses, but once they fled, they had to learn to do for themselves. They made it through the war, but according to Gram, her father never really recovered from the loss of her mother, and he died in Switzerland a few years after the war ended. After that, Gram came to this country." Dieter finished his dinner and rested his fork gently against the edge of the plate, wiping his fingers on the napkin that lay in his lap. "I've sort of monopolized the conversation," Dieter commented, as though he'd done something wrong. "Do you have family in town?"

Gerald snickered slightly. "Oh yes. My father is a lawyer in private practice in Mequon, along with two of my brothers."

"So the law is sort of a family business," Dieter said with a hint of mirth.

"You could say that. They're very successful, and my father wanted me to join their firm, but I wanted to make it on my own. I'm the youngest of five. One of my sisters is a doctor, and the other is a concert pianist." Gerald couldn't help laughing. "She's very talented, but a bit of a disappointment to my folks, but I think she's the bravest of us all. She had the guts to go out and do what she really loved regardless of everyone's opinion, and I admire her for that."

"Do you wish you'd done that?" Dieter asked him as their eyes met briefly, and Gerald felt a surge of desire that he worked to quash.

"That's the ironic thing—I did, sort of," Gerald explained as he tried to keep his thoughts on the conversation. "I love being a lawyer, and I like to think I'm quite a good one, or at least I will be. But I know I disappointed my father when I went out on my own rather than joining the family firm. Though I may eventually join them, I wanted to make it on my own first."

"That's very admirable. Plenty of people would have taken the easy way," Dieter told him, his eyes twinkling. "Although I've heard that working with family can be difficult, so maybe by going out on your own, you did take the easy way out." Dieter grinned teasingly, and Gerald laughed along with him. He'd often wondered that same thing himself.

The server came and asked if they'd like anything else before depositing the check on the table. Gerald reached for it just before Dieter did. "This is on me," Gerald told his companion, but Dieter shook his head, reaching for the check again, and when Gerald pulled it away again, Dieter acquiesced with a thank-you and a smile. Gerald placed his credit card with the check, and their server retrieved it. "I'll do some research and get back to you late next week," Gerald told Dieter, slightly relieved as he steered the conversation back to business, even as he felt disappointed that their time together was ending. He'd liked spending time with Dieter. Checking his watch, he found it almost impossible to believe that they'd been eating and talking for two hours.

"Okay. I'd really appreciate that." Dieter's gaze wandered around the restaurant, and Gerald knew he'd made him uncomfortable when he'd switched the conversation abruptly onto business, but Gerald knew he was becoming too friendly and familiar with a client, and that was not a good thing. It was okay to have friends as clients, under the right circumstances, but being attracted to a client the way he was attracted to Dieter was not particularly ethical, to Gerald's way of thinking. Thankfully, the server brought the slip quickly, and Gerald signed it before getting up to leave.

Outside on the sidewalk, Gerald wondered just what he should say. He was rarely at a loss for words, but the way he couldn't seem to take his eyes off Dieter frightened him a little. "Thank you for joining me for dinner," Gerald said, extending his hand.

Dieter took it. "No, thank you. It was good to get better acquainted," Dieter told him formally before releasing his hand. "Have a good night," Dieter added before walking down the sidewalk. Gerald turned before walking back toward the office where his car was parked in the underground garage.

Chirping open the doors as he approached, Gerald climbed into his car and headed for the exit, swiping his parking pass through the gate before turning onto the street. Gerald took the turn toward the freeway before turning once again, making his way toward Walker's Point and the clubby area of town. His attraction to Dieter had unsettled him a little. Figuring he just needed to get laid, he decided that maybe a visit to one of the clubs and a quick romp with a hot blond would take the edge off. "Christ," Gerald muttered to himself. He had to get Dieter and his blond hair and deep blue eyes out of his system.

Parking near one of the bars, Gerald took off his jacket and tie, laying them on the backseat before loosening his collar and getting out of the car. Normally when he came to the bars, he went to Triangle, but today he wanted something younger and maybe with more energy—it was Friday night, after all. Walking the block to Second Street, Gerald could feel the pulse of the music from Dance

All Night almost before he could hear it. Approaching the front, he saw guys entering the dance club as well as a couple leaving, their arms around each other's waists. Pulling open the black door, Gerald paid the cover to the bouncer near the door before entering the building, which pulsed with music, conversation, and enough sexual energy to send a zing of anticipation down his spine.

Gerald made his way into the already crowded club. It was still early, but that didn't seem to matter tonight. The low lighting and crowd of people seemed to reduce almost everyone except the bartenders to mere shadows of themselves. Making his way to the bar, Gerald ordered a beer and looked around at the men gathered in small groups throughout the bar area. No one seemed to notice him, which he pretty much expected. He wasn't dressed to capture anyone's attention. The men around him all looked like hip fashion plates with their strategically ripped jeans and skintight shirts—that is, those of them who were actually wearing shirts at all. Paying for the beer when it arrived, Gerald gulped it down in a matter of minutes before ordering another. Paying for it, he thanked and tipped the bartender before taking his beer toward a table that had miraculously opened up, reaching it just before a group of young club boys in see-through shirts. Sitting down, Gerald ignored the boys' comments and looks as he continued scanning the crowd. The dance floor was empty, but the flickering lights were still going full blast, lending an almost surreal aura to the rituals going on in the rest of the club.

Scanning the groups of men, he could easily pick out the posers, the ones that were there to be seen. They leaned against walls or in small groups, tight shirts straining over broad chests and thick arms. No one approached them except other guys that looked like them, because, after all, the muscle bunnies and gym rats only went for each other. It was as tight a clique as high school cheerleaders. There were also the club kids with their flamboyant outfits, the drag queens presiding over their courts, and of course the "regular guys" like Gerald who came just to have a night where they could be themselves around other guys. Sure, Gerald hoped he'd get lucky, but just unwinding and having some fun was the real order of the evening.

"You here alone?" A deep, slightly slurred voice crooned into his ear, and Gerald turned to see a rather tall man dressed all in black standing next to him with a definitely hungry leer. Without waiting to be invited, he pulled out the other chair, straddling it backward, presumably to give Gerald a glance at the goods on offer. "I'm Stan," he said, by way of introducing himself, "and you look like you could use a little company."

Good grief. Gerald could not believe the guy had used a cheesy line like that on him. "Does that really work for you?"

"What?" Stan asked, looking at himself and then around the room as though he was trying to figure out who Gerald was talking to.

"That line. It's old and really lame," Gerald replied, looking around himself to see if there was anyone he knew who could rescue him.

Stan smiled, the expression on his face softening, and he suddenly looked younger. "It got you to talk to me, didn't it?"

"I suppose it did," Gerald admitted with a nod, thinking that Stan—he doubted it was his real name for some reason—wasn't that bad-looking.

"Would you like another beer?" Stan asked him as he drained his own.

"No thanks, I'm good," Gerald replied, and Stan got up to go to the bar as the club suddenly became quiet, the pounding music that seemed to permeate the very walls of the building suddenly cutting out. "Gentlemen," a disembodied voice said through the club's speaker system, "your DJ for the evening is Randy, in more ways than one, so give it up for him and Dance All Night!" The crowd gave a cheer as the music started again, and boys began to move toward the dance floor.

"You wanna dance?" Stan asked him as he returned carrying two beers, one of which was already nearly empty just from the trip across the bar. Stan emptied the glass before placing it and the full one on the table. Gerald shook his head and began looking around and through Stan, figuring he'd eventually take the hint. A song ended and another began, and Gerald's attention shifted to the dance floor. A single man stood in the center, his body flowing and gyrating to each and every beat. Slender arms, powerful legs, and narrow hips all moved in conjunction with every nuance in the music. Gerald could only see his back, but what a backside it was. Butt and hips rocking and swaying, Gerald's eyes mimicked his movements as the dancer simulated the hottest sex Gerald could have possibly imagined, and there was no one near him.

A few guys approached and started to dance with him, but they quickly moved away when he paid them no mind whatsoever—he just kept dancing like he was lost in his own world. Gerald shifted in his chair, trying to get a better look at this gorgeous gazelle of a man, and as he glanced around, it looked like every guy in the club was trying to do the same thing, even the posers.

"If you're interested in him, good luck!" Stan slurred from across the table, yet another empty beer glass in front of him.

"Why?" Gerald asked without taking his eyes off the dancer, waiting for him to turn around. Gerald was already picturing the man's face, and he needed to see what he looked like.

"He only dances. Never with anyone else, and he never goes home with anyone. He only dances, for hours on end," Stan clarified, his eyes becoming glassy and unfocused. Lucky for Gerald, one of the bouncers saw him and made his way to the table and helped Stan away.

"He always does this," the bouncer explained as he helped Stan to his feet. "The man never knows when to stop." Gerald thanked him and asked if he needed help, but the huge bouncer shook his head and led Stan to what Gerald hoped was a safe place where he could sober up for a while.

Gerald looked back at the dance floor and saw that the dancer had turned around. Gerald saw big blue eyes and a head of blond hair, made red in the light, but he knew him. Finishing his beer, Gerald stood up and walked across the club as the music ended and the dancer stopped his movements, waiting for the next song. Gerald knew he only had a few seconds. "What would your Gram say if she saw you now?"

Dieter whipped around, the fire burning in his eyes quickly turning to pain and hurt. He'd only been teasing, but Gerald realized he'd accidentally hit on a source of pain. "Sorry, I was only kidding," he added hastily and saw Dieter's expression soften. "I only wanted to get your attention." It appeared he'd done that, and he'd also answered the question of whether Dieter was gay. He must have changed clothes, and Gerald took in the slim-legged jeans and tight shirt that hugged Dieter's frame. Dieter wasn't muscular, but what Gerald saw turned him on like nobody's business.

The music began again, and Gerald moved away, expecting Dieter to begin dancing, but he seemed to be following him. Of course the table he'd had was gone, so Gerald found a small area of unoccupied space. "What are you doing here?" Dieter asked, but he didn't seem upset any longer.

"I just needed to let off some steam, I guess," Gerald confessed. "I could ask you the same thing," he countered.

"Just dancing," Dieter answered matter-of-factly.

"Yeah, I saw," Gerald said almost yelling now over the music. "I'm sorry about my crack about your Gram. I didn't mean anything by it." He really hadn't.

"Thanks," Dieter yelled back. Gerald figured any sort of conversation was nearly impossible, so he stood there looking at Dieter, who looked back at him, as confused as Gerald was about what to do next. "Wanna dance?" Dieter asked him before practically pulling him toward the floor. Gerald had two left feet and couldn't dance to save his soul, but he let himself be led to the floor, and when Dieter began to move, Gerald went along, following his lead, trying not to embarrass himself too much. "Just move your body to the music," Dieter told him when they were standing close. "Don't be self-conscious and don't worry about what anyone thinks, because it doesn't matter. Just let yourself go." Dieter began to move, and Gerald closed his eyes, letting the music inside. At first, Gerald simply swayed to the music, but then he began to move more and more. When Dieter put his hands on Gerald's hips, Gerald forgot about everything but where those warm hands touched his body. Then he was dancing. It might not have been pretty or even very good, but Dieter smiled at him, and they danced.

Time seemed to move independently of them, especially since he spent the rest of the evening looking into Dieter's eyes and with a perpetual hard-on in his pants. Every time he felt Dieter's touch, a jolt of desire zinged through him, but Dieter made no move to do anything other than dance. Not that Gerald should have been surprised—it's what Dieter seemed to do, although judging from the puzzled and jealous looks of the other people in the club, it was true that Dieter usually danced alone.

The song ended and a bell sounded, the lighting in the club increasing. Gerald blinked a few times, having gotten used to the dimness, and he realized it was last call. Dieter stopped moving, standing on the dance floor as people moved around them, most of them trying for a last hookup before the night ended.

Gerald looked deep into Dieter's eyes and saw him lick his lips, that pink tongue making an appearance once again. Gerald leaned closer, wondering how Dieter's lips would taste and how quickly Gerald could move to sampling the rest of Dieter's mouth and everything else he could get his tongue, lips, and hands on. Right now, the whole thing about Dieter being a client was far from his mind. All he saw right now was the most enthrallingly sexy man he'd ever met in his life, and Gerald had rarely wanted anything as much as he wanted to get Dieter into his bed. And if the look he was getting were any indication, Dieter seemed to want that too. Gerald moved closer, his lips parting, and he saw Dieter's eyes drift shut and his head tilt ever so slightly.

Someone bumped into Dieter as they passed, excusing himself as he went by, and Dieter looked away for just a second, but it was enough to break the spell. Gerald realized what he'd been about to do, and Dieter seemed to as well. In the light, Gerald saw Dieter color and look away. Gerald stepped back to give Dieter some space. "I think we should be leaving," Dieter said, and Gerald nodded, not quite sure what he meant, but he felt a glimmer of hope well inside.

Dieter led the way to the door, and Gerald followed him outside. "Do you need a ride home? Or...." Gerald left it open-ended.

Dieter studied him for a few seconds before pointing and saying, "My car's over here, and I haven't been drinking, so I'm fine." Dieter began walking toward his car. "Good night, Gerald," Dieter called warmly.

Gerald watched him walk away, feeling unexpectedly disappointed. Once he saw Dieter turn the corner, Gerald walked to his own car. After driving home, he lumbered up the walk and into his small bungalow-style home. Placing his keys on the table, Gerald yawned wide, remembering to lock the door before padding to the bathroom. Gerald loved his house. It had been built in the twenties and had all the original unpainted woodwork, which had been a requirement when he was looking for a house. He'd bought it about a year earlier and was working to fix it up on the weekends.

After cleaning up, Gerald undressed, taking care of his dirty clothes before crawling into bed. He closed his eyes and tried to sleep. It should have been easy after a long workday, combined with the fact that it was after two in the morning, but sleep wouldn't come. His mind kept conjuring up images of Dieter dancing in the center of that club. Giving up on trying to sleep for now, Gerald pushed back the covers. Reaching to the nightstand, Gerald found the lube and squeezed a little on his hand before closing his eyes, running his hand down his frustrated length.

Dieter danced for him, but now, instead of in tight jeans and shirt, Dieter was naked, his swinging arms high above his head, stomach tightening. In his mind, Dieter turned around, swinging his tight butt for Gerald to see. His breath coming faster, Gerald stroked harder, faster, as Dieter crooked his finger for Gerald to come closer, and he imagined the feel of smooth, hot skin.

Gerald's stomach clenched and he came, clamping his eyes closed so he could milk everything from his fantasy before it faded. Opening his eyes again, Gerald reached for the box of tissues to clean himself up. Throwing the tissues away, Gerald pulled up the covers and closed his eyes, quickly falling to sleep, figuring he'd see Dieter dance for quite a while whenever he closed his eyes.

CHAPTER 3

DIETER fished his cell phone out of his pants, pulling his attention from the program he was working on just when he was close to finding the error that was causing him all the problems. "Hello," he answered quietly, so he wouldn't disturb the other people around him.

"Mr. Krumpf, I'm Carolyn with Prince, Graham, and Associates, and I'm calling for Gerald Young. He asked me to see if it would be possible for you to come into the office later this afternoon. He has an opening at five, and he'd like to speak to you about your case." It sounded to Dieter as though she were talking to him and doing something else at the same time because she seemed to pause between thoughts. "He knows it's short notice," she clarified.

"No. Five will be fine," Dieter said with a bit of relief. It had been almost two weeks since the evening he'd first met Gerald and gone to dinner with him, and later danced with him at the club, and he was curious to see if Gerald had something for him.

"Excellent. I'll add you to his appointment calendar. Thank you." She disconnected the line, and Dieter set the phone on his desk before returning to work, trying not to let his thoughts roam to the handsome man who'd danced with him that evening. Gerald hadn't been a graceful dancer, but he'd tried, and it looked to Dieter like he'd had a good time with him. He knew Gerald was interested in him, or at least he'd been interested in taking him home for the evening. But Dieter didn't do that, and if that was all Gerald wanted, then Dieter was relieved he hadn't given in. He'd thought about it but figured if

Gerald was really interested, Gerald could call him like a regular person—he had his telephone number. But he hadn't called.

"Who was that on the phone?" a familiar voice asked from behind him, and Dieter turned to face his friend. "Was that the attorney you danced with at Dance All Night?" Reed asked with a wry smile.

"No. That was his secretary making an appointment for this evening." Gerald could at least have called himself, but maybe that was too much to expect. They'd only danced together for a few hours. It wasn't as though anything else had happened.

"Oh," Reed said before moving closer so no one else could hear. "You like him, don't you? You must, you actually danced with him." Reed answered his own question the way he usually did. "Did he invite you home with him?"

"He may have, but I don't do that sort of thing, and you know it," Dieter retorted with a touch of anxiety. "I didn't approach him, he approached me. Besides, just because I like to dance and I'm good at it doesn't mean I'm some tart who'll go home with any guy I see," Dieter added accusingly, knowing that Reed wouldn't have hesitated the way Dieter had.

"Come on, you don't have to be mean." Reed pouted for a split second. "I just wish I'd seen this guy. He must be special if he's still got you riled up after two weeks," Reed teased, and Dieter sighed, knowing Reed was right. He usually was when it came to things like this.

"I wouldn't say he was that special. After all, he treated me just like all the other guys do," Dieter groused, his voice getting a little loud, and Reed reminded him to quiet down with a glance toward the offices in the corner.

"Dieter, there are times I regret that I ever took you there. I know you like to dance, but you turn on every guy in the place with the way you move. I know you don't mean to and that you're just having a good time, but you can't blame them if they want you."

"I suppose. But I guess I thought he might be different," Dieter confessed softly. "Anyway, I have an appointment with him after I leave the office," Dieter explained, and Reed smiled knowingly, then left Dieter's work area, walking back to his own desk, and Dieter went back to the offending computer program, trying to remember where he'd been.

At lunchtime, Dieter found Reed, and they ate together like they usually did. He'd met Reed when he'd started working at Sunbird Funds two years earlier, and he knew right away that he'd found a kindred spirit, or at least the only other gay man in the office. "Do you want me to go with you to your appointment in case he tries anything?" Reed asked after he swallowed a bite of his sandwich.

Dieter smiled. "No, Mom. I'll be fine. I think he's really a nice guy." Dieter would be happy if he could figure out why Gerald seemed to get under his skin, but he did, and Dieter would have to deal with it because he certainly wasn't going to do something as *L.A. Law*—as ridiculous as having an affair with his lawyer. He and Reed finished their lunch, talking about other things until it was time to go back to work, and thankfully the rest of Dieter's day was quiet, except for a few moments of excitement when he finally figured out what was wrong with the program he'd been working on.

Just before five, Dieter walked through the doors to Prince, Graham, and Associates, letting the receptionist know he was there and taking a seat to wait like he had before. "Dieter," he heard Gerald's voice say, "Come on back, please."

Dieter stood up and followed Gerald to his office, taking the same chair he had the last time. Gerald sat behind his desk and lifted the phone, making a brief call before hanging up again. "I explained what I found to Harold Prince, and he asked to be included in this meeting. He'll be about ten minutes if that's okay."

"Of course," Dieter answered and sat staring at Gerald, who fidgeted a little in his chair before getting up. Dieter followed him with his eyes as Gerald closed the door.

"I wanted to apologize for my behavior the other night. I hadn't expected to see you at the club, and you're a client. I certainly shouldn't have expected... or asked...." Gerald seemed at a loss for words, and Dieter sat quietly letting him struggle. "I shouldn't have...."

"What? Danced with me? That's all you did, you know. We didn't do anything else."

"I know. But I'm also sorry for my crack about how your Gram would feel if she saw you. I meant it as a joke, but it was in poor taste, and I'm sorry. I saw that it hurt you, and I didn't mean to."

"You didn't hurt me, just startled me, I guess," Dieter responded softly, grateful that they were at least talking about what happened.

"Did you ever tell your grandmother?" Gerald asked, and Dieter shook his head.

"Gram was very old-fashioned. I did tell Auntie Kate, though. I must have been seventeen, and I told her one afternoon after I'd had my first heartache. She hugged me and told me that I was who I was and that she loved me, and things like that weren't really important." Dieter smiled at the memory. Auntie Kate had always been supportive of everything he did, no matter what. "After that, she told me to sit down and brought me a plate of cookies, just like she always had. We both looked at each other, smiling through our shared secret. Then we both said at the same time, 'Don't tell Gram.'" Dieter's smile turned to a chuckle that faded quickly. "Gram was set in her ways, and she would never have accepted me as gay. I knew that very clearly, so I hid it from her and never told her who I really was."

"How do you know? People can surprise you," Gerald told him sincerely.

"Not Gram, at least not in this. She clung to some old ways and ideas. Heck, when she died, she still referred to guys with long hair as hippies." Dieter saw Gerald look at him in surprise for a second before laughing.

"You're kidding?" Gerald said though his chuckles.

"Nope. Gram was wonderful, and I know she loved me, but I know she would never have accepted me as gay. Oh, she wouldn't have kicked me out or anything, but she wouldn't have understood. I knew that, so I never told her. Does your family know?"

"Yes. I told them a while ago. I can't say they were thrilled, and it only added to my black-sheep reputation, but they know. Not that we ever talk about it. My family tends to see things the way they want to."

A soft knock on the door interrupted their discussion, and Dieter turned around to see an older, distinguished man walk into the office. Dieter stood up and shook the offered hand. "I'm Harold Prince and I knew your father very well," the man said before clasping Dieter by the shoulder. "You look so much like him."

"Thank you, sir," Dieter answered.

"There is one thing that puzzles me. I know you were just a boy when your father died. How did you know to call me?"

"Mark Burke recommended you. He said you'd been helpful to him. I didn't know you knew my dad. But maybe you could tell me about him sometime. I was four when he died and don't really remember much about him."

"I'd like that. Your father was something else," Harold started to say, and Dieter thought he was going to tell him a story about his dad, but he seemed to remember where he was and his expression changed, becoming more formal. "Why don't I have Gerald set up a day next week, and we can meet for lunch. I'd love to tell you about your dad. He was a good friend."

Harold took the chair next to Dieter's, and Gerald pulled a chair around to join them as they seemed to get down to business. "I did some research, and I have some good news and some not so good news for you," Gerald began. "First, I was able to verify that you are indeed the clear heir to your grandmother's family. That means that you have standing under the law, that you can indeed bring suit to recover the paintings, if you like." Gerald looked alternately at him and Harold. "However, since the paintings are in Austria, you'll need to bring suit there, and that's the difficult part. In order to bring this type of suit, you need to put up a bond that equals the value of the property in question."

Dieter gasped before swallowing hard. "I can't do that. Mark said those paintings are probably worth millions. I don't have that kind of money." He should have known this was a fool's errand, anyway. But he'd wanted to get those paintings back for his grandmother, and he'd allowed himself to hope. He should have known better.

"We know you don't," Harold said soothingly. "The issue is that we'd need to bring suit in Austria. We've requested copies of some of the records regarding the paintings from the Belvedere and the Austrian Cultural Ministry, and they are not cooperating. What we'd like to do is find a way to bring suit in the United States, but with the paintings physically in Austria, that's going to be problematic."

"So I should just give up?" Dieter asked. It sounded to him like that's what they were saying. "These people stole my family's legacy, and there's nothing I can do about it?" Dieter felt his temper rise. "There has to be something we can do. Even if I could put up the bond, is there any way I could get a fair hearing? No. They'd rule to keep the paintings where they are because they think they're theirs, but they're not."

"Dieter," Gerald interjected levelly. "We've not given up hope, and we're still looking into possibilities, but we wanted to tell you where things stood." Gerald didn't sound particularly positive, either.

"Well, I want to thank you both for looking into this for me," Dieter said as he stood up. "I'd like to take my photo album if I could." Dieter waited while Gerald opened a door in the credenza behind him, retrieving the album before handing it to him.

"Look, I wish we had better news, but don't give up hope." Gerald stepped around the desk.

"Will you send me the bill?" Dieter asked.

"Son," Harold said. "All the work we've done up till now has been on us. Your story was so compelling, and having known your father, I was hoping we could find a way to help." Dieter saw Harold look at Gerald and then back at him. No matter what their mouths said, their eyes said they'd given up hope, and that told Dieter all he needed to know.

"Thank you for trying." Dieter shook hands with both men before leaving the office, heading for the lobby. The glass doors closed behind him, and he'd called for the elevator when he heard movement behind him.

"Dieter." He turned to look at Gerald. "I don't know what we can do, but I'd like to find out some more about the paintings. I don't know if it will help, but I was wondering if you could arrange for me to meet this artist friend of yours. I could call him as your lawyer, but I think it would be better coming from you as a friend." The elevator door opened and Dieter looked at it, watching the door close again.

Dieter saw a touch of earnestness in Gerald's eyes and found himself agreeing. "I don't have a lot of money."

"Until we've figured things out one way or another, I won't charge you for my time. Since tomorrow's Saturday, if your friend agrees, I'll be happy to meet you at his studio or wherever you'd like."

"Why?" Dieter asked, clutching the photo album in front of him like a shield. "You don't know me very well. I'm really just some guy you saw dancing at a club." He wasn't sure what sort of game Gerald was playing, but Dieter wasn't going to play along.

"I like your story and want to do what I can to help," Gerald told him, but Dieter kept wondering what his angle was, and it must have shown on his face because he saw Gerald's expression change, becoming softer. "I went to law school so I could try to help people. And I do that, sometimes. But most of the time I end up arguing with other attorneys over stupid things like who gets the toaster or the television. Your case is bigger than that. It's about righting a wrong that was done to your family decades ago, and if I can, I want to help. It's why I became a lawyer."

Dieter was slightly shocked. Gerald seemed sincere, and Dieter wasn't quite sure how to react. "Okay. I need to call Mark and see if he's available. Can I call you and let you know?"

"Sure." Gerald smiled and reached into his jacket pocket. Pulling a pen from the receptionist's desk, he wrote on the card.

Dieter took the offered card. "That's my cell number. Please call me and let me know."

"I will. Thank you," Dieter said, turning to call the elevator again. The door opened and Dieter stepped inside, then the door closed and the car began to move toward the ground.

Dieter left the office building, standing on the sidewalk with the last of the office workers passing around him in their rush to get home or wherever they were headed to start their weekend. Dieter looked both ways before deciding to stop in at the wine store. He needed to talk to someone, and Sean was someone he trusted. Having decided, he hurried to his car, driving through town before luckily finding a parking space near Sommelier Wines.

The store was surprisingly quiet for a Friday night, and Sean looked anxious, the way he usually did when he expected to be busy and wasn't. "Evening, Dieter," Sean called as he strode over, before embracing him tightly. "How are you?" he asked quietly without releasing him right away. "It's been a few weeks, and I was beginning to get worried about you."

"I'm fine," Dieter answered as Sean's arms and warmth slipped away.

"You don't look fine," Sean countered before looking to Katie, who motioned to him.

"I'll call you when it gets busy," Katie told him. "Just send Laura out. We can handle it while you talk."

Sean led him to the back of the store, Laura already walking toward them. "Sean, I have a question about this invoice."

"Okay. Can it wait a few minutes? I'd like you to help Katie on the floor. We shouldn't be too long."

"All right." She headed toward the sales floor, still carrying the invoice. "Oh, Dieter, could you look at the computer before you leave? It's acting slow and cranky."

"I will," he promised before she disappeared through the door and they entered the office. Sean closed the door, and they sat down on the futon.

"So tell me what's got you flustered," Sean told him lightly.

"I met with the lawyers, and they didn't give me much hope about getting Gram's paintings back. They said I'd have to sue the museum and the Austrian government in Austria and that I'd have to put up a bond that would be a lot more money than I'll ever see if I wanted to do that."

"I'm sorry, Dieter. I know how much it means to you to get those paintings back."

"It's for Gram," Dieter clarified, "and it's my family's heritage." Dieter leaned forward nervously. "I knew I shouldn't have allowed myself any hope, but I did."

"I know. Did the lawyers say anything else?" Sean asked him in a very caring tone.

"Gerald said that he wasn't giving up and asked if I could arrange for him to meet with Mark. I don't know what he's expecting, but he wants more information. I think he's grasping at straws."

"How much is this fishing expedition costing you?" Sean asked him in a very fatherly way. After Gram died, Dieter had felt very alone for months, and over time, and Sean had become sort of the dad he never had.

Dieter shook his head. "Nothing. That's the strange part. Mark gave me the contact information for his attorney, and it turns out he and my dad were friends in school, so up to now, they've been doing the work for free. And Gerald, my attorney, says he's not going to charge me until they either give up or find something. Frankly, I don't know what to think."

Sean's eyebrows knit together in obvious suspicion. "Why would he do that?"

"I think he likes me," Dieter confessed, looking down at the floor. "Two weeks ago after I met with him, we went to dinner. And afterward, I had so much energy and couldn't sit still, so I went to

Dance All Night, and I saw him there," Dieter explained, and he saw the suspicion in Sean's eyes grow more pronounced. "I only go there to dance. When I saw him, I asked him to join me, and we danced together for hours. He's sort of uncoordinated," Dieter said, and he couldn't stop a grin, "but it was nice to dance with him."

"Did anything else happen?" Sean asked lightly.

Dieter shook his head forcefully. "No. I'd never!" Dieter swallowed hard. "I think he was sort of hinting that he'd like to go home with me or that we could go to his place, but at the time, I didn't really understand, and I'd never do anything like that."

"Why not?" Sean asked. "Not that I'm advocating anonymous sex. But why is it so bad that he'd like you or ask you to go home with him? You're twenty-four, and as long as you know what you're doing and take precautions, you shouldn't feel guilty for having a little fun. As long as you're not being hurt or hurting anyone else."

"I could never do that," Dieter said with a little more force than was necessary.

Dieter heard Sean sigh loudly. "Dieter, I'm going to say this, but I don't want you to take it the wrong way. I knew your Gram, and I liked her. She was quite a lady and a wonderful person. She raised you in an atmosphere of love that most people would kill to have. You never wanted for attention or affection. But your Gram could also be a bit of a snob, and some of those attitudes made their way into you." Dieter opened his mouth to argue, but Sean stopped him with a gentle touch. "I don't think you're a snob, but some of her opinions—and we both know your Gram was free with them—are still playing in your head."

"No, they're not."

"Dieter, I think they are. Your Gram had certain ideas about people and how they fit into the world. I think a lot of those ideas came from her early childhood, which was very sheltered, privileged, and quite narrow. Your Gram once told me stories of things I can barely imagine, balls and parties that boggled the mind, but always with the same people. But you realize she nearly had a conniption when I offered you the job here, because I was gay."

Dieter's eyes widened, and he shook his head. "No. Why would she?"

Sean smiled at him a little indulgently, and Dieter felt himself bristle slightly. "She was concerned that I would turn you gay."

"But she always liked you," Dieter countered.

"Yes, she did. But liking a shopkeeper who happened to be gay is one thing. Having your grandson working for him and in close proximity to him on a regular basis is quite a different story, at least in your Gram's mind," Sean explained, and Dieter wanted to refute what he was saying, but he knew his Gram, and what Sean was describing held a ring of truth he couldn't ignore. "I'm not faulting your Gram. She came around, but she never really understood."

"I know she had strong opinions about people, some of them not always good or right," Dieter confessed.

"Yes. You heard those views all your life, and they keep playing in the back of your mind. You can't live your life the way your Gram wanted you to. No one could. You need to be happy, and you need to live for you." Sean stood up as someone knocked on the door. Cracking it open, he said something quietly and then closed it again. "You shouldn't feel guilty for wanting to go dancing, and you most certainly have nothing to be ashamed of if you find someone attractive and want to dance with them. As for the rest, follow your heart and not the voice of your grandmother in your head," Sean told him with a knowing smile. "It's getting busy, and I need to get back out front, but we can talk again later if you want."

"No," Dieter said as he got up, and Sean pulled him into another hug. "Thanks, Sean."

"You're welcome," Sean responded before opening the door and striding toward the front of the store. Dieter followed behind and saw Sean hugging his son Bobby while Laura hurried back into the office, still carrying the invoice she'd had earlier. Knowing her, she'd probably been holding it the entire time for fear she'd lose it.

"Hey, Bobby," Dieter said as he approached, "are you working tonight?"

"No. Mark and I are getting together for an art slam."

"What's an art slam?" Dieter asked, visions of paintings being hurled against walls flashing through his mind.

"Not what you're thinking," Bobby told him with a mischievous grin. "Musicians have jam sessions. Mark and I have slam sessions. We get together and work through new techniques and just have fun. Would you like to come?"

"I'm no artist," Dieter countered, shying away.

"Don't have to be, we're just messing around with color. I've got some extra paint clothes in the car," Bobby coaxed with words and a smile.

"If you're sure," Dieter responded nervously. It sounded like fun, but he didn't want to intrude.

"Cool." Bobby practically dragged him out of the store, saying good-bye to his dad in his excitement. Sean waved as they left, laughing to Katie. "We'll leave your car here, and we can pick it up later," Bobby added as they climbed into his car and took off. "The extra clothes are in the backseat."

"Are you sure Mark won't mind?" Dieter asked as he reached into the backseat, retrieving Bobby's bag.

"Of course not. Mark and I both believe you don't have to be an artist to express yourself through art. Children do it all the time. It's only when we're older and get self-conscious that most people stop," Bobby explained, as they pulled up in front of Tyler's antique shop. Bobby turned off the engine and climbed out of the car. Dieter followed, carrying the bag, as Mark opened the front door.

"I see we have a new initiate," Mark called with a smile, and Dieter had his answer. Mark seemed genuinely pleased to see him. "I set things up out back. Come on in and get changed while I add another." Mark looked to Dieter as though he were going to burst with excitement. Dieter and Bobby went inside. Mark locked the door, and they walked through the fully lit store. "Tyler's upstairs, reworking some displays," Mark explained before standing at the base of the stairs. "We'll be out back. Don't come out without warning!"

"Okay," Tyler called back down the stairs, and they continued to the back door.

"Get changed and meet me outside," Mark instructed, and Bobby led him to Mark's studio, where he placed the bag on the bench.

"These sweats should fit you," Bobby said, and he tossed a pair of paint-covered sweats and a T-shirt to Dieter before beginning to change. "This should be a lot of fun, Dieter. I promise. So relax and enjoy. It's not every day that you get to make art with a famous artist." Bobby was right, and Dieter changed his clothes quickly, then followed Bobby out back. "You might want to leave your shoes so you don't get paint on them." Dieter looked down and saw Bobby wriggle his toes. "Bare feet work best for these things."

"Okay," Dieter said with a smile before slipping off his shoes and socks, following Bobby out behind the building. Three canvases stood on easels at the edge of a concrete pad near the building with a table across from them with what looked like squirt guns resting on it.

"I'm glad you could join us, Dieter. This should be a lot of fun. Each blast gun has a different color of water-based paint in it. Dieter, you're on the far end, and Bobby, you're in the middle. The trick is not to try to control the paint, but let your feeling and emotions show through the gun. You'll be surprised how what you're feeling will show on the canvas. There are only three rules: keep the paint on your own canvas, put the gun back where you got it, and have fun!"

Mark had labeled the colors on the table, and Dieter reached for the blue, not quite sure what to do. Bobby had already grabbed the yellow, squirting the canvas with lines of color, his face suddenly serious, eyes a little vacant, like he was seeing something that wasn't really there. "I'm not sure what to do," Dieter told Mark, who set down his gun.

"Just let yourself go and think about what you're feeling. What happened to you today? What strong emotion did you feel?" Mark took the gun from Dieter's hand and set it on the table. "Close your eyes." Dieter complied, listening to Mark's voice. "Think about a strong emotion, something recent and powerful. Concentrate, let it flow through you," Mark told him quietly, and Dieter nodded. "Now, what color do you think of?"

"Red," Dieter answered without hesitation.

"Then pick up the red and go," Mark told him, and Dieter barely opened his eyes enough to pick up the gun before he was squirting at the canvas like mad. Then, barely thinking, he grabbed the black and squirted in long diagonal lines, slashing with the gun at the canvas, color upon color, alternating red then back, his movements big and bold as the frustration and anger about the paintings, Gram, and everything else came pouring out of him. He hadn't realized he was making noise, but after a while, he heard some yelling and screaming and realized it was him.

Once the anger abated, Dieter set down the gun he was holding. Breathing hard, Dieter opened his eyes and looked around. Mark and Bobby had both stopped and were looking at him and then at his canvas. "Do you feel better?" Bobby asked just above a whisper.

"Yeah," Dieter swallowed and then colored with embarrassment. "I'm sorry."

"There's nothing to apologize for," Mark told him. "Look at the canvas." Dieter had been afraid to, figuring it would be ugly. Well, it was, but not in the way Dieter feared. All the frustration, repression, anger, and self-loathing he'd felt for years was there staring him in the face.

"Wow," Mark said. "That's amazing. You can tell exactly what you were feeling—it jumps off that canvas. The slashes of paint are so strong."

"But what about this up here?" He pointed to one of the few areas with no paint.

"Don't touch anything," Mark told him. "It's perfect just the way it is." Mark walked to his canvas, taking it down from the easel and placed it inside the door before taking down the other two canvases. "The light's fading, so we'll only do one more." Mark brought out three fresh canvases, setting the easels close together. "This time all of us will use all three canvases. We'll create three pieces together that represent all of us, and we'll do it in two minutes. Don't think, feel. Go!" Each of them grabbed a gun and paint flew, color streams hitting one another, making new colors and designs. Fast and furious they worked, dropping one gun and picking up another. "Done!" Mark called, and they stopped, each looking over their joint creation.

"It looks great," Bobby said, stepping back slightly.

"It does," Mark agreed with a grin. Dieter wasn't sure, but he liked it. "I'll put these aside to dry, and you two can pick up your work and one of the three we did together tomorrow. Did either of you eat dinner?" Dieter looked at Bobby, who looked at him and shrugged. "Okay. I'll get Tyler, and we'll meet at our place for dinner. Bobby, you call Kenny and see if he'd like to join us when he gets off duty." Mark looked down at himself and then at them. "I think we all need to clean up and change."

They all helped bring in the supplies before washing everything out in the industrial sink. Dieter cleaned himself up before changing clothes. "I'm going to go talk to Tyler," he told the other two before walking into the antique store and up the stairs. "Hey, Tyler," he called from the top of the stairs.

"Hi, Dieter," Tyler said as he set a lamp on a table. "How did it go?"

"Great," Dieter answered with a smile. "It was a lot of fun."

"Good." Tyler moved a table around a display before moving back to take a look at the display.

"I wanted to talk to you about the rest of the stuff in the attic," Dieter said, stepping closer. "I'm ready to clean out the rest of it. A lot of the stuff up there I liked, so I moved things around, but there's way more than I'm ever going to use."

"You're serious?"

"Yup. Come over anytime and take what you want. I trust you to give me a fair price," Dieter said, and they shook on it. "It's not doing anyone any good up there, and I have some of Gram's things I'm ready to see to. I need to make the house my own."

"Excellent. I'll let you know if I find anything really extraordinary and take care of the rest," Tyler told him with a grin. Over the past few years, Dieter had sold Tyler a few pieces in addition to the trunk they'd originally found, using the money to fix up the house. But Dieter had held off on anything else.

"Thanks, Tyler. I appreciate that."

"Are you two ready?" Mark called, his voice carrying up the stairs.

"Yes," Tyler answered, as they walked toward the stairs, descending to the main floor. They agreed to meet at Mark and Tyler's house. Bobby drove him back to his car, and Dieter drove home, singing along with the radio at the top of his lungs. He hadn't felt this good, this free, in a long time. Parking in the driveway, Dieter took his things in the house, putting them away before walking over to Mark and Tyler's with Bobby. Dieter rang the bell and instantly heard barking. Mark opened the door, and Jolie ran up to Dieter, rolling onto her back to get her belly scratched.

Dieter knelt down, scratching her belly until she rolled back over and raced back through the house. "Come on through. Dinner's almost ready," Tyler said before leading them through the entrance hall and into the kitchen. "Mark's out back grilling the steaks," Tyler explained before pulling the cork out of a bottle of Cabernet. "It shouldn't be much longer." Tyler poured and handed them both glasses. The back door opened, and Kenny walked in, giving Bobby a hug and kiss before picking up his own glass.

"How were things today?" Bobby asked his partner softly.

"Quiet, thank God." Kenny sighed before turning to Dieter and setting down his glass to exchange brief hugs. "Damn protestors who made big announcements about protesting a military funeral didn't actually show up. Not that I'm really complaining. No family who lost their son overseas should have to deal with those assholes, but we were on alert for trouble all day." Kenny took a gulp of his wine before sliding an arm around Bobby's waist, obviously happy to be with his lover.

"I heard about that," Dieter commented. "That group from Kansas is really screwed up."

"Yeah, they are," Kenny agreed. "Let's talk about something better. How's the house coming?" Kenny asked him.

"Really good. I spent last summer painting the outside, and last winter I got most of the inside rooms repainted and the carpets pulled up. The floors underneath were in great shape. All I needed to do was clean them and put down a coat of finish. Lately I've been doing some landscaping."

"I saw," Bobby said after lowering his glass. "It's looking really good." The back door opened, and Mark came inside carrying a tray of steaks, setting it on the counter. Tyler set a huge bowl of salad on the counter, as well as some fresh fruit, and everyone filled plates as conversation filled the room.

"By the way, Mark, I almost forgot," Dieter said once everyone was seated, cutting into the perfectly done steaks. "I met with the lawyer today, and he asked if he could meet with you. He had some questions he hopes you can answer." Dieter didn't know what good it was going to do, but he was determined to do whatever he could to try to get Gram's paintings back.

"Sure. When did he want to meet?"

"Will Saturday work?" Dieter asked.

"Sure, about four?"

"He gave me his number. Let me call him and ask." Dieter pushed back his chair and stepped away from the table so he wouldn't disturb everyone as he placed the call. "Gerald, it's Dieter. I'm with Mark, my artist friend, and he was wondering if four o'clock tomorrow was okay?"

"The sooner the better," Gerald answered. "I'm free most of the day," he offered.

"At Mark's studio?" Dieter asked, and Gerald agreed. Dieter told him where the studio was located before disconnecting the call. He'd wanted to ask how Gerald was doing and make small talk, but he didn't think that was appropriate. Putting his phone back in his pocket, Dieter rejoined his friends. "He'll meet us at the studio at four," Dieter told Mark.

"What's the attorney for?" Bobby asked, and Dieter explained about the paintings and that they were seeing what could be done.

"No way! *The Woman in Blue* is your great-grandmother? That's so cool!" Bobby exclaimed in excitement.

"I guess it is, but the uncool part is that the painting, along with some others, probably belongs to my family. The lawyer's looking into getting them back," Dieter explained.

"How's it going?" Mark asked, and Dieter explained what the lawyers had told him already. "I don't think they have much hope at this point, but Gerald is trying to be thorough," Dieter explained.

"So this attorney, is he gay?" Bobby asked.

Dieter chuckled, thinking of the night at the club. "Yes."

"Is he cute?" Bobby pressed, and he jumped when Kenny poked him in the ribs.

"I think he's good-looking," Dieter answered, feeling himself color a little the way he usually did, but with Sean's words fresh in his mind, he didn't look away this time. "I sort of ran into him at Dance All Night a few weeks ago."

"Is he interested in you?" Bobby asked him, and Dieter glanced around the table, noticing that everyone was watching him.

Dieter shrugged. "We danced at the club, and I think he's interested, yes."

"The important question is, are you interested in him?" Bobby asked, and Dieter shrugged, faking indifference, but his smile gave him away. "So you are interested," Bobby added, and Dieter nodded.

"It's so confusing."

"Not really," Tyler said gently. "Just follow your heart and try not to second-guess everything. You know, there is a really easy way to find out how he feels and what he wants," Tyler told him as he reached for the salad. "Ask him."

CHAPTER 4

GERALD left his house half an hour before he was to meet Dieter and his artist friend. He had looked Mark Burke up on the Internet and found out that he really was quite well known. It both surprised and pleased him. Not that Gerald held out much hope that this meeting was going to come to anything, but Dieter had seemed to need some sort of hope, and Gerald prided himself on being thorough. Although he knew this was more than just being thorough—he liked Dieter and found him interesting.

Carrying his briefcase, Gerald walked to his car. The drive wasn't long, and Gerald was soon parked in front of the antique store. Entering, he spoke to the man seated behind a desk, who directed him to the back of the building. Gerald walked around dozens of near breathtaking pieces of furniture, stopping at an antique desk. As he looked it over, he silently told himself he'd get one of these when he made partner.

"Gerald." He looked up when he heard his name and saw Dieter walking toward him. "Mark's studio is back this way," Dieter told him with a smile. God, he loved it when the man smiled. His face lit up and his eyes radiated warmth. Gerald followed Dieter, watching his butt sway in tight jeans. Dieter turned around to look at him, and Gerald averted his eyes, but he knew he'd been caught looking. Thankfully, Dieter said nothing. They walked through the back of the store, through a small seating area, and into what was definitely an artist's studio. Paintings with bold colors leaned against the walls. "Gerald, this is Mark Burke," Dieter said, to introduce them, and

Gerald automatically handed Mark one of his business cards after he'd shaken his hand.

"Dieter said you had questions about *The Woman in Blue*," Mark prompted.

"Yes. I've done some basic research, but I was hoping you could tell me more about what makes this painting important and some of what's behind the facts. You never know what small fact a case may hinge on, and if one exists here, I want to see if I can find it."

Mark pulled a couple stools from under the counter, and Gerald took one while Dieter sat on the other. "*The Woman in Blue* was a complete departure from Pirktl's previous work. Up till then, he was largely following an impressionistic mold, but something changed with this picture. It's often been speculated that he was in love with his subject, but there's no proof of that other than the painting. Her face is incredibly lifelike, and yet the rest of the painting seems to blend together, so much so that it's hard to see where her dress leaves off and the background begins. The only clue is in the style of brush strokes and patterns in the paint. The effect was completely new and quite startling. Everything in the painting seems designed to draw attention to the face, to focus the eyes there, and yet you can't help taking in the rest of the painting as well. Whenever I look at it, my eye refuses to settle—there's so much and yet nothing to see."

"Why is the painting so important?" Gerald asked as he continued taking notes on the pad he'd pulled out of his bag.

"Art scholars will always come up with reasons why one painting versus another is important. But I tend to believe that's a bunch of BS. In my opinion, a painting becomes important because it moves regular people. Some works of art are important because of their age, some because of technique and because they break new ground. I think this painting is important because it speaks to people and captures their attention, just like the *Mona Lisa* does. This painting is also important because the Austrian people have adopted the image as part of their identity. It was painted by an Austrian, hangs in an Austrian museum, and is widely regarded as one of the most important works of the early twentieth century." Mark slipped off his stool and walked to the cabinet. Opening one of the doors, he pulled out a long tube of paper. Gerald watched as Mark tacked the top corners to a corkboard before unrolling it and placing tacks near the bottom.

Gerald stared at the image, and he could see what Mark was talking about even from the poster. The image was amazing and so detailed. Standing up, he stared into the woman's beautiful face. Out of the corner of his eye, Gerald saw Dieter step forward, moving slowly, and it hit Gerald all at once. This wasn't a painting for Dieter, some abstract image of beauty—this was his great-grandmother, a relative. In essence, this was a family portrait, and Gerald turned his eyes away, because looking at this with Dieter seemed almost intrusive. Gerald swallowed and on reflex placed his hand on Dieter's shoulder. "We have to figure a way to get her back," Gerald mumbled under his breath.

"It's been widely known in artistic circles that the painting has a bit of a checkered past with its association with the Nazis. But many paintings in museums today do. The Metropolitan in New York recently returned paintings that had been in their collection for decades to the rightful owners once it had been proven they were looted art."

"But those were in a US museum, and the museum returned the works on their own because it was the right thing to do. I don't see the Austrian government doing that," Gerald said softly, his hand still resting on Dieter's shoulder.

"Neither can I," Mark agreed, both of them watching Dieter stare at the portrait. "You can take that if you like," Mark added, and Dieter nodded before looking toward Gerald and then at Mark.

"Thank you," Dieter said softly, and Gerald let his hand fall away before taking down the poster for him and starting to roll it back up.

"What is it? Why'd you stop?" Dieter asked, and Gerald looked up from where he'd been staring in near disbelief at the bottom of the poster. "Is something wrong?"

"No," Gerald said and began to roll the poster out on the table. "Have you got a magnifying glass?"

"Tyler does out front. I'll get it." Mark walked away as Gerald continued studying the poster, a smile forming on his face.

"I'll explain in a minute, Dieter," Gerald promised. "I just need to be sure of something." Gerald could feel himself vibrating as Mark returned. Using the magnifying glass to enlarge the small print at the bottom of the poster, Gerald let out a whoop. "Yes! I think this is it."

"What's it?" Dieter asked, leaning over the poster to take a look. Gerald handed him the glass and let him see what he was looking at. "I don't get it," Dieter told him, setting down the magnifying glass.

"It says at the bottom that the image is copyrighted by the Belvedere Museum and reproduced with their permission," Gerald explained. "What it means is that the Belvedere made money on this poster, and since the Belvedere is owned by the Austrian government, they in essence made money on the sale of this poster."

Dieter looked at him like he'd grown two heads. "I don't get it."

"What it means for us is that the Austrian government made money on *The Woman in Blue* in the United States. Since they made money here, we can try to sue them here. This may just give us the edge we need. I don't want to get your hopes up too high. This is going to be an uphill challenge, but this could work." Gerald felt a surge of adrenaline and excitement as he saw the surprised look on Dieter's face, followed by a smile, and then the man began to twirl and dance around the room like he had that night at the club.

"I take it you're excited," Mark said to Dieter, and Gerald watched as he bounced toward him, grabbing onto Gerald's hand, swinging him around the studio to the beat of music that it appeared only Dieter could hear. Dieter didn't answer, he just moved more and more. Gerald could feel the energy in the room rising, and without thinking he grabbed Dieter, pulling him toward him, hugging him for a few seconds before Dieter bounded away again.

"This doesn't mean we're going to win," Gerald tried to caution him, but Dieter was hearing none of it, and Gerald gave up, letting

Dieter's excitement take over. Soon, both of them were laughing, and Gerald had forgotten all about Mark as Dieter's energy surged through the room, making the air almost crackle.

Eventually, Dieter began to wind down, and both of them collapsed onto the stools, with Mark watching them, shaking his head slightly like they were both crazy. "So what do we do next?"

"We need to build a case, and that takes a lot of research and time," Gerald said, his mind already racing with ideas.

"Is there anything I can do?" Dieter asked earnestly, and Gerald smiled as he tried to think what Dieter could do.

"I'm not sure yet. But I know I'll need your help."

"Oh." Some of Dieter's excitement faded.

"It's not that I don't want your help, but I need to start with really boring legal research. However, I think we need to figure some things out. I was wondering if you'd like to come over. I could make some dinner, and we could talk things over. There are things you need to know before we move forward with this," Gerald explained.

Dieter stared holes through him for a split second before nodding his head slowly. "Okay." For a second, Gerald wondered what was going through Dieter's mind, but then he smiled. "Thank you, Mark, for everything." Dieter pulled Mark into a tight hug, and Gerald felt a tug of jealously that Mark got to hug him so freely.

"You're welcome, Dieter. Call us tomorrow. I know Tyler's going to get up in your attic and go through everything."

"I'll call," Dieter replied as Mark released Dieter from the hug. "I'll stop and talk to Tyler on my way out." Dieter stepped away, and Gerald shook hands with Mark, saying good-bye. Dieter picked up the rolled poster, and after thanking Mark once again, he led them back through the store.

At the front, Dieter introduced him to Mark's partner, Tyler, before kneeling down to pet a small dog that climbed out of her bed to say hello. Gerald extended his hand to her. "That's Jolie. She's really sweet," Dieter told him as he lightly stroked down her back. Dieter and Tyler talked for a few minutes, and Gerald tried not to eavesdrop, but he heard that Dieter was selling things to raise money, and it concerned him.

Dieter and Tyler finished talking, and Gerald stood back up, watching as Jolie ambled back to her bed. "Do you want me to follow you?" Dieter asked once they were on the sidewalk.

"That'd be great," Gerald responded, giving Dieter his address before walking to his car.

"I'll be right behind you," Dieter told him, and Gerald went to his car, taking his time before backing out slowly, seeing Dieter waiting for him. Gerald drove carefully, not wanting to lose Dieter. Yes, they had a lot to discuss, but this was totally new for him. Dieter was a client, and Gerald had never brought a client home before for any reason, but he was also very attracted to Dieter and very much wanted to get to know him. Constantly checking his rearview mirror, Gerald made sure Dieter was still following as they approached his neighborhood. Parking in front of his house, Gerald waited for Dieter before approaching the house and unlocking the door.

In his living room, Gerald turned on lights and opened the windows to let in the evening air. "Please make yourself comfortable. I'll start dinner and we can talk."

"Can I help?" Dieter asked as he looked around the room.

"Sure," Gerald answered with a smile. "The kitchen's this way." As they walked through the house, Gerald saw Dieter looking at everything as he passed.

"I love your house," Dieter told him, and Gerald saw Dieter run his hands over the woodwork. "It's so warm feeling."

"Thanks. I bought it a few years ago and put as much time as I could into fixing it up. I have to do the kitchen yet, so understand that it's still a work in progress. You can help with the salad if you like," Gerald said as he opened the refrigerator, pulling out raw vegetables of every description. "I like everything, so just put in what you like." Dieter moved the vegetables to the small counter area, and Gerald placed a bowl next to where he was working before handing Dieter a cutting board.

"Why are you doing this?" Dieter asked as he began tearing lettuce.

"Doing what?" Gerald asked as he pulled out some chicken breasts he'd been marinating. Gerald had originally expected them to last for two meals, but he was more than willing to share for some pleasant companionship. "Having dinner?" Gerald's mother had always said he had a smart mouth, and it chose now to come forward.

"You know what I mean. Why are you helping me like this? You met with Mark on a Saturday and you haven't charged me anything for your time, which must be very valuable," Dieter commented, and Gerald heard the sound of the knife on the cutting board as vegetables were chopped. When Gerald didn't answer right away, he heard the sounds dwindle and stop, feeling Dieter staring a hole in his back.

Gerald turned around, staring back at Dieter. "I'm working on your case because it's extremely exciting. Harold asked me to take it as a favor, and because no one else in the office wanted it. They thought there probably wasn't much merit. Instead, it's turning out to be one of the most compelling and interesting legal cases I've come across." Gerald set the chicken on the counter. "Nothing like this has been done before, and regardless of whether we actually win or not, this case will set precedent that other cases will rely on. I've been with the law firm for two years, and I've spent most of that time on insignificant cases that are relatively easy. I also get the jobs like drawing up wills and standard contracts. While those are valuable, they aren't very exciting. But this case could make my career," Gerald explained as excitement coursed through his body. "How many young lawyers get handed a case by accident that has the potential to make their career? Not too many." Gerald placed the chicken in a pan and set it in the oven.

Dieter's eyes hardened before he turned back to the vegetables, and Gerald lost sight of what Dieter was feeling. "Then I'm just a case to you?"

Gerald opened his mouth to respond before snapping it closed as the full implications of the question sank into Gerald's brain. Dieter was upset because he thought Gerald was here just because of the case. Dieter felt something for him. Part of Gerald wanted to do the dance of joy right there in his kitchen. "No, if you were just a case, then I would have met Mark during the week and in a more formal atmosphere. Also, if you were just a case, you wouldn't be here right now, because I never bring clients home." Gerald stepped closer and saw Dieter slowly turn toward him. "I like you, Dieter."

"Why? I get the guys at the club, because they just want to get in my pants, and I guess I can understand that. But I don't understand you." The confused look on Dieter's face puzzled Gerald.

"Have you ever had a boyfriend before?"

"Not really. Not a real boyfriend. One of the guys at the club said he wanted to be my boyfriend once, and we went out for coffee, but he really just wanted to get me back to his place. So I don't think that counts. The closest thing to a date that I've had since I was in high school was our dinner a few weeks ago."

"Why?" Gerald asked, and Dieter shrugged his shoulders before turning back to the vegetables again. Gerald stepped closer, placing his hands on Dieter's shoulders, feeling the heat and tension radiate through Dieter's shirt. "You have nothing to be afraid of or ashamed of." Dieter nodded slowly, and Gerald felt him turn slightly, their eyes meeting. "Nothing is going to happen unless we both want it to."

"That's what the man at the club said when he asked me on a date," Dieter said quietly.

"Did the man at the club do this?" Gerald turned Dieter gently, looking into his eyes as he leaned forward, touching their lips together in a tentative kiss that was just deep enough for Gerald to get the slightest taste of Dieter's mouth. He didn't linger too long, even though what he really wanted was to kiss Dieter until his knees buckled.

Dieter blinked at him a few times, and Gerald wasn't sure if the reaction was good or not. That is, until Dieter's fingers touched his lips and then he smiled. "No."

Gerald stepped back. "Okay, I'm sorry."

"Not that," Dieter said with a near giggle, "I meant, no, the man at the club didn't do that."

"You little shit," Gerald said, chuckling as he put some vegetables in the microwave.

"So, if you like me, does that mean you want to date or something?" Dieter asked, and Gerald nodded. "Won't that be some kind of conflict of interest or something?"

"No. As long as I'm up front about it and don't try to hide or lie." Gerald had checked on the firm's policy, and it was surprisingly quiet. He made a note to talk to Harold about it once he got the chance. "And I won't. Coming out was hard enough. I won't ask someone to hide or lie about a relationship." Gerald's tone sounded a little firmer than he intended, but Dieter either didn't notice or seemed to take it with the conviction Gerald felt.

"So, what do we do next as far as the case is concerned?" Dieter changed the subject, and Gerald didn't press him.

"I need to see if I can find anything I can use as a precedent. It would also help to know what records the Belvedere has on the paintings. Maybe I can check to see what kind of records-access laws they have. It would be nice to know the case they're going to try to make."

Dieter finished making the salad, placing it on the small table near the windows, a pensive look on his face.

"What is it?"

"Gerald, how am I going to afford this? A case like this is going to be very expensive. Your time isn't cheap, and I don't expect you or anyone to do this for free. I don't have a lot of money. I have the house that Gram left me, and I still have some money from my parents as well as some of Gram's. But a lot of what I had went into fixing up the house. I don't have the tens of thousands of dollars that a case like this could cost." Dieter leaned against the table, looking a bit stricken. "So I'm not really sure that all your work up to now can come to anything."

"Do you know where Harold Prince started his career as a lawyer?" Gerald asked, and Dieter shook his head. "Legal Aid. He worked there for two years. When I asked him why he did that, he told me it was because the law should be about justice, and generally the people who come to Legal Aid were people who deserved justice more than anyone else. Yes, he runs a very successful law practice, but he also understands justice and what's right. I'll talk with him."

"I don't know what good that's going to do. This is going to be expensive." Dieter swallowed, looking very worried. "And what if we lose? I could spend all kinds of money and still not be any closer to getting back my family's legacy."

"You need to decide what you want to do. There is the possibility that we could lose. There's also the possibility that we could win. But we'll never win if we don't try. You're the last person in your family who could possibly try to get these works of art returned. So the decision is yours and yours alone. You don't need to make any decisions about how you'd like to proceed until I can get all the facts together. At that time, we'll go over them, and you can make your decision."

The microwave dinged and Gerald took out the vegetables, lightly salting them before adding butter and placing them on the table. The oven timer went off as well, and Gerald took out the chicken, placing a portion on each of their plates. "Would you like a beer?" Gerald asked.

"Please," Dieter answered as he sat down, and Gerald placed the plates and drinks on the table, along with some forks and knives. "Smells good," Dieter commented, and Gerald passed the vegetables and salad to his guest first before taking a helping for himself. "Do you really think we have a chance to get the paintings back?"

"I don't know. If we have a good case, the Austrians may try to offer you money as part of a settlement, but first we have to do our research, build an airtight case, and then file suit and drop as big a legal bomb on them as we can. That means we need to keep this as secret as we can."

Dieter looked at him mirthfully. "I'll be sure to check my attic for Austrian spies."

"Don't laugh," he said, although Gerald couldn't help himself. "Loose lips sink ships. And once we've filed the suit, it could take months, or years, before the case actually comes to court."

"I know, but it's the only way I'm ever going to get back the portrait of my great-grandmother," Dieter responded as he took a small bite of the chicken. "This is really good," he added once he'd swallowed.

"You sound surprised."

"I guess I figured a busy attorney like you wouldn't have time to cook." Gerald saw Dieter snicker at him.

"My mom taught me how to cook. She made all of us learn because she wanted us to be able to eat at home every once in a while. In college I always had people who wanted to room with me because I could cook. I don't do it much because of time, but I enjoy it," Gerald explained. "Do you cook?"

"A little. Gram was pretty old-fashioned, so I didn't get much time in the kitchen. I took a cooking class in school, though. Gram tried to stop me until she realized it was a class they'd geared to boys. Otherwise she never would have allowed me to take it."

"Your Gram had a huge influence on your life, didn't she?" Gerald asked between eating and watching Dieter eat, or more accurately, watching Dieter's lips. Damn, he wanted another taste— the kiss earlier had only whetted his appetite for more.

"Yes. She, along with Auntie Kate, were the only parents I had, and she was a very powerful personality. Although I'm starting to realize that I've let her influence areas of my life that I probably shouldn't."

That sounded interesting to Gerald. "How so?"

"I keep wondering what Gram would think whenever I do anything. I know I should live my own life, but it's hard when you've had her preaching to you your entire life. I haven't dated or been with anyone. I haven't even explored being gay other than to go dancing.

Like I said earlier, the closest thing I've had to a date was our dinner the other week."

"Well," Gerald said with a grin, "then let's consider this a second date. You even got a kiss, and if you're good, you'll get another one."

"What if I'm bad?" Dieter asked with a wink. Jesus, Dieter was flirting with him and doing a dang good job of it too.

"Then you'll get two," Gerald flirted back, watching Dieter's cheeks redden. God, he loved it when Dieter got flustered. He was totally adorable. Innocence had never been a particular turn-on for him before. He'd always gravitated toward partners who knew what they were doing, but Dieter's blush and smile had him nearly painfully hard at the dinner table.

They laughed and flirted lightly as they finished eating. Gerald cleared the dishes, placing them in the sink before ushering his guest into the living room. "Would you like to watch a movie or something?"

"Sure," Dieter answered before sitting on the sofa. Gerald put in a DVD and sat next to him. He felt like a kid in high school and actually thought of extending his arm on the back of the sofa, but said to hell with it and moved closer, pulling Dieter into a loose hug. At first Gerald felt him tense, but then Dieter relaxed against him, and they watched half the movie without moving, simply being together.

"Would you like a snack or another beer?" Gerald asked.

"A snack would be nice, but I shouldn't drink any more. I have to drive home."

Gerald wanted to tell him he could stay, but that probably wasn't a good idea. He needed to take things slow, so he paused the movie and made some popcorn, returning with a huge bowlful and a couple sodas. Taking his seat once again, Gerald restarted the movie, and they munched for a while. Once the popcorn had been reduced to kernels, Gerald sat back, and they watched the rest of the movie with Dieter curled next to him.

The movie ended and Gerald turned off the player and the television, but neither of them moved. Not that Gerald had any intention of moving—as long as Dieter would let Gerald hold him, he would. "You're worried about something," Gerald commented quietly. "I can feel it in how tight your muscles are."

"I'm worried, Gerald. I'm worried that I'm on a fool's errand. I could spend everything I have and not be able to get my family's legacy back. I don't have a lot, and what I do have came from Gram's estate."

"I heard you talking to Tyler about selling some things. I don't want you to do that. Not for the sake of the case. I'll work something out with Harold." What, he wasn't sure. But there had to be some options other than Dieter selling the things he got from his grandmother.

"Gramps was a bit of a collector. I never knew him, but Gram said he used to go to all kinds of sales for years. She said he dragged home some of the most God-awful stuff she'd ever seen." Dieter turned his head so their eyes met, and Gerald saw Dieter smile a happy, contented smile he hadn't seen before. "Gram must have had him put the stuff she didn't want in the attic, because I found it loaded with stuff after she died. Gram never let me go up there when I was a kid and always kept the door locked. After she died, I found the key and went up there. The place was full to the gills. Tyler's been over a few times and found some interesting things that he's bought, and I've used the money to fix up the house, but I was still in school when Gram died, and I've spent most of my spare time the last few years working on the house and deciding what I wanted to do. Now I think I've gotten out what I want to keep, so I want Tyler to take anything that he thinks he can sell, and I'm going to either donate or yard sale the rest."

"I'm glad you're not selling your things to finance the lawsuit." Gerald squeezed Dieter a little closer.

"I'll admit it wouldn't be a bad thing to find a dragonfly Tiffany lamp up there, but I'm expecting there will be some things of interest and the rest is probably junk. But who knows? Just to clarify, I'm not selling off the important things from Gram and Gramps because of the lawsuit, although I'm not really sure where the money is going to come from. I have the house, which Gram left me free and clear. I could mortgage it, but Gram would roll over in her grave." Dieter became quiet and settled next to him.

After watching the younger man for a few minutes, Gerald lightly kissed his forehead, feeling exceedingly protective. Dieter lifted his face, and Gerald moved closer, giving Dieter time to move away before kissing him softly, just a light caress of their lips that made Gerald's heart race. Deepening the kiss slightly, he felt Dieter's lips move against his, and to his surprise, Gerald felt Dieter's tongue slide along their lips. Tugging him tighter, Gerald cupped the back of Dieter's head in his hand, the last of his control slipping away as Gerald feasted on Dieter's mouth. He thought he might have gone too far when he felt Dieter stiffen against him, but a small moan reached his ears and then he felt Dieter's arms around his neck. It took him a second to realize that he was being kissed back with just as much intensity and earnestness as he'd ever felt from anyone.

Dieter tasted like the spices from dinner and the saltiness from the popcorn, and then those flavors faded and the sweet tanginess that their first kiss had hinted at burst through, driving the kiss deeper. Pulling away so he could gasp for breath, Gerald shifted his weight, and Dieter fell back on the cushions as Gerald kissed him again. He'd wanted this every single time he'd seen Dieter. Hell, he wanted so much more. Images of Dieter dancing in the club flashed behind his closed eyes, and Gerald moaned softly as his hands slid along Dieter's body.

Gentling the kiss, Gerald let his lips pull away from Dieter's as he looked into his unfocused eyes. Breathing heavily, his heart pounding, Gerald's body throbbed with desire, especially when Dieter moved beneath him and Gerald felt Dieter's hardness against his hip. "You are so beautiful," Gerald murmured as he stared into Dieter's eyes, watching as they began to focus and then seeing Dieter blush before he tried to shift away. "You have nothing to be ashamed of," Gerald soothed. "I like that I can make you excited."

Dieter swallowed, blinking in surprise. "But...."

"No. It's amazing, wonderful, and absolutely nothing to be embarrassed about," Gerald said reassuringly before lifting himself off Dieter and righting himself and then helping Dieter back to a seated position.

"It's just so hard to get my mind around. I've wondered what it would be like to be held and kissed, but that was just dreaming," Dieter said very softly, and Gerald moved closer to kiss him again.

"You aren't dreaming now, are you?" Gerald asked, and Dieter smiled shaking his head.

"I should be getting home, though," Dieter explained before standing up. "It's getting late, and… and I want to do things I shouldn't."

Gerald felt his heart jump slightly. Dieter was truly attracted to him. He'd felt his body's reaction when they were kissing, and now he'd told him in a roundabout way. The idea seemed heady and thrilling. "I'd like to know if you have plans for next Saturday evening."

"No. Not that I can think of," Dieter replied tentatively.

"Then I'd like to take you out on a proper date. Can I pick you up at your house at six?" Gerald asked rather formally, but if Dieter hadn't dated much, then he wanted to make this special, he needed to make this special. He wanted Dieter to remember the time they spent together.

"All right," Dieter answered with a grin. "What are we going to do?"

"That's part of the surprise." Gerald returned the smile, catching some of Dieter's excitement and energy. Walking his guest to the door, Gerald hugged and kissed Dieter good night before watching as Dieter walked to his car. He saw him look back, and Gerald waved as Dieter started his car and drove away. Shutting the door once Dieter was gone, Gerald straightened up the living room, carrying the dishes to the kitchen, where he did the dishes and made sure the house was clean and put to rights before cleaning up and getting ready for bed. *What a day*, Gerald thought as he opened the bedroom windows to let in the cool breeze off the lake. He'd found an angle in Dieter's case that could possibly make his career, but even better than that, Dieter liked him, really liked him—that was the best thing of all. Now he just had to figure out how he was going to make it all work.

THE rest of Gerald's weekend had been very low-key. He'd worked a bit, getting his ideas together for Dieter's case as well as reviewing the rest of his cases before his Monday-morning meetings. He'd called Dieter on Sunday afternoon just to talk to him and tell him he'd had a wonderful time with him. He knew he probably shouldn't have called right away, but he wanted Dieter to know he was thinking of him. Sunday he'd gone to bed early, and on Monday morning, he got up early, almost beating everyone else into the office. The ideas were racing, and he wanted to get them down on paper. A small alarm next to his computer dinged, and Gerald wrapped up what he was doing so he could get ready for the morning case briefing with the partners.

In the meeting room, Gerald took his usual seat, sitting as still and normally as he could. Harold entered and started the meeting. Gerald listened to the other attorneys talking about their cases. When it came time for the junior associates, the other two were called on first, and they gave their updates. When it was Gerald's turn, he gave an update on his other cases. "Are there any developments in the Krumpf case?" Harold prompted.

"Actually, there are. I've been able to establish standing as well as verify through multiple sources that *The Woman in Blue* is Mr. Krumpf's great-grandmother."

"But aren't the paintings in question in Austria?" Linda Thomas, one of the partners, asked him. "I don't know why we're pursuing this when it's obvious that the painting is in Austria and the bond required to file suit in Austria is way beyond the client's means." Harold nodded at her assessment and turned his attention to Gerald.

"We're not planning to file suit in Austria. We're going to sue in the United States," Gerald said, but before he could explain, Linda jumped on him again.

"What grounds? Wishful thinking?" It sounded really bitchy, but Gerald kept his cool, knowing she was doing her job for the firm. It wasn't personal.

"The Belvedere Museum is owned and operated by the Austrian government. So in order to bring suit, we need to sue the Austrian government, and we can do that in the United States because of this." Gerald pulled out the copy of the poster he'd purchased on Sunday at the Milwaukee Art Museum store and unrolled it onto the table. "The Belvedere, and by extension, the Austrian government, made money selling this poster of the painting in question here in the United States. Since they made money here, we can sue them here."

"But you can only sue up to the amount they made in the United States," Linda said, her voice a little less sure than it had been.

"Actually, no. In this case, since they made money directly off the property in question, then we can sue for the property itself. There are other works of art involved, but *The Woman in Blue* is the primary property involved. Furthermore"—Gerald was just getting started, and everyone in the room was totally enthralled—"the US government has shown a willingness to enforce these judgments. Four years ago, the US Customs Service impounded four paintings that were part of an exhibition in New York so they couldn't leave the country when the true owners brought suit claiming the works were looted Nazi art and belonged to them. I understand this could be precedent-setting, but it's also justice. These paintings were looted from our client's family not once, but twice: first by the Nazis and then by the Austrian government." Gerald stopped, figuring he'd said enough, and the other attorneys looked a little shocked.

"Is there anything else?" Harold asked, looking around the room. "If not, we're adjourned. Gerald, I'd like to speak to you in my office." Harold got up and walked out of the conference room. Gerald followed the others out of the conference room.

After Brian went on his way to Harold's office, one of the partners put his hand on Gerald's shoulder. "You did great. That's an amazing legal strategy, and it might just work."

"Thanks," Gerald said, smiling as he continued toward Harold's office, knocking lightly before entering.

"Sit down and close the door," Harold told him, and Gerald wondered what he'd done wrong. "That was an interesting presentation in the meeting and very effective. The question is, can you pull that off in federal court, because that's what you'll need to do."

"Yes," Gerald answered with confidence and excitement. "This case could be precedent-setting."

"Yes, and it could give our firm a national reputation. The thing is that I think this case needs to be handled by one of the partners now," Harold said, and Gerald felt as though all the wind had been let out of his sails.

"I thought you'd be pleased, and instead you're taking this case away from me." Gerald battled to hold his emotions in check. Every fiber in his being wanted to lash out, but he managed to keep his cool. "Besides, there may not be a case. Dieter isn't sure he can afford to go forward with this. He knows it's going to be expensive, and he doesn't have that kind of money. He most certainly doesn't have the money to be able to afford one of the partner's hourly rates. I was going to speak to you about that this morning. There is a huge potential payoff in publicity alone if we can win this case. The paintings are worth tens of millions, possibly hundreds of millions, and are sure to be newsworthy. Even if we lose, people will be flooding us with business. And if we win, while I doubt Dieter would be willing to actually sell the paintings, there are many possibilities that could be explored where they would generate income to pay our fees."

Harold leaned back in his chair. "What are you proposing?"

"Can I speak freely?"

Harold smiled at him. "You'd better."

Gerald swallowed and thought carefully before speaking. "I like Dieter, a lot. He's someone I could possibly care for a great deal."

Gerald met Harold's eyes to make sure he understood what Gerald was saying. "And I think he likes me."

"So you're saying the client is probably going to want you to handle the case," Harold clarified.

"Yes. But if I thought I couldn't handle this, I would step back because that would be right for Dieter. I told him I was going to be talking to you because of the money issue to see what your ideas were. But I know I'm the attorney to handle this case. It's going to take someone who can think differently, and I've demonstrated already that I can do that." He wanted this case for so many reasons he could taste it, but mostly he wanted it for Dieter. Yes, if he won, it would make his career, but winning in this case was getting Dieter's family legacy returned to him.

Harold sat back without moving or talking, and Gerald nearly held his breath. He probably could have pushed to let Dieter decide, but that would have alienated Harold. Yes, he was taking a gamble, but he also knew how to read people. He just hoped he was right this time.

CHAPTER 5

DIETER looked at himself in the mirror, checking to make sure he looked okay, keeping the butterflies in his stomach at bay. Harold Prince himself had called yesterday to invite him to dinner at his home. He'd said he had some things he wanted to discuss with him and he thought dinner would be a better venue than the office. Dieter wondered what it could be and had thought of calling Gerald, but wasn't sure if that was proper since Mr. Prince had called him directly. Mr. Prince had specified that the dress was casual, but somehow Dieter figured that didn't mean jeans, so he was taking the time to make sure he looked properly casual, but not too casual. Giving up, he made sure his hair wasn't too unruly before heading downstairs. Carefully picking up the flowers he'd gotten to bring along, Dieter left the house, locking the door behind him.

The drive to the northern suburbs took a little time since Dieter stayed off the freeway, taking city streets out of Milwaukee and into Shorewood. Following the directions he'd been given, he pulled into the driveway, checking the numbers on the house before getting out of the car. The house was very nearly what he'd been expecting, imposing stone exterior, maybe not as large as he would have thought, but classic and elegant.

Mr. Prince opened the door to Dieter's knock. "Come in," he said warmly, ushering Dieter inside and closing the door as a stunningly elegant woman entered the hall. "Dieter, I'd like you to meet my wife, Christine."

"It's a pleasure to meet you," Dieter said rather formally as he handed her the flowers.

"Thank you," she replied with a smile, sniffing the colorful blooms. "I'll put these in water. Harold, we're in the summer room this evening."

Mr. Prince led him through the house, past beautifully decorated rooms that looked as though they were rarely used. "Would you like anything to drink?" Mr. Prince asked as they arrived in an outdoor-type room with stone floors, floral-print furniture, and large plants and greenery. It felt like an extension of the garden, though indoors, the breeze through the open windows cooling the room perfectly.

"Iced tea would be very nice. Thank you, Mr. Prince," Dieter answered as he took the seat he was offered.

"Please call me Harold," he said as he handed Dieter a tall glass with ice clinking. Dieter heard the Westminster chime doorbell and then heard footsteps. Realizing there were to be other guests, he stood up, waiting. Gerald entered the room, shaking hands with Harold before smiling at Dieter, shaking his hand as well. Dieter smiled and some of the butterflies he'd been feeling floated away.

"Are you going to talk business for a while?" Christine asked from the doorway. "Dinner will be ready in an hour, so get the business out of the way," she added with a smile before disappearing into the house, leaving the three of them alone. Dieter sat back down on a comfortable wicker sofa, and after Harold got drinks for Gerald and himself, Gerald joined him with a quick look and a smile while Harold sat across from them in a matching chair.

Harold sipped from his martini before beginning. "Part of the reason I asked both of you here tonight is to talk business. Dieter, your case has caused quite a stir in the office. Every attorney in the firm, including the partners, would like to be the attorney on your case."

"Gerald is my attorney," Dieter said softly as he looked at Gerald, wanting to touch him for his own reassurance, but he refrained. He didn't want anyone else. "Gerald understands what this case means to me and why I'm thinking of pursuing it. He also understands my limitations and why I may have to decide to let it go for now." Dieter took a sip of his tea to tamp down his nerves and give his hand something to do. "I trust him," he added once he'd swallowed. Harold sat quietly, and Dieter glanced at Gerald briefly, but he looked relaxed, so Dieter returned his gaze to Harold. "What's going on?" he asked both of them, wanting to move closer to Gerald.

"As I said, it seems your case has caused quite a stir, and I'll be honest with you, when I asked Gerald to look into it, I never realized it would be this complex or this potentially important. My first thought was to transition this case to a more senior attorney."

"As the client, don't I get to choose my attorney?" Dieter asked, and he saw Gerald smile slightly in his peripheral vision.

"Yes, you do," Harold answered, "but when you hire my firm, you hire our entire firm along with our combined expertise and reputation. As I said, at first I thought to transition this case to another attorney, but Gerald has convinced me that, with the proper support, he can handle this case as lead attorney, and he's promised me that if the case became too much or if he thought he couldn't do a better job than anyone else, he'd step back. I don't believe that will happen. It's obvious that Gerald has your best interests at heart," Harold said. "I need to caution both of you about some things. First, it's obvious that you have feelings for each other. I'd have known even if Gerald hadn't told me. I do have concerns about that, so all I'm going to say is that I trust all my attorneys to conduct themselves in a professional manner at all times." Harold seemed to be addressing his remarks to Gerald, who nodded solemnly. "I also have a concern that involves both of you. If this case progresses to court, and it might, I want to caution both of you. If I can pick up on the feelings you have for each other, so can any opposing attorney, and they'll use it against you and the case if given the chance. Do both of you understand that?"

Dieter nodded unconsciously. "I hadn't realized," he said softly.

"There's nothing to be ashamed of, son," Harold said. "It could be a problem if the opposition was able to use it. So be careful about what you let others see." Harold's expression changed to what Dieter had always imagined a father would look like. "We're attorneys, we like to win, and so does the other side, so we don't want to give them ammunition." Harold drained his glass, setting it on the table next to his chair. "Gerald and I have talked over the issue of our fee, and I believe we've come up with something that might work. Gerald, would you care to explain?"

Dieter shifted and saw Gerald smile at him. "Harold and I agreed that a positive outcome in this case is good for both you and the firm. So, he and the partners have agreed to take a bit of a chance. You will pay what you are able to for the hours incurred. Because of our relationship, you and Harold will work out the details. If we win or settle the case, then we are entitled to a percentage. Harold can explain that further when you discuss the fee agreement," Gerald told him, and Dieter could see him suppressing a smile. "Basically, it shares the risk and the reward."

"But you'll be my attorney?" Dieter asked for clarification.

"Yes," Gerald answered with a huge smile, "I'll be your attorney. We've developed a strategy and a plan to develop our case, and it looks like I'll be going to Vienna to do some research in the Belvedere archives."

"When are you leaving?" Dieter asked, disappointed that Gerald was going to be gone.

"We have to decide that," Harold answered.

"We're trying to find someone who can act as a research assistant who speaks German—no one in our office does—but the sooner the better." Gerald added. "The Austrians recently announced that they were opening the archives at a number of institutions to qualified researchers, and my graduate degree in international business qualifies me, so I don't have to let them know I'm a lawyer, but they could change their rules at any time."

"I speak and read German as well as Austrian German. There are slight differences. Gram taught me when I was a kid. I also took advanced classes in college and studied for a year in a special program from visiting German professors. I was originally going to be a German teacher, but the thought of being in a classroom with thirty high-school kids gave me hives, so I changed majors and discovered an aptitude for computers. I'm not a lawyer, but I'm sure I can read most documents we find." The thought of going to Vienna had Dieter excited. Maybe he could find the house Gram had grown up in. "How long would it take?"

"If the archives are catalogued, it could take a few days. If they're not, longer," Gerald explained.

Dieter scoffed. "Catalogued. They probably have them catalogued and cross-referenced eight ways from Sunday. They're Austrian, after all, and the Belvedere is an old museum that has kept records for decades. If you want me to go, I'll need to take time off from work, but at least it's a way I can contribute to the case."

"It is unusual, but not unheard of," Harold commented. "We'll call tomorrow to arrange a schedule and a time you can come in so we can review the financial details."

Christine stepped into the room, indicating that dinner was ready. "That's enough business talk, gentlemen. I want to remind you, Harold, that part of the reason you invited Dieter here this evening was so you could tell him about his father." She smiled brightly at Dieter as Harold got up, and together they led them to dinner.

The table was beautifully set, with the flowers Dieter had brought in a crystal vase in the middle of the table. Dieter sat where Harold indicated, with Gerald directly across from him. "Please help yourselves," Christine said, and Harold began passing dishes around the table.

"Your father and I were quite a pair," Harold began almost as soon as the serving dishes settled back on the table. "He and I went to a private high school, and we used to love to trick the newbies. Along one edge of the campus was a retaining wall, and in the fall, leaves always collected at the base of the wall. It was my job to befriend the new kid and show him around campus. Somehow," Harold said, chuckling knowingly, "we always ended up sitting on the edge of the wall talking with our feet dangling over the edge. Your father used to hide in the pile of leaves at the base of the wall, and at the prearranged signal, he'd reach up and grab the newbie's leg." Harold began to laugh and Dieter laughed along. "They'd nearly jump out of their skins, and after they got over it, they'd beg us to let them scare the next kid. Last I heard at an alumni board meeting, they were still doing it."

"Did you know my mother too?" Dieter asked after he swallowed. "I have few memories of either of them. Most of what I know came from Gram or Auntie Kate."

"Not very well, but I was at your parents' wedding. Your dad and I remained in touch almost until he died. You look a lot like him, but you seem very different. He was loud and boisterous, where you seem much quieter. I think you got that from your mother." Harold began to eat.

"Was my dad a good student?"

"Your father was the class clown. He was smart, but he also liked to be the center of attention. The things he did almost got us both expelled more than once. Like the time he put shaving cream on all the toilet seats in the faculty restrooms," Harold explained through chuckles that rippled through everyone else as the image hit home. "Or the time he decided to use a chemical fire extinguisher as propellant for a desk-chair rocket for our science-fair project. It took us two days to clean up the mess." Dieter began to laugh, pleased to know something more about his father.

"I met your father just once," Christine said with a smile. "He took my hand and bent forward. 'It's a pleasure for you to meet me,' he said before bringing my hand to his lips, turning it at the last minute to kiss his own hand."

"Do you know if my parents liked to dance?" Dieter asked once the smiles faded.

Harold looked puzzled for a few seconds. "I don't know about your mother, but your father had two left feet."

"Dieter's a wonderful dancer," Gerald explained with a slight wink.

"Harold used to take me dancing when we first met," Christine commented. "We haven't been in years. It's one of the reasons I love weddings, because we get to dance." Harold said nothing in response, but Dieter could almost see Harold's mind working, and Dieter had little doubt that Christine was going to be taken dancing soon.

The stories about Dieter's father continued through dinner and into dessert. Dieter took in all of them he could, committing them to memory as though they were precious jewels. By the time they were done eating, Dieter had formed a picture of the father he never really knew, one of a man who loved fun, was fiercely loyal, and a practical joker above all else. By the time they left the table and returned to the summer room, Dieter wished that he'd been able to meet his father, because he thought he'd probably have liked him. Relaxing in the cooler evening air, the four of them talked for a while after dinner.

At the end of the evening, Dieter said good-bye to his host and hostess, thanking them for a lovely evening, and waited for Gerald to do the same before they left the beautiful home together.

"Were you serious about helping with the research?" Gerald asked once they were outside.

"Sure, and I've done research in Germanic libraries. They use a different system than here in the US. I'm not sure what sort of system the museum uses exactly, but I think I can be of help, if not with the research itself, then the language, at least," Dieter explained as they walked to the cars. "Are we still on for Saturday?" he asked.

"Definitely," Gerald answered as he opened his car door. Dieter wanted to kiss him good night, but wasn't sure that was a good idea in front of Harold and Christine's house. After getting into his car, Dieter was about to start the engine when he heard a tapping on his window. He lowered the glass, and Gerald leaned into the car, giving him a kiss good night. "I wish it was Saturday already."

"Me too," Dieter answered, his body tingling from the energy in the kiss. Gerald moved away from the car, and Dieter pulled out of the driveway and onto the street, smiling the entire drive home.

DIETER had done his best to keep himself busy, but he'd been looking forward to Saturday all week and it was finally here. "Tyler, would you like something to drink?" Dieter asked as he pushed open the attic door, carrying a couple sodas.

"You're a godsend," Tyler told him as he took the cold drink Dieter offered and began gulping it almost before he'd opened the can. "I placed the things I'm interested in near the door, and here's a list of what I'm willing to pay for each item. I've still got half the attic left. Your Gramps had an amazing eye. I've found boxes full of Baccarat crystal and some amazing pieces of Roseville pottery." Tyler pulled another box from the row he was working on, setting it on the work table he'd brought with him, and began unpacking, letting out a whistle when he pulled out a vase painted with an angel. "Look at this. It's porcelain, hand-painted, probably nineteenth century, European, signed, and absolutely exquisite. This wouldn't have been looked at twice twenty years ago, but now I'd sell it for two thousand dollars and I'll have customers fighting over it." Tyler handed the vase to Dieter. "You don't want to sell this. Put it in your living room. You'll never see another one as long as you live."

Dieter took the vase out of the attic, placing it in his Gram's old room for the time being before returning to the attic, where Tyler had moved on to yet another box. Dieter started going through the things Tyler had set aside, making sure there wasn't anything he wanted. "We'll need to wrap this up in about an hour," Dieter explained as he peered down the list of items Tyler had made, his eyes widening at some of the values Tyler was going to pay him.

"That's fine. I'm about done for today. I set aside a few things I want you to pay special attention to before letting them go." Tyler motioned to a few boxes off by themselves. "What are you and Gerald doing this evening?"

"I don't know. He said it was a surprise," Dieter answered as he heard the phone ringing downstairs. Hurrying away, he answered the phone in the upstairs hall.

"Dieter, it's Gerald. I'm sorry to spring this on you, but...." Dieter felt his stomach sink. "I'd planned to take you out, but my mother called and the family has decided to get together for dinner, and my presence is strongly requested. I was wondering if you'd like to go with me. You don't have to, and I'll understand, but I'll be in hot water if I don't show." Gerald didn't sound particularly happy. "My dad's celebrating winning some big case, and all the little ones have to be there to prop up his fragile ego." Dieter chuckled at Gerald's mocking tone.

"Of course I'll go," Dieter answered, a little disappointed that he wouldn't be alone with Gerald, but he would get to meet his family. "Are you still going to be here at six?"

"A little earlier, if that's okay?" Gerald asked, and Dieter said that was fine before hanging up and returning to the attic.

Thankfully, Tyler was finishing up, and Dieter helped him carry down the things he was willing to buy. After making multiple trips down the stairs, Tyler had him make a final check of each item, and they agreed on the price, haggling a little over a few items. "Just drop a check by when you get the chance."

"I will, and if there are any items in the area I set aside for you that you would like to sell, let me know. Of course I'll give you a good price, but I think you'll be pleased you held onto them, especially the desk set."

"Thanks," Dieter said. He really had no idea what these things were worth, and he knew Tyler was being very fair. "I'll help you carry these to your truck, and then I need to get ready. Gerald is coming early, and I'm going to meet his family," Dieter said nervously, remembering that Gerald's family were all lawyers and doctors. He hoped he fit in.

"Don't be nervous," Tyler told him reassuringly. "You're going to be just fine, so have fun tonight and don't worry about it."

"I'll try," Dieter promised before helping Tyler carry out the boxes. After saying good-bye, he hurried inside to clean up and get ready for his date.

Jumping in the shower, Dieter thought of Gerald, wishing he were with him right now. With soapy hands rubbing over his skin, Dieter closed his eyes, wondering how Gerald's hands would feel on his skin. He'd longed to feel the touch of another man, to know if what he'd imagined could be made real. His hands became Gerald's hands, touching him, stroking his skin and stoking his desire. Why Gerald enthralled him so he couldn't say, but he did, and Dieter found himself thinking of little else when he was alone. Dieter's hand slid along his shaft, stroking, grip tightening just the way he liked it. In his mind, Gerald knew just perfect ways to touch, to tease. Dieter's other hand stroked down his back, palm caressing his butt, finger teasing at the tender, sensitive skin of his opening. Warm water sluiced over him as he imagined Gerald touching and stroking instead of his own hand. Stepping out of the water, Dieter opened his eyes, stopping what he was doing. The real Gerald was taking him to meet his family, and afterward Dieter intended to invite him home, hopefully to see if the real Gerald was better than his imagination. Concentrating on his washing, rather than other things, Dieter finished his shower a bit frustrated, but definitely eager for his date with Gerald.

After turning off the water, Dieter stepped out of the shower, still excited and more than a little nervous. Drying himself, Dieter walked to his room, dressing carefully. Gerald had said that the partygoers included his family, and Dieter wanted to make a nice impression, but he also wanted to be comfortable in the summer heat. Choosing a light pair of slacks, he stepped into them and pulled on a light blue shirt. Checking the clock, Dieter picked up his pace as he realized he was very nearly late.

Once he'd finished dressing, he made a quick pass through the house and his bedroom as he heard the doorbell ring. Smiling, he answered it, and was immediately greeted with an equally pleased smile as well as a kiss. "I'll be right back," Dieter said, retrieving a small box before leaving the house with Gerald. "What is your family like?" Dieter asked once he was seated in Gerald's passenger seat.

The driver's door closed and Gerald started the car, pulling away from the curb. "My oldest brother, Angus, thinks he's the family conscience and the harbinger of all that's right and proper. He can be downright sanctimonious and thinks he knows what's best for everyone. He can also be one of the most generous people I know, but it always comes with a price. My second brother, Henry, is quiet and thoughtful. Getting an opinion or anything out of him is like pulling teeth, but when he does offer an opinion or thought, it's usually incredibly insightful. My sister, Doreen, is a doctor of internal medicine and incredibly gifted, but takes after Angus and my father in that she knows everything." Gerald looked across the seat at him, swallowing hard. "I'm afraid I may be throwing you to the wolves, but I know they'll all like you, especially my youngest sister, Mary. She's the one I'm closest to, and she's the most talented of all of us."

"She's the concert pianist?" Dieter asked as Gerald entered the freeway and the car sped up, heading north toward the suburbs.

"Yes. She loves it and she's making quite a name for herself. There's also my father, Gene, and my mother, Elora. I know I talk about my family as though they're harsh, but they really aren't, just a bit driven. I guess that's the best way I could describe them. I know they're all going to love you," Gerald told him, and Dieter wanted to believe it.

They rode quietly for a while until Gerald exited the freeway and began weaving through suburban streets. Gerald made a final turn down a residential street, pulling into the driveway of a huge modern house that made Dieter gasp. Nothing looked right about it, all angles and sharp lines. "Is this your parents' home?" Dieter asked as he turned to Gerald.

"No. This is where Angus lives. My parents still have the house we grew up in, but it isn't big enough for my brothers and sisters, their wives, and children. In addition to knowing what's best for everyone, Angus has to be the center of attention," Gerald said, and Dieter heard him sigh as he opened the car door. Dieter got out of the car, still carrying the small box, and right away, two boys about eight years old ran up to the car.

"Uncle Gerry, look what we found," they chimed delightedly, each holding up a large frog before turning to Dieter. "Who's this?"

"Kyle and Peter, this is Dieter," Gerald said with an indulgent grin. "These two are Henry and Joanne's twin sons."

Dieter said hello, and both boys looked at him as though they were trying to figure something out. "Are you Uncle Gerald's boyfriend?" one of the boys asked, the other nodding as though he wanted to know as well.

Dieter looked to Gerald, not quite sure how he should answer, as both boys looked at him with muddy faces and big blue eyes, waiting for an answer. "Yes," Gerald answered, "Dieter is my boyfriend, and you two better get those frogs back where you found them and your faces washed before your mother or grandmother see you. You both know what your mother will say." Both boys nodded and raced toward the edge of the property, where Dieter could see tall grasses and what looked like a pond of some kind. "They're great kids," Gerald commented softly as they watched them for a few seconds before walking up toward the house.

As they approached, Dieter heard laughter and music drift around the gray wood-sided house, and he followed Gerald around the side to the backyard. "Gerald," an older woman said, rushing toward them. They hugged warmly, and Dieter stood out of the way, not wanting to intrude.

"Mom, this is Dieter," Gerald said, and Dieter stepped forward, shaking her hand before giving her the small box.

"Thank you," she said taking the box. "It's nice to meet you," she told him genuinely before peeking into the box, her eyes widening. "These look lovely, thank you. That's very thoughtful."

"It's a pleasure to meet you as well, Mrs. Young," Dieter responded, pleased that Gerald's mother liked the chocolates. He'd originally planned to give them to Gerald, but changed his mind when their plans changed.

"Please call me Elora," she replied warmly, and Dieter felt himself smile.

"Gerald, you finally made it," a deep voice said from behind them, devoid of mirth.

"Dieter, this is my father, Gene," Gerald said. They shook hands, but Dieter noticed that other than nodding to one another, there was no other greeting. Elora took her husband's arm, guiding him away as Gerald was nearly knocked off his feet by a small wisp of a woman.

"Gerry," she squealed as she hugged him. "Thank God, you're here. The know-it-alls are driving me crazy," she stage-whispered, looking at one of the umbrella-shaded tables before turning to Dieter.

"Dieter, this is my sister, Mary," Gerald said happily. Dieter found himself being hugged exuberantly, and he returned her embrace carefully. She was so slight, he was afraid he might hurt her.

"It's nice to meet you," Dieter said while he was still being hugged, looking at Gerald over her shoulder.

"Mary, he's my boyfriend, so you can't steal him away," he teased, and she giggled softly. "She tried once."

"I did not. I just thought Hank was cute, and I'd had a little too much to drink." She colored and the giggles got louder. "I know I shouldn't have sat on his lap," she added as the giggles died away. "So, how did you meet my brother?"

"We met at Dance All Night a few weeks ago. Dieter is an amazing dancer, and he caught my attention right away," Gerald answered for him, throwing a look that said, "I'll tell you later." Gerald touched his back lightly, and Dieter moved slightly closer, liking the way Gerald's hand felt. "I suppose we should take the plunge and introduce you to the rest of the family." Gerald guided him toward the table Mary had indicated earlier.

As they approached, the conversation dwindled off and heads turned in their direction. For a second Dieter shifted under their gazes, feeling uncomfortable. "This is Dieter," Gerald began.

"Yes, we heard, your boyfriend," a woman scoffed, and since she looked a bit like Gerald, Dieter assumed it was Doreen, the other sister.

"I didn't know they taught bigotry in medical school," Gerald retorted, "or did you simply major in closed-minded arrogance." Gerald's retort was fast and biting. Dieter nearly winced, but did his best to ignore the remark. Maybe this was a thing among Gerald's family. Dieter turned and saw Gerald glaring at his sister. "The welcome wagon is Doreen, and the man next to her is her husband Jules." He stood up, and Dieter shook hands with the darkly handsome, tall man. "This is my brother Henry and his wife, Joanne. We met their sons earlier." Again, Dieter shook hands and exchanged greetings. "The man at the grill is my brother Angus." Gerald waved, and Dieter saw the man half wave in return. "His wife is probably inside, and last, but not least, is Mary's fiancé, Reggie."

"It's nice to meet you, Dieter," Reggie said as he stood up and shook Dieter's hand. "There are drinks in the coolers over by the door," Reggie explained, walking over to show them. "Don't let Doreen bother you," he said as he opened the cooler lid. "She was catty to me when I first met her too. Now she's just an icy bitch," Reggie added, and Dieter had to stop himself from putting his hand over his mouth. As it was, he turned away so he could laugh quietly.

"That's my sister you're talking about," Gerald said seriously before breaking into a smile. "But it's accurate." They each got beers and sat at another table to talk.

"I'm surprised you brought Dieter," Mary said as she sat down next to Reggie. "It's either really brave or really stupid."

"I'm starting to think stupid," Gerald said, looking over at the other table. "What's gotten into her, anyway? She's bitchy even for her."

"She applied for the head of internal medicine at the hospital, and they gave the job to someone else," Mary said with a hint of amusement. "Like anyone would ever want to work there with her as a boss."

"Didn't you get along as kids?" Dieter asked before looking around. "I'm sorry, that's none of my business," he added quickly. He'd always been alone and had often wondered what it would be like to have had brothers and sisters. "It's just that I always wanted someone to play with when I was growing up."

"As long as they were like Gerry, it would have been great," Mary said, turning toward the other table. "Henry wasn't bad, just quiet, but the other two were always lording it over us somehow, and it's never really changed," Mary said, and Dieter saw her shoot daggers at her sister. Dieter looked at Gerald, confused and a little worried, as he wondered just what he'd gotten himself in the middle of. Gerald's family looked like they were a little nuts.

"So, little bro, you made it." Dieter turned, looking up at Gerald's brother Angus.

Gerald stood up, shaking his brother's hand, and Dieter stood as well. "This is Dieter," Gerald said, and they shook hands, but beyond that Angus seemed to look past him, and Dieter sat back down, wondering who ever taught these people manners. If he treated anyone like that, Dieter knew his Gram would rise out of her grave and snatch him bald, as Auntie Kate used to say.

"So, when are you going to quit that place you're working and join the family firm?" Angus asked coldly.

"I'm not. I like what I'm doing, and I've got some interesting cases."

"You do, huh?" Angus pulled out a chair. "We could really use you. We're getting so many clients right now that we could use another attorney. Granted, you'd be doing the junior work at first, but you'd be helping the rest of us."

Dieter seethed inside at Angus's condescending attitude toward his brother, and Dieter reached under the table, touching Gerald's leg lightly.

"I don't need your castoffs, Angus. I have my own cases and clients. I'm happy where I am, and I intend to make it on my own instead of riding Dad's coattails."

Dieter saw Mary snicker behind her hand before bursting into all-out laughter. "I guess he told you, Aggie," she said.

Dieter turned to Gerald and saw him glaring at his brother, who returned the stare, both of them looking like they were waiting the other one out. "That's enough, boys," Elora said as she approached the table. "Angus, go on back to the grill before the steaks burn," she instructed, and Angus turned without saying a word. "Do you have to antagonize your brother?" she asked, turning to Gerald.

"Mom, Aggie was doing the antagonizing," Mary explained. "Gerry just put him in his place." She stood up, and Dieter watched the two women walk back into the house, their rather heated conversation fading away.

"I'm sorry about all this," Gerald said. "My family expects me to fall into line and be what they want me to be, and I guess I feel like I have to fight them because I want to do things my own way."

"It's okay," Dieter reassured him as he watched the kids throwing a ball out in the yard. After finishing his beer, Dieter got up and began walking to where the twins were playing, watching as they ran, chased, and tumbled in the grass to the sound of giggles, yells, and laughter.

"Uncle Gerry, will you play too?" one of the boys called. Dieter wasn't sure which. Turning around, he saw Gerald jogging toward him.

"Would you like to play?" Gerald asked.

"Sure, I guess," Dieter replied, not sure what Gerald had in mind, but he found out soon enough when the ball was kicked over to him, and he began dribble-kicking it around the yard, passing the ball to one of the boys, who kicked it to Gerald. Soon, a sort of impromptu game of soccer sprang up among the four of them, with the ball going all over the place. By the time they were done, both Dieter and Gerald were covered in grass and dirt, both of them laughing as the boys had a ball.

"Dinner," someone called, and they all raced toward the deck, with Gerald and Dieter letting Kyle and Peter win, to whoops and high fives.

Gerald showed him where he could wash up, and after getting off the worst of the dirt, they returned to the patio, where the food had been set up, and after filling plates, they joined Mary and Elora at a table, while the rest of the adults talked at the other. Kyle and Peter brought their plates so they could sit next to their grandmother.

"It's always like this," Mary said to him when Dieter peered toward the other table. "They're talking business. They always do."

"Gerald said you were a pianist. That's sounds lovely. I wish I'd learned to play when I was growing up."

"She plays beautifully," Gerald explained, and Dieter saw Mary blush a little.

"You're totally biased," Mary countered.

"True," Gerald retorted, "but that doesn't make it any less true."

Dieter cut a small bite of his steak and began eating as the conversation continued. They asked what he did and where he lived and listened as Dieter explained all the things he'd done to fix up the house. "Gram left it to me, and I wanted to restore it as much as I could."

"Did you do the work yourself?" Elora asked between bites of potato salad.

"Most of it. There were things like electrical work that I couldn't do, but mostly I liked doing it. It let me do something creative with my hands."

Once dinner was over, the tables were cleared, and everyone sat and talked until the sun began to set. Everyone seemed to rise to leave at the same time. Dieter made sure to thank and say good night to everyone, shaking hands with the men and getting hugs from some of the ladies before following Gerald to his car.

"Can I ask you something?" Dieter inquired once they were moving, and Gerald nodded slowly. "Why did you tell them we met at Dance All Night instead of at your office?"

"I didn't want them to know you were a client," Gerald answered.

"Oh."

"It's not that I'm ashamed of you or that you're a client. It's just that I wanted them to meet you as my boyfriend and not as a client," Gerald explained. "I know it doesn't make much sense, but if I introduced you as a client, I guess I thought my family would treat you differently." Gerald sighed loudly. "I'm not explaining this very well, but for today, I wanted you to be my boyfriend and nothing more. I hope that's okay?"

"I like that you said I was your boyfriend. I just don't understand why you left out that I was a client too."

"Because sometimes things have to be kept separate. At the office, you're a client, but I hope that at other times, you're my boyfriend," Gerald said as he turned onto the freeway. "I know it's confusing, and I don't mean for it to be. It's just that there are things that I have to keep separate if you want me to be your lawyer. Besides, I didn't want your case talked about with my family. It's really none of their business."

Dieter nodded and sat quietly for a while. "I like your mother and sister. They were really nice, and your nephews were fun."

"They loved you, they really did," Gerald said, and Dieter saw him smile.

"Will you come back to my house with me? As my boyfriend?" Dieter said, still not fully understanding, and he became quiet as he mulled things over. "I guess I don't really understand," he said as they continued through town. "Should you not be my boyfriend and my lawyer?" He really didn't want Gerald to stop being either, but he also didn't want him doing anything wrong.

"We've both spoken to Harold, and as long as we behave properly, it's okay," Gerald said as the streetlights cast moving swaths of light as they rode beneath them. "I didn't mean to make you feel bad. I just wanted you to know why I didn't mention that you were a client, because what was important was that you're my boyfriend." Gerald parked the car in front of Dieter's house, and neither of them made a move to get out even after Gerald turned off the engine. "If I hurt you, I didn't mean to."

"You didn't. I was just curious," Dieter said with a hard swallow, looking toward the dark house. A gentle hand touched his cheek, and Dieter turned his head slowly to look at Gerald.

"Dieter, you're the first person I've ever brought home to meet my family. They're a tough crowd, and I've never cared enough about anyone to actually bring them to meet my family."

Dieter watched as Gerald's face moved closer.

"The important people really liked you, and that means a lot. As for this client/boyfriend thing, I'll tell you this, if there's a conflict, I'll turn your case over to another attorney before I'll let you go." Dieter heard Gerald swallow hard. "I want to do the absolute best I can for your case because I care for you, but you're so much more than a client."

Dieter felt Gerald's lips touch his, and the questions he had flowed away. All the stuff about boyfriend and client became instantly unimportant as Gerald kissed him. The seat made crunching sounds as Gerald shifted closer, and Dieter felt Gerald's hand cradle his head, the kiss deepening slightly and then gentling again before Gerald's lips slipped away. Dieter blinked a few times, wanting Gerald to do that again, but instead Gerald got out of the car, and Dieter opened his door as well.

Inside, Dieter turned on a few lights. "Would you like to see the house?" Dieter asked, and Gerald stepped closer, hands cupping Dieter's cheeks before kissing him gently.

"I'd love to," Gerald told him as he took Dieter's hand. "So this is the house you grew up in?" Gerald looked around. "It's really something. I always drove by the homes in this area of town and wondered what they looked like on the inside."

"Gram maintained it as best she could, but after she died, I realized I couldn't live here and have it look the same as it always did. It was too painful, and the house needed work. I stripped the walls of all of the old wallpaper and pulled up the carpets. Thankfully Gram liked the woodwork natural, so she didn't paint any of it."

"This is beautiful," Gerald said as he ran his hand along the smooth banister. "I bet you used to slide down this as a kid."

"Auntie Kate used to say it was butt polished," Dieter explained with a smile, remembering how Auntie Kate would scold him when she caught him sliding down the banister. Dieter knew it was only for show because Gram didn't like it at all. "Look at this," Dieter said, walking to the woodwork under the stairs, moving one of the panels to the side. "I doubt Gram ever knew this was here." Dieter turned the hidden knob and opened the door. "I played in this house for years and never knew about it. The door locks, but thankfully it wasn't when I found it because there's no sign of the key, but isn't this amazing? When the door is closed, there's no sign of it at all." Dieter stepped back and let Gerald peer into the empty space.

"This is cool," Gerald exclaimed as he walked into the small, angled roofed space. "Why would they build this?"

"Pirates?" Dieter quipped, laughing. "I suspect the person who built the house wanted a place to hide things from his wife or the servants. I doubt we'll ever know, but it's really fun." Dieter closed the door and slid the panel back over the knob.

"Did you refurnish the house?" Gerald asked, as they wandered from the living room to the dining room.

"Somewhat. I kept some of Gram's things and used some of what I found in the attic. I needed to make things different," Dieter explained, and he felt Gerald's arms slide around his waist, Gerald's chest pressing to his back. Dieter leaned into the embrace, soaking up the warmth and closeness. "Would you like to see the upstairs?"

"I want to be with you," Gerald whispered into his ear, and Dieter shivered when he felt Gerald's lips on his neck. He didn't want to move, especially with Gerald holding him, doing those things to his neck that made his knees shake. "Will you take me upstairs?"

Dieter nodded, and Gerald's lips slipped away from his skin. Dieter moved out of Gerald's embrace, feeling the loss of closeness as he turned off the lights before leading Gerald upstairs.

Excitement and nerves warred for dominance as Dieter climbed the stairs toward the single light at the top. He could hear Gerald's footsteps behind him, and for an instant he wondered if he was doing the right thing. Was he rushing? Should he wait? At the door to his room, Dieter hesitated for a second and felt Gerald take his hand once more. Opening the door, he walked inside, switching on a small light on the dresser. When he turned around, Gerald embraced him, pressing them close, their eyes meeting. "I've never done this before," Dieter explained softly, his voice steady in spite of his nerves.

"I know," Gerald told him as he stroked his cheek. "We'll take it slow and easy. Nothing is going to happen that won't feel good and right for both of us, I promise," Gerald said in a soothing, gentle tone that calmed the butterflies almost instantly. "Just relax and let me take care of you."

Dieter looked toward his bed, the same one he'd had for years with its handmade quilt and embroidered pillow cases. "Do you want me...." Gerald's hand gentled over his skin, and his voice drifted off.

"Wherever you're comfortable," Gerald told him, and Dieter moved away, folding back the bedspread before turning down the covers. His arm shook and he hoped Gerald didn't notice. Gerald's hand soothed down his back, and Dieter turned into the touch. Gerald pulled him close and kissed him, lips touching his softly. "You're a stunning man," Gerald said as he pulled Dieter's shirt out of his pants before tugging it up. Dieter lifted his arms, and his shirt slipped away before falling to the floor. Gerald's kisses continued as Dieter's pants fell to the floor, and Dieter nearly fell backward when he tried to take his shoes off.

"I'm sorry."

"Relax, honey. There's nothing you can do wrong," Gerald soothed as he kissed the skin of Dieter's shoulder. "Everything is right because it's us together. You can't possibly do anything wrong, so relax and be happy."

Somehow Gerald helped him get his shoes off, and Dieter stepped out of his pants, standing in front of Gerald in only his white underwear that barely hid his excitement from view. Feeling a bit on display, he looked around for something to cover himself. Then Gerald touched him, fingertips skimming over his chest, the touch barely there and yet enough to make him ache in a way he'd never felt before. "Gerald," Dieter said with a giggle as he tried wriggling away when Gerald lightly tickled his side. Moving close once again, Gerald held him, hands stroking his back while Dieter was kissed—a deep, achingly incredible kiss. Then he was moving, propelled in Gerald's powerful embrace toward the bed. of what happened until the back of his legs bumped the bed, and Gerald guided him down onto the sheets. "It's not fair," Dieter groused lightly. "I want to see you too."

"You will," Gerald said, lifting his lips away. Dieter propped himself up onto his elbows, watching as Gerald pulled his shirt over his head, his long, lean body stretching, and Dieter wanted to reach out and touch. But before he could move, Gerald's polo shirt joined the small pile of clothing on the floor. A light dusting of dark hair ran down the center of Gerald's chest, disappearing into the waistband of his pants, which Gerald's fingers opened, parting the fabric. Then they fell and Gerald got his shoes off, stepping away from his pants, wearing nothing but clingy, heavily tented black briefs.

Gerald stalked closer to the bed, and Dieter saw heat in his wide eyes. At first, he slid back on the bed, not sure what the look meant, but then he recognized it as desire and the realization took him by surprise—that look was for him. He did that to Gerald. The bed tipped slightly when Gerald joined him. Then Dieter was kissed, hard, fully, Gerald's tongue exploring, devouring his mouth, and Dieter hugged Gerald, holding on like he was starting to fall and couldn't stop. Then Gerald's skin touched his, their chests pressing together, and Dieter sighed, relishing the feeling of skin-to-skin touch.

At first, returning Gerald's kisses was all he could do. Holding Gerald tight, he put himself in his lover's hands, letting him lead where he would as his mind floated on the pleasure of new sensations. "Scoot back," Gerald said as he guided him back onto the mattress, his head resting on the pillow. Dieter took the opportunity to place his hand on Gerald's chest, fine hair lightly scratching his palm, and he thought he could feel Gerald's heart thundering beneath his hand. "What would you like?" Gerald asked, and Dieter shrugged.

"Not sure what to ask for," Dieter explained, a little overwhelmed, but in a good way.

"When you were alone in your bed at night, what did you think about? What did you dream about?" Gerald asked him, and Dieter turned away, not able to look into Gerald's eyes. He felt a light touch roll his head back. "There's nothing to be ashamed of. All you have to do is tell me."

Dieter didn't know how to answer—his fantasies seemed so boring compared to having the real, live Gerald with him. "Did you dream about this?" Gerald asked before swiping his tongue over one of Dieter's nipples, and Dieter's breath caught in his throat.

"Yes," he hissed softly in response, and Gerald did it again, longer this time, sucking lightly, and Dieter gasped softly.

"How about this?" Gerald asked before kissing his way down Dieter's chest and stomach, tongue and lips tasting his skin before skirting just above the waistband of his briefs. Dieter inhaled and stilled, holding his breath as he willed Gerald to go further. "Is that what you dream of?"

"More," Dieter begged softly, and Gerald stroked a finger along his now-throbbing length. "Gerald, you're being mean," Dieter gasped when Gerald's fingers slipped beneath the cotton fabric, gently sliding near his cock, but not actually touching it.

"No, I'm not. All you need to do is tell me what you want. What is it you always wanted to know?" Gerald questioned as he tugged away Dieter's underwear, leaving him naked and panting.

"I want you to use your mouth, please." Dieter thrust his hips forward a little to accentuate his point, spreading his legs, his breath coming in shallow pants. "Gerald, please touch me." Gerald's fingers closed around his length, and Dieter gasped and moaned softly at the first intimate touch of another person. His hips thrust, and Dieter's eyes drifted closed, his body already reveling in the sensation. "Yes!" Then the fingers slipped away, and Dieter groaned, his eyes flying open as Gerald kissed him hard.

"I know what you want," Gerald told him, his lips and tongue teasing Dieter's lips before pulling away. Dieter tried to muffle his cry, but failed as Gerald's tongue swiped up his length from base to tip. Dieter didn't know what to say or do. His hands needed to grab something, so he clutched the bedding in his fists, swallowed hard, and waited, his breath stuck in his throat, and then he whimpered pitifully.

"Jesus, do that again!" Gerald did, again and again, before taking him into his mouth and sucking hard. Dieter thought his head would explode, and he didn't know what to do, with anything. Was it okay to move? Should he touch Gerald's hair? Should he moan or cry out? Dieter had no idea, but when Gerald took him deep, Dieter did it all. Running his fingers through Gerald's hair, he thrust forward and made some unclassifiable noise that he could hardly believe came out of him. Gerald took it all as encouragement, sucking harder and deeper until Dieter could take no more. Letting go of the last of his control, Dieter clamped his eyes closed as his release built. He must have made some sound, but Dieter heard nothing. All he could see and feel was Gerald making him happy, showing him pleasure he'd never known. Opening his mouth, Dieter threw back his head and let his release wash over him.

When Dieter became aware of himself again, Gerald was lying next to him, Gerald's hand stroking his forehead. "You okay?"

"What happened?" Dieter asked, snuggling closer to Gerald.

"You zoned out for a few seconds," Gerald explained before smiling. "It's okay. It happens sometimes."

"Oh," Dieter said, letting Gerald hold him. "I didn't freak out, did I?"

Gerald chuckled a little. "No. You were amazingly gorgeous and sexy. I've never had that happen before. You were perfect." Gerald kissed him, and Dieter realized that Gerald was still wearing his underwear.

"What about you?" Dieter asked, shifting so he could look at Gerald.

"Honey, you don't have to do anything you aren't ready for."

"But what if I want to?" Dieter said with a smile before kneeling on the bed and launching himself at Gerald. They fell backward, laughing, with Gerald holding him close, and Dieter kissed the nearest patch of skin, then he did it again, and Gerald relaxed back on the mattress. Dieter felt as though he'd been given a plate at the Gerald buffet.

"I'm all yours," Gerald told him, his voice deep. At first, Dieter wasn't sure what to do, but then he figured Gerald had done to him what he liked, so Dieter mimicked the way Gerald had touched him. Soon Gerald was whimpering, and Dieter was smiling. Tapping Gerald's hip, he tugged away Gerald's briefs, throwing them onto the floor and taking Gerald's length into his mouth. Gerald's flavor burst on his tongue, like when they kissed, only more intense. Being careful, Dieter took what he could, holding and caressing as he licked the length. Gerald made these little noises that drove Dieter wild because he knew he was the cause, that he was making Gerald happy. "Dieter, I'm gonna come." Dieter stroked harder, watching the most incredibly blissful look come over Gerald's face as he came with a small cry.

Hurrying to the bathroom, Dieter returned with a towel, wiping Gerald quickly before turning off the light, scooting into bed, and hugging Gerald close. "Will you stay?" Dieter asked, angling for a kiss and getting two.

"How could I possibly say no?" Gerald answered, kissing him yet again as they settled together. Dieter held Gerald as tight as he was held, not wanting to let him go. "Good night and thank you for meeting my family. It meant a lot," Gerald said, obviously pleased, and Dieter kissed his new lover, letting warmth and sleep wash over him.

CHAPTER 6

GERALD woke with a smile, Dieter's warm body curled right next to him in the air conditioned room. It didn't seem to matter if the room was warm or cold, Gerald had quickly discovered that when they spent the night together, Dieter spent the entire night curled as close to him as possible. It almost seemed like he was expecting Gerald to disappear in the middle of the night. Actually, Gerald thought it nice that Dieter wanted to be close to him. He'd had previous boyfriends who never spent the night with anyone, and those who, after sex, rolled over and went right to sleep without so much as a hug. Selfish pricks.

Two, no, three weeks had passed, Gerald realized, since he'd taken Dieter to meet his family, and unfortunately, he'd been so busy most days that he'd gone home and fallen right into bed. Gerald made a point, no matter how tired he was, to spend at least one evening a week with Dieter, and they got together on the weekends, but he wanted more, and Gerald could sense that Dieter did as well. But in order to make sure Dieter's case progressed, at as little cost as possible, Gerald would do his normal work during the day, and almost every evening he'd work for a few hours on strategies and research for Dieter. He'd made excellent progress and had even begun the outlines and ideas for a basic brief, but as they expected, the information Gerald needed now was in Austria, hopefully in the archives of the Belvedere Museum.

"Gerry," Dieter mumbled softly, burrowing closer, "go back to sleep."

"I'd like nothing better, but we need to get ready to go to the airport," Gerald explained, holding Dieter to him. "I'd love to stay in bed with you, but we need to be at the airport in less than an hour." Gerald kissed his adorable lover before slipping out of bed, figuring he'd get cleaned up and let Dieter sleep for a few more minutes. Padding to the bathroom as quietly as he could, Gerald shaved and brushed his teeth before turning on the shower. Stepping in, Gerald pulled the shower curtain closed and let the hot water wash over him. At five thirty on a Saturday morning, his body and mind wanted nothing more than to go back to bed with Dieter.

The bathroom door opened, and Gerald heard Dieter moving around outside, and then the curtain opened slightly and Dieter slipped in behind him. Gerald was now instantly awake in more ways than one as Dieter pressed to his back, hands gliding over Gerald's chest. Over the past few weeks, a lot of Dieter's reticence had slipped away, and it showed when Dieter's hands moved lower before encircling Gerald's hard cock. "Feels good," Gerald said quietly, stifling a groan when the hand disappeared only to return a few seconds later all slippery and soapy as Dieter washed his back for him. When they stayed over, a morning togetherness shower was one of the highlights. Sometimes they had sex, but more often than not, their morning showers were an exercise in quiet, luxurious intimacy that Gerald had never had with anyone before.

"Do we have time?" Dieter asked, his voice deep as his fingers lightly caressed Gerald's balls.

Gerald groaned in a mixture of pleasure and frustration. "I wish, but we have to be at the airport to catch our shuttle in less than an hour, and the cab will be here soon." Dieter's hand slipped away. "Turn around and I'll wash your back," Gerald told Dieter and let his soapy hands roam over Dieter's back and down to his butt before both of them rinsed off.

After stepping out of the shower, Gerald dried quickly before leaving the bathroom and pulling on his clothes. He knew if he stuck around, he'd get distracted by Dieter, and there were things that had to be done. Once he was dressed, Gerald packed the very last things before hauling his suitcase into the entry. "Dieter, the cab will be here anytime," he reminded him lightly before making a pass through the house, verifying that all the doors were locked. When Dieter was ready, Gerald took his suitcase to the hall as well, and as the cab pulled up, they were hauling their suitcases to the curb.

The ride to the airport took ten minutes, and they waited another ten minutes for the shuttle to O'Hare, and less than two hours later, they were in line at the international terminal for their flight to Vienna. Dieter could barely stand still, jumping from side to side to see what was happening around them. "You have your passport?" Dieter nodded, still bouncing with excitement as they approached the desk.

"Is this your first trip to Europe?" the ticket agent asked Dieter when she saw his excitement.

"You never told me that," Gerald said, and the agent smiled at them as she typed before checking and taking their bags. Handing them their boarding passes, she told them their gate and wished them a pleasant flight.

Security was a nightmare, with a line snaking down the hall for what seemed like half a mile, and it moved as slow as molasses. Thankfully, they had time, and eventually made it through and down the concourse to their gate with only a quick stop so Gerald could buy a snack for the flight: Garrett's caramel corn and cheese popcorn. "I can't stop in Chicago without getting some," Gerald explained to Dieter as they stood in line. "You'll love it."

They made it to the gate, and their flight began boarding a half hour later. At the end of the Jetway, Gerald showed the flight attendant their seating stubs, and she directed them toward the front of the plane where they found themselves seated in the wide seats of business class. In order to help save money, Gerald had booked economy-class seats, and all he could figure was the ticket agent had decided to give Dieter a special flight.

Dieter could barely settle next to him, and thankfully, the flight attendant brought around champagne and Gerald handed Dieter a glass. "Drink this. It'll calm you down a little," Gerald said with a wink and a smile.

"I'm okay," Dieter protested.

"You're so excited that the plane could take off on your energy alone," Gerald said before leaning closer to whisper, "Not that I really mind, but you'll be more comfortable when you're calm, because it's going to be a very long flight, and if you can sleep, you'll be better off."

Dieter drained his glass and smiled at Gerald. "Happy?" Gerald laughed, and the flight attendant took away the glasses as the doors were closed and announcements began. Then the plane began to move, and Gerald watched as Dieter's excitement ramped up again as the plane picked up speed and they lifted off the ground. Once the plane leveled off, Dieter settled down somewhat. "Okay," Gerald said quietly after he'd gotten out his laptop, "here's the plan. We'll arrive on Sunday morning, and we're expected at the museum at nine Monday. I was able to secure us most of the day, which probably won't give us enough time, but we'll have to find what we can. They wouldn't commit to more time than that because, they claimed, of the availability of people to retrieve the materials."

"Do they have a catalog online?" Dieter asked as he leaned over to look at what Gerald had already.

"Some things are online, but they aren't what we need. I was able to find some documents a few days ago," Gerald said before pulling printouts out of his case and handing them to Dieter. "But I'm not sure these will help us." Gerald watched as Dieter scanned the documents, handing back two of them quickly, but he gasped when he read the third. "What is it?"

"This appears to be the documentation regarding an appeal Gram made twenty-five years ago." Dieter flipped the page as he continued reading. "They found that there was insufficient proof that the paintings belong to my family. It also says that the paintings were left to the museum by Anna Meinauer. There's a copy of a letter that my great-grandmother wrote saying that she wanted her portrait to go to the Belvedere, and they consider the matter closed." Dieter turned, all the wind gone from his sails, the excitement from earlier gone.

"Is it a letter or a will?" Gerald said as he looked at the document, kicking himself that he hadn't researched these documents earlier, but he'd just found them yesterday and had only printed them on the chance that they were meaningful. He felt like such a newbie. He should have checked everything.

Dieter showed him a copy that was attached to the report. "It looks like a handwritten letter."

Gerald breathed a sigh of relief. "First thing, it isn't a will, so that argument should be easy to dispel, and from what we understand, the painting wasn't hers to give away, anyway. It belonged to your great-grandfather. It was his money that paid for it, regardless of whether Anna commissioned it, and hopefully we'll be able to prove that. But this is better than I thought because it gives us a clue as to what they will argue, and we'll need to be able to refute that."

The flight attendant asked if they wanted more champagne, and Gerald motioned for a glass for both of them. "We need to keep our heads cool and our brains engaged. I know this is very emotional for you, but if we're going to do a good job, we need to leave those emotions behind so we can think clearly. That's the only way we're going to find what we need." Gerald watched closely as a lot of different emotions flashed behind Dieter's eyes.

"I guess this is going to be more emotional than I thought," Dieter explained.

"There's nothing wrong with that. I just don't want you riding a roller-coaster. The chances are that we're going to find things that will help us and hurt us. The important thing is to know what can hurt us so we can minimize it."

"So this doesn't hurt us?" Dieter asked, still holding the document.

"Actually, it may help us, because it could help show a pattern of disregard for their own laws as well as international property rights, because this is very plainly not a will and yet they have used it as such. Hopefully we can find something within their own records that disputes this, and then we can paint them as putting their own interests ahead of the rightful owners. Courts really hate that." Gerald could feel himself getting excited now.

Dieter smiled at him. "You really are a total lawyer. You take everything and change it to suit what you want it to."

"That's what we do, and hopefully the end result is justice."

The flight attendants came around with warm towels and began serving fruit and nut appetizers to everyone. Dieter got out his book and began to read while Gerald continued making notes and getting his thoughts on paper. After dinner, the lights in the cabin dimmed, and Gerald continued working for a while before reclining his seat and covering himself with a blanket to try to get some sleep. The seat was comfortable, but thoughts of the case and Dieter kept running through his mind. Eventually Dieter turned out his light and tried to sleep as well.

Gerald must have slept because when he woke, the cabin was still dark and quiet. Dieter's eyes were closed in the seat next to him, and he snuffled lightly, the way he always did when they slept together. Gerald closed his eyes again, and thankfully, the next time he opened his eyes, the flight attendants were serving breakfast. Reaching over, Gerald gently woke Dieter. He wanted to wake him with a kiss, but refrained and woke him with a gentle caress instead. Dieter blinked at him a few times before pulling the blanket up over his head. A few seconds later the blanket slipped down again, and Gerald was treated to one of the most beautiful sights he knew, Dieter's sleepy eyes blinking up at him.

"Would you like an omelet or a fruit plate for breakfast?" the flight attendant asked, and they ordered one of each, figuring they could share. By the time they'd eaten and their trays were taken away, the tone of the plane engines had changed and Gerald felt the telltale pressure in his ears as the plane began to descend.

Tray tables were stowed and seats returned to their upright positions, and they landed half an hour later and deplaned. Going through immigration and then customs, they moved through the airport to the train station. They could have taken a taxi, but Dieter wanted to ride a train and Gerald had already researched the route and knew how easy it would be to take the City Airport Train right into Vienna. The best part was seeing Dieter's excited bouncing again. Exiting at their station, they walked to their hotel, looking at the buildings. "I picked this hotel because it was one of the few non-chain hotels that had air conditioning," Gerald explained as they walked, but Dieter wasn't paying attention, which didn't bother Gerald at all.

"Is this it?" Dieter asked, mouth open, standing in front of their hotel, looking up at the façade of the eighteenth-century home now converted into a small hotel. Gerald had probably paid more than necessary for their room, but he wanted Dieter to stay someplace special, and since they were staying together for more than a single night for the first time, he sort of wanted to impress.

"Yes. I hope you like it," Gerald said, but from the look on Dieter's face, he knew it was a hit. "Let's go inside," Gerald prompted, and Dieter looked both ways down the sidewalk.

"Can we see things?" Dieter asked, practically jumping out of his skin.

Gerald nearly groaned out loud, but stopped. Dieter had so much energy, but their time in Vienna was very limited. They were scheduled to leave again early Friday morning. "Sure. Let's get checked in and our things up to the room, then we can explore a little." God, he loved Dieter when he was this happy. The man practically glowed with energy and excitement.

Picking up the bags, Gerald led the way inside and walked to the small front desk in what had once been a grand living room. Gerald rang the bell, and a middle-aged man appeared through a door behind the desk. "Guten Morgen," he said and began speaking in German, only parts of which Gerald understood. Turning to Dieter, Gerald noticed that he wasn't behind him, and he craned his neck and caught sight of him just outside in the hallway.

"Guten Morgen," Gerald replied, "I'm afraid that's about the limit of my German."

"Do you have a reservation?" the man inquired, switching to near perfect English.

"Yes, one room under the name Young."

"Yes. We're expecting you," he said, handing Gerald a reservation card. "Your room will not be ready until 1400 hours this afternoon. We can hold your bags for you and put them in the room when it is ready," he explained pleasantly, and Gerald thanked him before filling out the registration card and handing him a credit card and his passport. Dieter rejoined him, still looking around, and after signing the credit slip, they placed their bags in a small room before leaving the hotel, heading to the subway station.

"Where are we going?" Dieter asked as they descended beneath street level.

"How about visiting a palace?" Gerald asked before buying their tickets and making their way to the train.

He and Dieter spent most of the morning and early afternoon touring Schönbrunn Palace, the gardens, and grounds. Both of them stared open-mouthed as they stood in the middle of the ballroom, looking up at the frescoed ceilings, glittering gold walls, and massive crystal chandeliers. Once they'd toured the palace itself, they played hide and seek in the hedge maze, climbed the hill to the fountains, and then walked farther to the Gloriette on the hill. "This is beautiful," Dieter commented as they stood on the roof of the Gloriette looking down at the gardens, palace, and then the whole city beyond. "To think, from one of the pictures in Gram's album, Anna and Joseph stood right where we are now."

Gerald slipped an arm around Dieter's waist, squeezing him lightly. "I hope they were as happy as I am to be here with you." Heedless of the people around them, Gerald leaned to Dieter, kissing him to accentuate his sentiment, and the sun, which had been absent for most of the day, hidden behind low clouds, chose that moment to break through, bathing them, the gardens, and the golden palace in showers of light that seemed to reflect off everything.

They ate a late, light lunch in the Gloriette café before walking back down the hill. Gerald took as many pictures as he could, some of a couple on their honeymoon in front of the Neptune fountain, and the couple returned the favor. By the time Gerald and Dieter left the palace grounds and rode the subway back, they were exhausted, and the final walk to the hotel seemed to take forever.

Their room was ready when they got back, and they found their bags already waiting for them. Gerald's body screamed for sleep, but he forced himself to stay awake through the rest of the afternoon. After eating dinner in the small restaurant around the corner, Gerald convinced Dieter to take a walk before going to their room and falling into bed, where Dieter curled next to him in the cool room. Gerald slept like the dead, waking only to use the bathroom before falling right back to sleep, and as far as he could tell, Dieter never moved a muscle the entire night.

Gerald's traveling alarm woke them in the morning, both of them having difficulty waking up, but they made it to breakfast and left the hotel on time, arriving at the Belvedere Museum as they opened the doors. Gerald told the woman in the information booth who they were there to see, and she asked them to wait and quietly made a phone call. "Can we see the paintings before we leave?" Dieter asked softly.

"Without a doubt. We just need to get as much research done as we can," Gerald answered.

"Herr Young," a woman in her midthirties said as she approached. "Guten Morgen, I'm Hanna Weis," she said by way of introduction.

"Guten Morgen," Dieter answered, continuing the conversation in German. Gerald caught their names in the conversation, but that was all, and she shook hands with both of them.

"We can speak English if you prefer," Hanna explained as she led them through controlled doors to utilitarian portions of the building that the public never saw. At another door, they paused at a desk where they were instructed to sign in and their passports were checked. Badges were issued, and then Hanna swiped her card and the door opened and closed behind them. The air felt instantly cooler and drier as they passed through metal detectors before being led through another door and into what looked like a catalog room. "Some of our more recent records have been computerized, but many are still cataloged in these card files and record books."

"We understand you are interested in records involving art transferred to the museum during the Nazi period," Hanna said as she pointed them to that portion of the catalogs, and Gerald felt his eyes roll when he realized the amount of material they would need to search. "I can assure you that there is no art in the museum's collection that does not belong. We have researched everything extensively," she explained proudly. That was almost equivalent to a statement he'd read on the Internet when the records were opened a few years earlier.

Gerald glanced at Dieter to make sure he was okay, and his only reaction was a hard look in his eyes that only Gerald would probably understand. "We understand that. What we're hoping to find are some interesting stories that will help add life and interest to our work. Many works of art make quite a journey before they arrive home, and it's some of those stories and the facts behind them that we're interested in." Gerald felt the bullshit flow off his tongue like water off a duck's back. He knew if he let on to their true purpose, the archive doors would close and lock faster than a stripper could remove his Velcro pants.

"There are some things I can help you with," Hanna explained as they got settled at one of the tables. "When the Nazis entered a country, they'd done their research. They already knew what was in the museums and they also found out where the important private collections were located. Two of the largest collections in Vienna at the time were the Mintz and the Meinauer collections. While the soldiers were parading around the Ringstrasse, teams were already entering those residences to confiscate the art. We could start there. Some of the works ended up here. The works from the Mintz collection that were in the museum's collection at that time were returned to the family after the war. The works from the Meinauer collection were left to the museum, so they remain here." She walked to the catalog and pulled out a drawer. "I believe we have the inventory lists from a number of these private collections," she explained and began to search for a few minutes. "I'll be right back. These lists might be a place for you to start."

As soon as she was gone, Dieter moved to sit in the chair next to Gerald. "You lied to her," he whispered.

"No, I didn't. I just bent the truth a little. We are researching the journey of looted art, just the trip of some very specific pieces. She doesn't need to know that," Gerald cautioned.

"But she seems so nice," Dieter countered innocently.

"She probably is. But she's also an employee of the Ministry of Culture, the same ministry that denied your Gram's claim. And if she had an inkling of why we were really here, she'd tell her supervisors, and we'd find ourselves outside this room and this building in no time flat," Gerald told Dieter a little more harshly than he meant and saw him flinch a little. "Sorry. Remember that we're here for your case, and I'm here as a lawyer doing research. I may have to say things or do things that you may not agree with, but know I'm doing them for your benefit."

"Can I ask you about them?" Dieter inquired, biting his lower lip nervously, and Gerald wondered if bringing him along was such a good idea.

"When we're alone, you can ask me anything at all."

Hanna returned, wearing gloves, carrying a book. She gave each of them a set of gloves that she had them put them on before setting the book on the table and carefully opening it.

"These are some of the German records from 1936 to 1940 that relate to their artistic endeavors." She carefully turned the pages until she found what she wanted. "Here's the list of items from the Mintz collection and their disposition." She pointed down the handwritten page. "These eight works ended up here because they weren't of interest to the Germans. These were taken into the Reich collection. That was their euphemism that meant they ended up with Goering, Himmler, or one of the other officials, and these two were presented to Hitler himself. It also lists all pertinent information about the work."

"Would it be possible to get a copy of this list?" Gerald asked, seeing a flicker of confusion in Dieter's eyes.

"Of course. I need to make them on a special copier so it doesn't degrade the paper. If this is for research, would you like an official copy? Each one is five Euros."

"That would be fine."

"Would you like to see the other lists?"

"If I could," Gerald replied, hiding his excitement.

Hanna slowly turned some additional pages. "This is the list of items from the Meinauer collection," Hanna explained, and Gerald saw Dieter perk up and he shot him a quick warning glance. "You can see the disposition of these paintings as well. There are twelve still in the collection, and the others were taken into German hands. Would you like a copy of this as well?"

Gerald explained that he would, and they continued through another, smaller collection and Gerald had a copy made of that list as well. When Hanna left, Gerald smiled at Dieter before concentrating on the tack he wanted to take. Hanna returned with the copies, each bearing an impressed seal, and Gerald handed Dieter the lists. "Let's pick one of these and see what we can find." Gerald hoped Dieter would get the idea, and he seemed to, shuffling through the pages before handing her the page that listed the work from his family's collection. "If we can get what we need from this today, we can move on tomorrow," Gerald explained, hoping Dieter understood.

"I'll see what I can find," Hanna said, and hurried to check the catalogs before entering something in a computer. "It'll be a few minutes because the materials are not bound like these." After awhile she left the room, and Dieter scoured the list of his family's collection.

"I feel dishonest," he said softly.

"Shhh," Gerald said. "Remember, we'll talk later."

They waited quite awhile this time, and Gerald asked Dieter questions about the paintings from his family's collection that were still in the museum and made notes so they could be researched further. When Hanna returned, she brought another man with her, and he sat at another table and began asking her questions. Eventually Hanna brought a folder to them, setting it on the table before explaining to them the rules for handling the documents.

Following her instructions, Dieter opened the folder and carefully removed the first document. "This is the detailed description of each artwork," Dieter explained before turning the pages slowly, one after another.

"We'll need those," Gerald said, thankful he had plenty of Euros in his pocket, because the bill for copying was going to be enormous. "What's that?"

"The letter from Anna," Dieter answered his hand shaking slightly as he held the letter in his great-grandmother's handwriting.

"Read it if you like, but we have a copy already," Gerald explained, reminding himself to add that letter to the lawsuit as well.

"No, this one is different. There's a second page that wasn't copied, and it seems rather personal," Dieter explained softly, adding the letter to the documents to be copied before carefully looking through the rest of the file.

There was plenty of information, but other than the additional paintings they hadn't been aware of, they hadn't found anything that would really aid their case. When they'd looked through the files, Hanna returned, and they asked for copies of what they needed, and when she returned she informed them that she would be going to lunch in an hour and that the research library closed for the day at that time.

Dieter began asking her questions in German, and at first she shook her head, but then Dieter must have hit on something because she nodded and went to the catalogs once again.

Dieter explained to Gerald, "I asked her if the information was filed under the paintings rather than the family. At first she said no, but when I asked if they kept records by artist, she agreed to look. I don't know if there is anything, but we can try."

Hanna helped the others in the room, and they waited, the clock ticking down until closing time. Finally, she returned with another folio. "These are some documents on our Pirktls. I'll be back to make any copies you need in fifteen minutes, and then I have to close."

Gerald nodded. "Danke," Gerald said with a smile as Dieter began looking through the documents. There wasn't time to read them in detail, but Dieter said that some of the documents appeared to reference *The Woman in Blue,* so Gerald made a command decision and had the entire folio copied, knowing he was probably throwing away the money, but what the hell. They could come back tomorrow to follow up on anything else, and they needed to look into the other collections to maintain their cover. Gerald knew that even though Hanna was being professionally helpful, she was also monitoring every document they looked at. Hanna made the copies, and Gerald paid her almost two hundred Euros for them before thanking her and placing the copies in his case.

By the time they left, both he and Dieter were shivering from the temperature controls in the research room, and Gerald turned his head toward the sun when they reached the street. "Let's get something to eat, and then we can visit the museum." Gerald knew Dieter was anxious to actually see his great-grandmother's portrait.

"What about your bag?" Dieter asked. "Shouldn't we take it back to the hotel?"

"I can check it at the museum," Gerald said as they walked toward what appeared to be a business district nearby and found a small restaurant for lunch.

Inside, Dieter took over, speaking to the maître d', and they were seated near the window. The menus were in German, so Dieter translated for him. "I'd like the schnitzel," Gerald told Dieter, and he ordered for both of them when their server came to the table.

"I ordered you one of the local beers too," Dieter said, and the server brought tall glasses of a light-colored beer that went down smoothly when he tasted it. "How do you think it went?" Dieter asked when the server was gone.

"Pretty well, I think. We got a lot of information, but we'll need to figure out what we have so we can determine what we need to try to find tomorrow." Gerald took another drink of his beer. "Is there anything you want to talk about?"

"Yes, but I'm not sure how," Dieter told him, looking concerned. "I know you were being a good lawyer, but I have difficulties when I see you act like the hard-edged lawyer because I can't reconcile it with the sweet, caring man I slept with two nights ago." Dieter took another gulp of his beer, and Gerald could see the conflict behind Dieter's eyes. "You're doing this for me, I really do know that, and you're trying to get me what I want, I know that, too, but I sort of wonder which is the real you." Dieter set down his glass, and Gerald felt Dieter's gaze bore into his eyes.

"They're both me, sort of. The caring person you know is very much me, as is the lawyer. I guess the best I can say is that the lawyer in me loves to win, and the rest of me feels like he already has," Gerald tried to explain. "I want you to think about this. I told Hanna a story based on the truth today. I did it so we could get the information we needed. I understand that you may not like what I did, but we found out a number of things. Your grandmother appealed to the Ministry of Culture to get back what was rightfully hers, and they used only part of the story to deny her claim. What we're trying to do is get the rest of the story." Gerald lowered his voice, not that anyone was listening, but he didn't want to appear harsh. Dieter's questions were valid, and he needed to know the truth. "We're not asking for access to information that isn't available to other people, and we're not stealing it. We just need to know what they know. And we got some good news today. They have more than just the five paintings, and the so-called letter that they're basing their claim of ownership on is a little note from Anna to Joseph explaining her wishes. It's not legal or binding. Joseph was free to decide what he wanted, and he never donated the paintings, so their claims are pretty weak."

"I guess you're right," Dieter said, but he didn't sound very convinced. "You've never treated me in any way but wonderfully."

"And I promise I'll always try to treat you that way. But there will be times when I go into lawyer mode, though I'll try not to do it when it's just us." Gerald reached across the table and lightly touched Dieter's hand. "You don't have to be afraid."

"I'm not really afraid. It's just that everything's so new, I keep wondering if it's for real. It seems so easy, too easy, maybe," Dieter said, but he didn't continue when the server brought their plates. "Let's eat and we can go back to the museum. And when we get back to the hotel, we can take a look at those papers we had copied." Dieter took a bite of his veal, and Gerald tried his own dish as well. "I shouldn't be so sensitive."

Gerald swallowed and took a drink of beer. "You're a good person, and you see that same goodness in others. It's one of the things I really like about you. So don't change, just try to understand, and I'll do the same," Gerald explained.

"Okay," Dieter replied with a half-smile, and they continued their lunch. "Is there anything planned for this evening?"

"Once we've reviewed the documents, the time is ours. I thought we could take the subway to the city center, and I thought we could walk part of the Ringstrasse one evening. I'm really going to need your help with these documents. I have no idea what they are, and unless we can determine what we have, I can't figure out what we need."

"Then after we look through the museum, let's go back to the room and get the work done. That's why we're here, after all. Once we're done, we can look around the city. The lawyer's right," Dieter said, giving him a wink, "we need to get the work done first. Just don't get a big head and start thinking the lawyer's always right."

Gerald smiled. If Dieter could joke, then maybe he was beginning to understand. Dieter was his boyfriend and his client; maybe that wasn't the most ideal situation, but he wasn't willing to give up either one of those right now. They continued talking as they finished their lunch.

"I'm so full, I think I need to walk around for the next few hours," Dieter commented happily, a huge, satisfied smile on his face as they left the restaurant.

"Are you feeling better?" Gerald asked, still a little unsettled about their earlier conversation. He was a good attorney, he knew that, and he also knew from some of the stories in the office that the job could take over your life. He could feel a bit of that threatening already, and he was determined not to let that happen. He liked having someone wonderful in his life, and he was becoming convinced that his Mr. Wonderful was Dieter. He also knew that he had to be who he was. He just hoped that Dieter could accept that.

"Yes. I think so," Dieter said as they walked back toward the museum, "and I'm beginning to realize that there's more to you than just the kind person I know. Not that I'm disappointed. In fact, I should have expected it. We met in your office, and I wanted you on my case because you cared and because you're a good lawyer. I shouldn't fault you for doing your job well."

"I know it can be difficult. Half the people in my office are divorced, some more than once. I asked Steven, one of the partners, about it once, and he told me that success comes with a price," Gerald explained as he moved closer to Dieter. "I've always hoped I wouldn't be one of those people who paid that price and sold their soul for their job."

Dieter stopped walking and turned toward him, an unreadable look on his face. "What if I'm the price?"

"Then it's too high," Gerald said, the words tumbling out before he could think about them. Other people walked around them on the sidewalk as Gerald stared back into Dieter's eyes. He seemed to be looking for something, and Gerald hoped he found it.

"You're serious," Dieter commented softly.

"Yes. I won't lie to you or just tell you what you want to hear. That's not who I am. I may have to bend the truth sometimes in order to help my clients, but I don't lie, and I won't lie to you," Gerald said firmly, but with a slight smile he hoped softened the message. Gerald wasn't angry with Dieter, he just hoped he would understand. "Would you like to go inside?"

Dieter nodded and they climbed the steps, entering the museum once again. This time, Gerald stood in line to check his case, making sure it was locked before handing it over, and after paying the entrance fee, he and Dieter walked into the museum.

Like the Louvre, this museum had once been a palace, and the setting for the Austrian paintings was spectacular, with baroque decoration of the walls almost as breathtaking as the art. They walked through room after room, quietly looking at each painting before moving on. With each room they saw, Gerald could feel Dieter's expectations and excitement rise until they walked into the room with four Pirktl landscapes hanging on the walls.

Dieter stopped, staring at each painting in turn. "They're beautiful," Dieter murmured so softly Gerald barely heard him.

Gerald had purchased a guide and he opened it, finding the pages that explained the paintings. "It says these landscapes were commissioned by a prominent Austrian family and that they were the only four landscapes he ever completed. The scenes are from the wood outside Vienna where the Meinauer family once had property. Each painting depicts the same stand of trees from different angles at different times of year." Gerald stopped reading as he joined Dieter in staring at the canvases. They weren't massive, by any means, but they weren't small, and having seen where they originally hung in one of Dieter's photographs, Gerald knew they had been painted for a specific location.

"Can you imagine the lights, music, glittering jewelry, and gorgeous gowns as people danced in the ballroom where these paintings hung?" Gerald looked away from the paintings and saw that Dieter's eyes were closed, as if he were imagining the scene, and slowly Dieter's head began to nod, his eyes sliding open the way they did first thing in the morning.

"They're spectacular. I thought the portrait would be moving, but I wasn't expecting these to be so beautiful. They're the same and yet different," Dieter told him without taking his eyes off the canvases. "It's the same group of trees, and each painting is serene and you can almost hear the wind and the rustling of leaves or the muffled sound of the snow, and yet, each one is different. The vibrancy of spring, the lushness of summer, autumn's last burst of color, and winter's quiet beauty. I know it sounds cliché, but it's not."

Dieter tilted his head, looking at the depiction of spring. "It looks like the trees are happy, sort of dancing, and in summer, look at this limb, you can almost imagine it swinging back and forth, sort of like the trees are fanning themselves from the heat. They're almost playful." Gerald stepped next to Dieter, afraid to touch him or disturb him in any way. Eventually, he felt Dieter move closer, and Gerald touched his arm lightly. "I think I'm ready to move on," Dieter said, but as they left the room, Gerald saw Dieter look back at the paintings.

Together, they wandered through a few more galleries until Gerald felt Dieter stop in his tracks. Turning, Gerald saw it: *The Woman in Blue,* or *Portrait of Anna* as it was properly called, the face hauntingly beautiful. In real life, the blue looked like one of those mythical colors that legend says existed but was lost to time. The canvas shimmered as they moved farther into the gallery. Gerald stayed behind, watching as Dieter moved closer, his gaze never wandering from his great-grandmother's portrait. The other people in the room turned to look as Dieter slowly moved closer, stopping just a few feet away. Gerald was surprised, after having seen the large-format landscapes, that the portrait wasn't particularly big, but the impact of the image was monumental. At least it felt that way to Gerald, like the woman was looking off the canvas and into his soul. He suddenly knew why it was so important, because if a painting's worth was in its ability to move the viewer, then this was worth more than any work of art Gerald had ever seen.

Dieter hadn't moved, and Gerald saw a woman look at Dieter, then at the painting and back at Dieter once again. Seeing the portrait in person, Gerald realized that Dieter had his great-grandmother's eyes and facial structure. He looked like her in some ways, and the woman in the gallery had seen that as well. "Young man," the woman was saying as Gerald approached. "I can't help noticing that you look like her." The woman continued to look from Dieter to the painting.

"Thank you, but I'm not as pretty as she was," Dieter said lightly, and the middle-aged woman smiled.

"I think you're prettier," she said. "Would it be all right if I take your picture next to her?"

"Okay," Dieter said, and he stood near the painting as the woman snapped a picture.

"You couldn't be related, could you?"

Dieter's gaze flashed to Gerald, and he felt himself shaking his head lightly. "I don't believe so," Dieter lied before stepping away from the painting, and the woman thanked him before moving out of the gallery. Gerald joined Dieter, and they looked at the portrait together. A few times Gerald thought he might have heard Dieter say something, but he couldn't make out what it was, and he figured he'd allow Dieter his privacy.

"Are you ready to go?" Gerald asked, and Dieter nodded his head slightly. Leaving the gallery, Gerald expected Dieter to turn for one last look, but he didn't, he simply led the way through the museum. At the exit, Gerald retrieved his case and they stepped out into the sunshine. "Are you okay?"

"Yes," Dieter answered. "I told her who I was and what I was trying to do. I didn't get an answer, of course, but I told both her and Gram." Dieter rushed ahead and stopped walking when they reached the corner of the wide boulevard that ran next to the museum. Turning back to him, Dieter grabbed him and hugged him tight.

It took Gerald a few seconds before he realized Dieter was crying. Soothing him as best he could, Gerald rubbed Dieter's back softly. "It's going to be okay," Gerald kept saying, looking around, wondering how he could get Dieter back to the room.

A taxi pulled closer and Gerald signaled. Once the car stopped, Gerald ushered them both inside and gave the driver the name of the hotel. The driver looked over his shoulder when he saw Gerald holding Dieter, but he said nothing, and Gerald wasn't in the mood to offer any sort of explanation.

CHAPTER 7

THE ride wasn't too long, and by the time they reached the hotel, Dieter had gotten hold of himself, and they exited the taxi. Gerald paid the driver, and they went inside and right up to their room. "Do you want to lie down for a while?"

"No," Dieter answered, "I want to look over those papers so we can see what we've got."

"Dieter, that can wait a few minutes," Gerald said as lightly as he could, concerned about Dieter.

"I'm okay. I let myself get worked up when I was looking at my great-grandmother's portrait, and when that woman wanted to take my picture. I should have declined, but I didn't see how it could hurt." Dieter sighed loudly. "I feel like a bit of a fool, actually." Dieter pulled a tissue out of his pocket, wiping his eyes before blowing his nose and throwing the tissue in the trash.

"There's no need. You're allowed to feel however you want. I found the portrait incredibly moving, so I can't imagine what you must have felt," Gerald said, hoping Dieter would talk about it.

"I guess I hadn't expected to be as moved as I was," Dieter explained, motioning to Gerald's case. Unlocking it, Gerald pulled out their copies and handed them to Dieter. "We should organize these so you know what they are. Do you have any Post-it Notes?"

Gerald found some in the bag and handed them to Dieter.

"Let's number each document, and then you can make a list describing each document, referencing each one by its number." Dieter started writing numbers on the Post-its, attaching one to each page. Gerald booted up his laptop and opened a file. "Document number one is the list of Meinauer art works," Dieter dictated, and Gerald typed as fast as he could.

"I think I can make out most of that document," Gerald said, and Dieter set it aside, moving to the next.

"Two, three, four, and five are the detailed descriptions of the Meinauer works. Number six is the letter from Anna to Joseph." Dieter picked up the next document, setting it aside. "I won't bother numbering the documents we copied to maintain our cover," Dieter explained, setting aside a few copies. "Now, let's see. These are the documents we copied right at the end. Number seven appears to be a document detailing the condition of the *Portrait of Anna* in 1965." Dieter continued through the documents, none of them of any use other than as background material. "Number thirty-nine is a letter from"—Dieter stopped talking, and the room became quiet as he read the document—"what appears to be someone from the Ministry of Culture." Dieter kept reading silently while Gerald typed, occasionally glancing at him. "I'm not sure who he was, but do you have Internet access? Maybe we can find out."

Gerald did indeed have Internet access and he opened a browser window. "What's the name?"

"Georg Mitterval," Dieter said, spelling the first and last names.

Gerald searched and turned the laptop so Dieter could see it. "I don't see what I'm looking for. Can I try?" Dieter asked, and Gerald moved back as Dieter typed and searched. "That looks better. I added the official name of the ministry, and it looks like we found him." Dieter opened the page and began to read. "It appears he was a lawyer in the fifties and he was employed by the ministry." Dieter picked up the letter. "Yes. He was employed by the ministry from 1957 to 1964, and he wrote the letter in 1960." Dieter went back to the letter. "There's a lot of legal stuff here I don't really understand." Dieter's words began to run together as he spoke, his energy level spiking, and Gerald felt his own pulse begin to race. "I believe it says that he doubts the Belvedere's claims to ownership of a list of paintings—" Dieter stopped, and Gerald watched him scan the document. "Holy crap!"

"What is it?" Gerald asked, automatically trying to see, even though he didn't understand a thing.

"You'll need to get this translated properly by someone who knows the legal terminology, but as near as I can tell, it lists a number of works of art, including the five Pirktls, and says that he doubts that the museum's claims of ownership will hold up to serious scrutiny, and in this part of the document"—Dieter pointed to the section—"he also says that the Ministry of Culture should attempt to locate remaining family members and return the paintings to their rightful owners."

"Hot damn," Gerald called, jumping to his feet, "this is fantastic." Gerald grabbed Dieter, twirling him around as the paper fluttered to the floor.

"I don't understand," Dieter said, but Gerald cut him off with a fierce kiss. When they came up for air, both of them breathing heavily, Gerald met Dieter's eyes and gasped as Dieter pounced on him, sending him backward onto the bed. Dieter's energy felt like a live wire, and Gerald could not get enough. Usually, Dieter's kisses were soft and tender, but today they were hard and filled with a passion and excitement that blew Gerald away.

Gerald let Dieter have his way as Dieter's body vibrated with uncontrolled energy on top of him. Gerald's shirt was practically torn from his body as Dieter attacked his skin, licking and sucking so hard Gerald had no doubt he'd have marks all over. Not that it mattered in the least. He'd handle a few marks, because Dieter this excited had his dick throbbing in his pants.

"Lie on the bed," Dieter said, and for a second, Gerald wondered what had happened to the lover who never forgot his manners. "I think it's time to celebrate," Dieter said as Gerald repositioned himself on the bed, and Dieter opened his belt and pants before tugging them away. Then he pounced again, and Gerald did his best to get Dieter's shirt off.

Gerald hissed softly when Dieter roughly clamped his lips around a nipple, sucking and even using his teeth. It was almost too much. Cupping Dieter's head in his hands, Gerald brought their lips together in a searing kiss that left him breathless. As soon as their lips parted, Dieter practically jumped off the bed, tearing off his remaining clothes before nearly attacking Gerald again. There was no gentleness like there had been the previous times they'd made love. This time Dieter was all excitement and need. Whatever was driving him, Gerald knew he had to let it play out. Dieter needed to get it out of his system, and Gerald was determined to go along for the delicious ride.

"Dieter," Gerald said softly to get his attention, but then words and thought failed him as Dieter took him deep. Over the past few weeks, Dieter had honed his oral skills and was quickly turning into a master. "I love your mouth," Gerald whimpered softly as Dieter, sweet, well-mannered Dieter, attacked him with a ferocity Gerald had never seen in him before, with anything, and damn if it wasn't the hottest thing Gerald could ever remember.

"I love your dick," Dieter responded, and Gerald widened his eyes. Dieter had never shown the slightest interest in dirty talk before. Gerald hadn't done it at all because he wasn't sure how Dieter would feel about it, and here was this man with a nearly angelic face and body talking dirty to him. Gerald groaned as his cock throbbed in Dieter's mouth just before Dieter's lips slipped away. "Was that bad?" Dieter asked sheepishly.

"Fuck no," Gerald answered, and Dieter grinned as he slid his lips down Gerald's shaft. He'd unleashed a monster, a hot, sexy little monster, and there was no way Gerald was going to complain in the least. Especially when he was surrounded by the hottest wet heat he could ever imagine. Gerald tried not to thrust, but he couldn't help himself, Dieter was driving him wild, and his body screamed down the fast lane to a climax. Dieter must have sensed it somehow because he backed away, and Gerald groaned loudly before opening his eyes, peering down at a suddenly tentative lover. "What is it? What do you want?"

"I'm not sure how to ask," Dieter replied. "I want you to… to…." Dieter swallowed. "Fuck me," he whispered. Now that was the Dieter he knew. The man wanted everything, but saying the words was the difficult part.

"Okay," Gerald said softly even as his body went into excitement overdrive, and he had to take a deep breath before restraining himself as he got off the bed to get the supplies from his kit. "Lie on your belly," Gerald said softly when he returned, and after climbing on the bed, Gerald set the supplies on the table before stroking lightly over Dieter's back. Dieter twitched and muscles bunched with excitement beneath Gerald's hands. "You need to relax or it'll hurt, and that's the last thing I want. Let me soothe you. Breathe deeply and evenly," Gerald said as evenly as he could, trying not to let his own anxiousness show through.

Gerald kissed his way down Dieter's back, trailing his hands as he used both to try to calm Dieter, but it didn't seem to be working—with every touch, Dieter became more of a live wire, and Gerald decided to use that excitement. Kissing and licking his way lower, Gerald caressed Dieter's butt cheeks and heard a soft rumble from Dieter's chest. Parting the milky-white cheeks, Gerald licked along Dieter's cleft and got a surprised gasp from Dieter that continued when he blew on his wet skin. "What are you doing?" Dieter asked, as he propped himself up on his elbows, looking over his shoulder at Gerald.

"Getting you ready for me," Gerald answered with a sly smile before flicking the skin of Dieter's opening with the tip of his tongue. Dieter whined softly, pushing back, and Gerald let him, swirling his tongue around the puckered skin before teasing the opening. "You need to relax, sweetheart," Gerald said, before deciding the only way that was going to happen was if Gerald made it happen. So he rested some of his weight on Dieter's legs to hold him in place, thrusting his tongue deep and hard into Dieter's body. Dieter tried to thrust back again, wanting more, but Gerald held him in place, working the muscle until the tension slipped away and the muscle finally relaxed. Then the mewling and moaning started. Gerald knew when the realization of the pleasure hit Dieter, because he gasped softly, flopping onto the bed, fists gripping the bedding, and Gerald probed deep within his lover. Adding a single finger, Gerald slowly worked it into his lover's body, listening for any signs of discomfort. There were none, only soft moans and ripples that seemed to run through Dieter's muscles like a wave through water.

Crooking his finger, Gerald searched for just a few seconds until he found just what he was looking for. "Jesus!" Dieter cried as his entire body jerked.

"Like that?" Gerald asked, already knowing the answer as he rubbed the spot, feeling Dieter vibrate as he worked a second finger into Dieter's body. The heat and pressure were incredible, and Gerald found it hard to catch his breath as Dieter whimpered and moaned beneath him.

"Please, Gerry," Dieter begged, and Gerald continued getting Dieter ready, taking it slowly, not willing to hurt him in any way.

"Get on your hands and knees, sweetheart," Gerald said, massaging the spot inside to encourage Dieter to do what he wanted.

"Want to see you," Dieter gasped, and Gerald let his fingers slip out of Dieter's body, helping him roll over and placing a pillow under his hips.

"Give me a minute, okay?" Gerald said after giving Dieter a kiss and reaching to the supplies on the table. Tearing open a condom packet, which wasn't easy with slick, shaky fingers, Gerald managed to get the package open and the condom rolled onto himself before squeezing some slick onto his fingers. Coating both himself and Dieter's crease, Gerald locked eyes with Dieter, and as carefully as he could, pressed his cock to his lover's opening.

At first, Dieter's body resisted, and Gerald, afraid to push too hard, nearly backed away, but then he felt Dieter's resistance fade and his body opened, letting him inside a tight heat that nearly took Gerald's breath away. Deeper, hotter, Gerald slowly entered his lover's body, joining with him, Dieter's expression a mask of surprised bliss: mouth open, eyes huge, their initial joining almost a surprise to both of them. Sinking further, Gerald reached the bottom, fully buried in his lover. Stopping, he waited, watching Dieter's face as he gave him time to adjust to all the new sensations. "Are you okay?" Gerald asked between his heaving breaths.

"Yes," Dieter said through clenched teeth. "I feel so full."

"I know. Just relax a little and breathe steadily. Let everything relax a little," Gerald explained as his body tried to rebel against his own advice because it wanted to pound into Dieter, claiming him for his own. Gerald's eyes widened at the thought. He'd never felt possessiveness like that before, but right now, with Dieter's blue eyes locked onto his, their bodies joined, each and every of his lover's heartbeats echoed through Dieter's body and into his.

Pulling out slowly, Gerald heard Dieter groan through the entire motion. Then he pressed forward again, sliding back into Dieter's furnace-like heat to the accompaniment of a low, deep moan.

"Do that again," Dieter told him, and Gerald complied, moving very deliberately. The speed was driving him insane, and carefully he picked up the pace, his strokes still deep and long. Repositioning Dieter's legs so Dieter's heels rested on his shoulders, Gerald felt some of the tension leave Dieter's body, and he picked up the pace of his movements even further as he watched Dieter's head roll back and forth on the pillow, a steady stream of moans coming from deep in his chest.

Gerald loved that Dieter seemed to be getting more vocal during their lovemaking, and he decided to try to see just how vocal he could get. Stroking deep, Gerald stopped, his cock throbbing and jumping inside his lover. "Gerry!" Dieter whined.

"Gonna love you so good," Gerald said as he ran his hands along Dieter's legs. "I want you to tell me what you like." Gerald pulled almost all the way out of Dieter's body before driving back inside and holding.

"Yeah, that. I like that!" Dieter cried, and Gerald did it again, a thrill zipping up his spine. "Oh God!"

Dieter's cries and moans only fueled their mutual desire, and soon Gerald drove deep into Dieter's body, his own cries joining those of his lover, all control gone as instinct and passion seemed to take over, driving them both to ever higher and higher planes of ecstasy. Gerald saw Dieter stroke himself, and he felt his lover's body tighten around him as Dieter nearly screamed, shooting ropy lines onto his own hand and chest, with Gerald following right behind him, barreling through his own release.

All tension left Dieter's body as he lay beneath Gerald, covered in sweat, breathing like he'd run a marathon. "Is it always like that?"

"I think it is when you love the other person, yes," Gerald answered without thinking, and then realized just what he'd said. Yes, he knew he was developing feelings for Dieter, and he had known for some time, but he'd been hesitant to vocalize them. He'd spoken the truth now, and he wasn't about to take it back or try to explain it away.

"You love me?" Dieter asked, his lips curling in a beatific smile that rivaled the late-day sunshine streaming through the windows.

"Yes," Gerald answered as he felt their bodies separate, and he let Dieter's legs fall to the bed before leaning forward to capture Dieter's lips in a kiss Gerald hoped reinforce the truth of his feelings. Words were cheap, Gerald knew that better than anyone, but he also knew you couldn't hide your true feelings when you kissed, and in the first seconds of that kiss, he felt Dieter's feelings coming right back to him. He knew at that instant that he was one of the lucky people who loved and was loved in return. Gerald's heart soared, and he shifted on the bed, trying not to break their kisses, and he told Dieter over and over again that he loved him without saying a word.

When they stopped to breathe, Gerald took that break to retrieve a towel, cleaning up both of them before returning to what was now the most important thing in the world. "I love you too, Gerald," Dieter told him as he nestled close. Gerald lost all track of how long they held, petted, and kissed one another—an instant, minutes, hours—time seemed to fly around them, leaving them untouched and unaware.

A muffled ringing sound that stopped and then started again invaded Gerald's bliss. Blinking a few times, he realized it was his phone. Listening to Dieter's half-asleep, snuffly groan, Gerald smiled as he fished around on the floor for his pants before pulling his phone out of the pocket. "Hello," he answered, hoping to God it was some sort of wrong number.

"Gerald," the familiar voice said, "this is Harold. I was wondering how you were making out?" Gerald instantly turned toward the bed, thinking, *We weren't, but we could be soon*, but stopped the thought.

"We found some useful information that highlights how weak their case really is. Tomorrow I want to research the process the Austrians used to return looted art to the rightful owners and why that process wasn't followed for Dieter's family."

"Good. I'm glad the trip is turning out to be productive," Harold said.

"I think it's more than that. We found out that there are seven other paintings in the collection, and they don't appear to have any legal claim on them at all. I got official copies of all the documents; they're even sealed."

"Excellent. Call me or Brian if you need anything, and I mean that. We're here to support you in every way we can."

"Thank you. I'll do that." Gerald disconnected the call and climbed back in bed. "Dieter, sweetheart, we should eat before we go to sleep." Gerald heard Dieter snuffle before getting out of bed. They ate a light dinner at a café and then returned to the room, going right back to bed.

ARRIVING at the museum the following morning, Gerald once again gave his name to the same woman at the ticket window before sitting down to wait like they had the morning before, expecting Hanna to get them like she had. Instead, a tall man in a suit approached them. "Herr Young?" Gerald stood up and nodded. "I'm sorry, but you cannot visit the archives today."

"Can you tell me why?" Gerald asked, looking concerned at the very official way the man handled himself.

"The ministry has closed the archives to all but ministry personnel while a thorough review and cataloguing is made of all the contents," he said, his accent heavy, his tone clipped. "I am sorry, but I have to ask you to allow me to look in your bag to make sure you are not carrying any unauthorized materials." The man glared at Gerald, and Gerald could feel Dieter shifting around nervously behind him.

"No. You cannot search my bag or either of us. All the materials we removed from the archives yesterday were official copies that we purchased, and I have a receipt. Those copies are ours, and we paid for them, so unless you have something else, we will be leaving." Gerald stared at the man, and it was obvious he hadn't been expecting that answer.

"I will call the police," he said.

"You do that, and by the time they get here for such a foolish call, we will be at the American Embassy registering a complaint with our government and yours. I wonder what your superiors will think of an international incident." Gerald felt his words coming fast and sure, puffing himself up. He could see a small amount of doubt creep into the man's eyes, and Gerald knew it was now or never. "Come on, Dieter." Gerald stepped around the man and out of the museum with an iron grip on his case, walking fast.

"Where are we going?"

"The nearest subway," Gerald answered, continuing his fast pace. Once they reached the station, they descended the stairs. "I saw a post office in the large station near the city center, and I hope we can find some sort of business directory. I want to find a Federal Express office so I can send these copies to Harold."

"Why not just keep them with us?" Dieter asked as they ran their passes through the gate and descended to the track.

"I'm probably being paranoid, but Hanna checked our passports. She didn't copy them, but she did have our names, so the sooner these are out of our hands, the better. I don't want to explain them at the airport. Besides, they can't get from us what we don't have." The train arrived a few minutes later. Exiting the train at the city center station, they didn't find a post office, but there was a DHL Express office. Fishing out his phone, Gerald looked through his phonebook, finding Carolyn's phone number. "She's going to kill me."

"Who?" Dieter asked as Gerald connected the call, but it was already ringing.

"This better be an emergency," Carolyn said as she answered the phone.

"I know what time it is, and I'm sorry, but I need the firm's DHL Express account number and I need it now. I promise I'll bring you flowers and European chocolates when I get back," Gerald said, trying to smooth the way. He heard her moving around, probably to get her planner.

"Okay, I have it." She read off the number, and Gerald wrote it down before thanking her.

"Yeah, yeah. Those better be some damned good chocolates," she told him before hanging up.

"Let's go in," Gerald said. "I just got the firm's account number, so no one should be able to trace the package to us."

"Why all this cloak-and-dagger stuff?" Dieter asked as he followed Gerald into the office. "It seems like overkill."

Gerald smiled to reassure him. "It probably is, but these copies could be the key to everything, and I'm not taking any chances. Would you take care of things for me? It'll be easier in German. Here's the account number," Gerald said, handing Dieter the slip of paper along with a business card. "Have it shipped to Harold's attention."

"Okay," Dieter said, not sounding convinced, but Gerald's insides were fluttering and his gut was telling him that this was the right thing to do.

Gerald waited inside the door, half listening to the conversation between Dieter and the shipping agent while his mind raced through possibilities. Had someone at the museum found out he was a lawyer? That wasn't particularly likely. Had he and Dieter stumbled onto something that got Hanna's attention? Probably. Gerald could just imagine her reaction when she discovered Mitterval's letter. She'd probably alerted her supervisor, who then raised concerns up the ladder, and the ministry had closed the archives. That didn't bother him as much as the demand that he return the copies he'd paid for.

"They're on their way," Dieter told him, and Gerald felt much better. "Now, can we relax and stop running around the city like spies?"

"Yes," Gerald answered as the tension that had been building since the confrontation in the museum suddenly slipped away. "I have a bit of a surprise for you today. Come on." Gerald took Dieter's hand, ignoring the people looking at them as he led his lover back toward the subway trains. "Let's see a man about a house."

CHAPTER 8

DIETER left his office, feeling very nervous and excited. Harold's administrative assistant had called and asked if he could come in to the office after work. After having shipped the copies home, Gerald had taken him to what had been his family's home in Vienna, but to Dieter's surprise, he'd felt almost nothing. It was just a building now. It wasn't even a home any longer, but some sort of exclusive hotel. At least he'd been able to go inside and look through some of the rooms, but none of them looked anything like they had in Gram's pictures or in his imagination, and he left feeling only disappointed. Dieter had spent much of their remaining time in Vienna helping Gerald with his research. They'd gone to various research libraries throughout the city. Much of what they'd looked at, Dieter hadn't understood the importance of, but Gerald had seemed excited.

The day before they left, Dieter went back to the Belvedere and walked the halls, staring at his great-grandmother's portrait as well as the set of four landscapes for the longest time before saying good-bye. He had no idea what was going to become of the endeavor he'd set for himself and Gerald, but in his heart, he knew it was down to him to bring his family's heritage home. What he'd do with them if he got them, he had no idea. He'd cross that bridge when he came to it.

Since he'd been home, Dieter had spent the past three weeks working and completing tasks on his house and spending time with Gerald, but Gerald had been so busy that they really hadn't had a lot of time to spend together. However, the amazing thing was that Gerald never failed to call him each evening, and on the weekends, they always spent their entire Sunday together. They didn't necessarily do a lot or even go out. Those days became about the time they had together. Dieter wished Gerald had more time to spend with him, but he knew Gerald was working so hard for him and to help him.

Driving to Gerald's office, traffic was the worst he could remember, and by the time Dieter parked and took the elevator up, he was feeling bad that he'd wasted both his lover's and Harold's time. When the mirror-polished stainless-steel doors opened, the lobby looked deserted, with only one light on. Dieter nearly turned around to leave when Harold walked through the doors. "We're in my office," he told him, and Dieter followed Harold through the dimly lit hallways to the large corner office, where Gerald waited for him.

"I'm sorry I'm late," Dieter said to both of them as he looked through the quiet work area. "I didn't mean to keep you waiting, but traffic was awful, and I got here as soon as I could." He felt terrible that he'd kept them both waiting after the office had closed.

"We know," Harold said with a smile as he shook Dieter's hand, picking up his briefcase before walking through the doorway. "I'll leave Gerald to give you the news. Have fun." The only sound Dieter heard from Harold's trip through the office was the outer door opening and closing.

"I don't understand," Dieter said as he turned back to Gerald. "I thought there was something he needed to discuss with me." Dieter hadn't heard much about the case since they'd gotten home, and he was getting a bit nervous and excited, hoping that something would happen soon.

"Well." Gerald stepped forward, taking his hand. "This morning I took the paperwork to the federal courthouse and got it filed," Gerald told him, "so we've officially sued the Austrian government and the Belvedere for the return of all twelve of your family's artworks. This is only the first step, and there will be a lot of ups and downs, as well as waiting, from here. But I wanted to take you out to celebrate." Gerald's smile lit the office, and Dieter wasn't quite sure how to react. He wasn't sure suing someone was a particular cause for celebration. "I know I've been busy for the last few weeks, and I wanted to do something to mark this occasion, because it's the first official step toward the eventual return of your family's legacy." Gerald stepped close, and Dieter met his gaze in the late-day sunlight coming through the office windows. "I know this probably isn't the best occasion for this, but I've sort of felt like we haven't had much time together, and I wanted that to change." Tilting his head slightly, Gerald kissed him, his lips sliding lightly over Dieter's and then backing away. "I'm yours for the entire weekend. All we need to do is go to your place to pack a bag and we'll be off."

Resting his head against Gerald's shoulder, Dieter hugged Gerald tight, feeling his warmth through their clothes. "You don't have to do this. I'd be happy if we went back to your place and never left the bed for two days." Dieter lifted his head and found Gerald's lips.

"Wonderful, because that's exactly what I had in mind: you, me, a bed, and no clothing in sight. I made reservations for a nice dinner, and then we'll go to my place for the rest of the weekend." Gerald tightened his grip, and it felt as though he was going to kiss him again when a sound from outside drifted into the office.

"I think we'd better leave," Dieter said as he looked at the desk, "because I don't think Harold would appreciate us doing anything in his office." Dieter couldn't stifle a soft giggle as an image of him flat on the desk with Gerald standing over him flashed through his imagination.

"What's going on in here?" Linda asked, walking into the office, looking fierce enough that Dieter jumped back.

"Harold knows we're here," Gerald retorted, and Dieter felt Gerald's arm slide around his waist. "We filed suit this morning, so Dieter and I are about to go celebrate the first step in a long journey." He sounded confident in the face of this steely woman, who continued glaring at both of them like she'd actually caught them having sex on the desk. Still watching them, she stepped back, and Gerald led Dieter toward the door. Dieter felt somewhat like when he was a child and Gram had caught him doing something he shouldn't. "Have a great weekend, Linda," Gerald called, and he held it together until the front door closed behind them before breaking into a fit of giggles that took Dieter along with him.

When they got it together, Dieter called for the elevator, and they stepped in as Linda opened the office door. The elevator doors slid closed, and Gerald kissed him. They mustn't have been quite fast enough because the doors slid back open. Dieter knew Linda was staring at both of them, but Gerald didn't stop his kiss for a split second. Dieter would have liked to have seen her face, but the touch of Gerald's lips on his drove everything else from his mind, and he was barely aware of the doors closing again or the movement from the elevator as they descended toward the ground, and it wasn't until the doors slid open again that Gerald broke the kiss. "Let's go to dinner, and then we'll come get your car."

Dieter nodded, and Gerald led him out of the building and down the block to Dimitri's. "Is this where we're eating?" Dieter looked through the large plate-glass windows at candles flickering on white linen-covered tables with dark accents. "It seems so nice."

"It's wonderful and special, just like you," Gerald said quietly as he touched the small of Dieter's back with a very intimate gesture that propelled Dieter through the doors. Inside, the restaurant was very quiet. Intimate seemed like a cliché, but it was the only word that came to mind. Everyone spoke in low tones, including the staff, and Gerald spoke very softly to the elegant hostess before they were led to their table in front of one of the windows, where they could see people walking on the sidewalk and the lights in the trees that lined the sidewalk. "I always wanted to bring someone special here," Gerald explained as he stood and waited for Dieter to take his seat. A few minutes later, a server approached, filling their wine glasses. "I hope what I've arranged is okay, but they do an amazing beef Wellington here. They only make it for two, and you have to place the order ahead of time."

"You planned all this for me?" Dieter asked, realizing the thought and care that went into this evening.

"Yes. You deserve this and so much more." Gerald lifted his glass and waited for Dieter. The glasses tinged a perfect note, and the sip of wine tingled Dieter's tongue before sliding down his throat to warm his stomach. Their table was small, and when he set his glass down, Dieter saw Gerald leaning forward. Dieter looked around and saw no one paying any attention to them and looked back at Gerald waiting for him. "I love you," Gerald mouthed. Dieter didn't need to hear those words, he knew them, how they looked, and how they felt when they were whispered against his skin as they made love.

"I love you too," Dieter said, the sounds dissipating around them, but the look in Gerald's eyes would have shot through time and space to find him. Dieter had seen that look before, and he knew what it meant and what it felt like, enough to make his entire body tingle with anticipation and warmth. Leaning over the table, he met Gerald's eyes as they got closer, heads tilting slightly as they kissed softly and tenderly, the taste of wine and Gerald's now-familiar lips filling his senses.

When they separated, Dieter licked his lips slightly, staring across at Gerald as they settled back in their chairs. The moment was broken when the server nearly silently set their salad plates in front of them. Dieter took a small bite, the sweet, tangy flavor of the dressing bursting on his tongue as the crisp greens and pecans added texture and crunch while gorgonzola cheese added a touch of salty richness. When their salads were done, Gerald leaned over the table again, and this time, their kiss was salty and tangy, but still there was the taste of Gerald beneath everything, strong and with a touch of sweetness that always seemed to be there.

This time when they separated, Dieter peered around and saw a few other diners looking at them, and he turned back to Gerald, feeling slightly embarrassed, but Gerald smiled back at him, ignoring everything and everyone in the room except him.

The server cleared their dishes and brought a creamy vegetable soup that had an amazing flavor and seemed like melting butter in his mouth. Then their entrée arrived, puff pastry filled with beef, a rich sauce, mushrooms, and just a hint of pâté. The server cut into the shell and the smells filled his nose as a portion was placed on a plate and set in front of him. Dieter waited until Gerald had been served and the waiter left before he took his first bite. The flavors melded on his tongue, and Dieter thought he'd never tasted anything so wonderful. When he opened his eyes, he saw Gerald gazing back at him, and he knew the last time he'd tasted something as special, and he colored at the memory. "I know what you're thinking," Gerald told him very quietly, and Dieter looked down at his plate because he knew Gerald was right.

"You're picking on me," Dieter said.

"No, I'm not. I was thinking the same thing about you." Gerald smirked slightly before returning to his meal.

"I'm sorry I've been so busy these last few weeks," Gerald said as they finished their meals, his eyes dancing with excitement. "Yours is the first really major case I've handled, and it took time to make sure everything was done correctly."

Dieter always wondered whenever Gerald said things like that if he was just a case to Gerald. So much of their time, conversation, and energy revolved around his court case, and he wondered sometimes if Gerald was with him because of the case. He hated even thinking it, but the notion wouldn't go away. Dieter knew he wouldn't really know until it was over if he was excitement enough for Gerald, or if their attraction was based upon the adrenaline and energy that his case generated. He hoped it was more than just the court case and that he was enough, because Dieter loved Gerald, he knew that, and Gerald really seemed to love him. "The flowers you sent Monday were beautiful," Dieter said after swallowing his bite of beef, trying to get his mind off the case and onto the other things that Gerald did for him.

"I was thinking of you and wanted to show it," Gerald said, and Dieter internally chastised himself for doubting how Gerald felt, but deep down, the worry still remained to a small extent. He ignored it, though, as he concentrated on the soft look in Gerald's eyes. "I haven't had much time, and I wanted you to know that I missed you," Gerald said as he reached across the table to touch his hand, and Dieter colored slightly, not because he was embarrassed by Gerald's display of affection, but by his own doubtful thoughts that just wouldn't seem to go away. Gerald began to pull his hand away, but Dieter held it and saw Gerald smile warmly.

They finished their dinner, and the server cleared their plates. Gerald asked if he'd like dessert, but Dieter was too stuffed to eat another bite. The server brought coffee, and they talked for a while, saying nothing really, the words not nearly as important as the fact that they were together and the rest of the world stayed outside those plate-glass windows. The server silently placed the check on the table, and Gerald put his credit card on it, barely looking away from Dieter's eyes.

"Are you ready to go?" Dieter asked softly, his doubts now seeming like a distant memory under Gerald's gaze, and he felt a bit foolish for even letting them come forward.

The server returned and Gerald signed the check. "Yes," Gerald answered, pushing back his chair to stand up. He waited for Dieter, and together they stepped out onto the sidewalk and into the sounds of the city evening. The restaurant had been so quiet, so intimate, that the street seemed like a cacophony of sound and noise. Walking back to where their cars were parked, Gerald held Dieter's hand until they entered the parking structure. "I'll meet you at my house," Gerald said when they stood next to Dieter's car. "Don't take too long."

Dieter nodded. "I won't," he said, with Gerald kissing him sweetly before walking to his own car. Suddenly in a hurry, Dieter got in his car and sped out of the structure. Traffic was still bad, and it took him longer than he'd hoped to get home, although as excited as he was, instantaneous would probably have been too long. Rushing into the house, Dieter sprinted to his closet and found a small bag. Throwing in a few changes of clothes and his shaving kit, he rushed back out of the house, barely remembering to lock the door behind him before throwing his bag in the backseat.

Driving to Gerald's, Dieter somehow managed not to get a speeding ticket as he made his way through the streets. After parking out front, Dieter picked up his bag from the backseat before walking to the front door. Knocking softly, he waited until the door swung open. As Dieter stepped inside, the door closed behind him, and Dieter found himself pinned against it, Gerald's insistent lips pressing to his. Caught between the door and Gerald's warmth, Dieter threw his arms around Gerald's neck, returning the kisses with gusto. Dieter's pants tightened, and he felt Gerald's excitement press to his, and Dieter gasped and moaned into the kiss, his hips pressing forward, grinding into Gerald's. He hadn't seen him all week, and his body craved Gerald's touch, his spirit needing him. The buttons on Dieter's shirt opened, and he felt the coolness of the room against his skin as the fabric parted and fell to the floor. He felt Gerald guiding him away from the door and onto the sofa.

Gerald's lips fell away as they sank onto the sofa, and Dieter gasped when Gerald sucked on one of his nipples, and he inhaled deeply when he felt Gerald's hand slip beneath the waist of his pants. "God," Dieter panted as warm fingers encircled his length. As Dieter thrust his hips forward, the sensations threatened to overwhelm him, and Gerald hadn't even removed his pants.

"Gerry, it's too soon," Dieter gasped, and the fingers and hand slipped out of his pants, lips moving to lick and suck his other nipple. Gerald's weight pressed him into the sofa cushions, and Dieter tried not to thrust his hips. It was happening so quickly, and he didn't really want to come in his pants like a teenager, but Gerald felt so good, and once Dieter managed to work Gerald's shirt off, the skin-on-skin contact nearly sent him over the edge and Dieter had to think unsexy thoughts to keep his body under control.

Dieter's stomach muscles fluttered when Gerald's lips moved away from his nipple, kissing down his stomach, Gerald's tongue swirling into his belly button. The giggle that threatened was cut off when he felt fingers opening his belt before the zipper slid down tooth by tooth. "Is this what you want?" Gerald asked, as Dieter felt his underwear being pulled down around him, and then he was engulfed in wet, sucking heat. Whenever Gerald sucked him, Dieter thought his head was going to explode, and this time was no exception.

Dieter's hips thrust forward, and Gerald took all of him deep. Dieter whimpered softly, trying to keep himself under some semblance of control, but he could already feel it fading fast, too fast. Gerald sucked hard, forcefully pinning Dieter to the cushions as he bobbed his head, driving Dieter quickly to the peak of need and desire until he couldn't control it any longer and he poured himself hard and fast down Gerald's throat before collapsing back on the cushions in a completely limp heap. "You're so good to me," Dieter said contentedly, his eyes still closed as he waited for the room to stop spinning.

Stretching his hands over his head, he felt Gerald's palms caress his skin from his elbows to his belly, warm lips kissing him there. Then Gerald's weight lifted off him, and he allowed his eyes to slide open.

"Come to bed with me?" Gerald asked him, his voice deep, and Dieter accepted his offered hand as he lifted himself off the sofa, pants falling to the floor before he could reach them. "Step out of them," Gerald said. Dieter complied and followed Gerald into the bedroom, already nearly naked. After slipping off the last of his own clothes, Dieter climbed onto the bed, watching as Gerald stripped. Dieter loved watching Gerald's body appear from under his clothing. Long legs and a strong chest drew him like a moth to a flame. Scooting toward the edge of the bed, Dieter traced his fingers along Gerald's hip before sliding them around his balls and along his length. "If you keep that up, I'm not going to last very long," Gerald told him through clenched teeth before bending forward and taking Dieter's lips in a searing kiss. Using the kiss as cover, Gerald climbed onto the bed, Dieter moving along with him, letting Gerald direct him to wherever he wanted him. "What do you want, Dieter?" Gerald asked between deep kisses.

He had no idea what to say. "Everything, anything, as long as it's with you," Dieter answered, drawing Gerald down on top of him, bringing their bodies into contact, chest to chest, cock to cock, lips to lips. The kissing began again, and Dieter lifted his legs, entwining them around Gerald's waist as their hips rocked together. "Love you," Dieter said against Gerald's lips before kissing him. He did love Gerald, there was no doubt in his mind, but he'd never been in love before, and he'd never had someone in his life like this before. There had always been just him, Gram, and Auntie Kate. He'd already lost them, and somewhere down deep, he was finding it hard to believe that he wouldn't lose Gerald too.

Gentle fingers skimmed down Dieter's hips, gliding over his butt before teasing the sensitive skin of his opening, and all other thoughts, except what Gerald made him feel, flew from Dieter's mind. "You like it when I touch you here, don't you?" Gerald asked breathily as he teased Dieter's opening with small, circular movements that provided just enough sensation to register, but not quite enough for Dieter to know exactly what he was doing. It was maddeningly delightful, and Dieter squirmed beneath his lover, trying to get him to give just a little bit more. "Gerry! That's so mean!" The fingers slipped away and Dieter groaned in frustration. "That's not what I meant," he whined against Gerald's lips.

"I know exactly what you want," Gerald told him, and Dieter felt him smile before he kissed Dieter again. This time Dieter jumped slightly when Gerald slid a wet finger into his body. "And I'm going to give it to you, sweetheart, I promise." Gerald curled his finger, and Dieter felt the fireworks go off inside his body. He had no idea how Gerald knew just how and where to touch him, but he did that every single time, driving Dieter nearly insane. Pressing against the sensation, Dieter tried to take Gerald deeper, but the finger slid over the spot again, and he cried out as a zing of supercharged pleasure shot up his spine. Then the finger slipped from his body, and Dieter whimpered at its loss.

Gerald's weight shifted above him. As he sat up, Dieter watched as Gerald got himself ready. Dieter saw Gerald's chest expand with each breath, his eyes, soft and bright blue, shining down at him. Dieter continued to watch every movement his lover made as he finished rolling on the condom and then leaned toward him, his lips once again finding Dieter's, the kiss searing as Gerald slowly breached his body. This was still new for him, and each sensation seemed almost like their first time together. Only now, he knew what to expect, and he relished the feeling of Gerald deep inside his body, every pulse and movement of the long thickness inside him seeming to touch at his very core. "Yes," Dieter hissed when he felt Gerald's hips against his butt, and he locked his feet behind Gerald's back to restrict his movement. Gerald lifted his head slightly, and Dieter locked eyes with his lover, stroking Gerald's cheeks. "You're so beautiful like this," Dieter mumbled, throwing his head back when Gerald made his cock jump inside him, touching that spot once again.

"I'm beautiful?" Gerald scoffed lightly. "You look like an absolute angel, a sweet, beautiful angel." Gerald slowly slid back, withdrawing from Dieter's body before pressing back inside, and Dieter saw two of Gerald as his eyes crossed and his breath caught.

"Yes, right there," Dieter cried, and Gerald adjusted himself slightly before pulling out and driving back into Dieter's body. Putting his arms around Gerald's neck, Dieter held on as Gerald drove into him, touching that spot, driving Dieter to the point where he could barely see straight.

Being connected to Gerald was an almost transcendental experience for Dieter, and all he could do was hold on and let his lover drive him to the very peak of pleasure. Dieter's head throbbed and his body shook, muscles quivering as he opened his heart and body to Gerald, and he felt Gerald playing both of them like a virtuoso. Dieter's cock bounced against his stomach, and a few times he tried to take himself in hand, but every time he let go of Gerald's neck, he felt as though he were falling and he grabbed on once again. Not that it mattered. Dieter could still feel his excitement building with each drive of Gerald's body, each time his length slapped against his tummy. "Gerry, I'm... I feel like I'm falling," Dieter said softly, trying to keep his mind from swirling around and around.

"I know the feeling," Gerald said with a hard kiss, "I've already fallen for you."

"Oh," Dieter gasped as his body reacted physically to Gerald's sentiment.

"Come for me, sweetheart. I want to see you come without touching yourself." Gerald groaned as he drove deep, and Dieter arched his back up against Gerald's body, his cock brushing lightly against Gerald's skin, but that was just enough to send him over the edge with a cry that filled the room and echoed off the walls, leaving Dieter feeling a little hoarse as his body throbbed and he felt his release from his head to the heels of his feet. Then he felt Gerald tense before burying himself deep into his body as his lover's orgasm overtook him.

Collapsing back onto the mattress, Dieter managed to keep his eyes open long enough to see the amazing smile on Gerald's face. Then his eyes slid closed, and he gasped softly when their bodies disconnected before settling back down against the warmth of the mattress. He felt Gerald kiss him, and he watched through half-lidded eyes as Gerald retrieved a cloth and, after a cleanup, climbed into bed with him. Dieter rolled onto his side, holding Gerald tightly to him as Gerald's arm settled around his back, a hand stroking lightly along his skin. "I love you, sweetheart," Gerald said, and Dieter angled his face toward the sound of Gerald's words, sleep already threatening to overtake him.

"I love you too," Dieter replied happily before receiving a gentle kiss. Then he settled his head against the pillow and began to fall asleep to the sound of Gerald's soft chuckles. "What?" he mumbled, snuggling a little closer to the warmth.

"You're so cute. You always cuddle close and fall asleep after sex," Gerald told him, continuing to gently rub his skin.

"You want to talk?" Dieter asked, trying to roll over and open his eyes.

"No. Go to sleep," Gerald said softly, and Dieter slid his eyes closed, his mind already floating on happy, contented clouds that blew apart at an annoying ringing sound.

"Make it stop," Dieter said, burying his head in the crook of Gerald's arm, trying to escape the noise. He heard another soft chuckle and then felt the bed shake as the warmth near him slipped away. Rolling to where Gerald had been lying, Dieter soaked in his residual warmth as he heard his lover answer the phone, his voice getting closer. He didn't really pay attention to what was being said, but he heard Gerald say good-bye and then soft laughter as he tried to get back into bed.

"You took my spot," Gerald said before tapping Dieter's hip, and he slid over as Gerald's warmth rejoined him in the bed. "By the way, that was your phone," Gerald told him. "The call was from Mark. He called because he and some friends were going dancing tomorrow night and he wanted to know if you'd like to come along. I hope it's okay, but I said it sounded like fun." Gerald settled on the mattress, and Dieter felt him spoon to his back. "I like holding you like this." Gerald kissed his shoulder, and Dieter made an unidentifiable sound as sleep overtook him again.

Dieter slept like the dead and woke to an empty bed. Stretching, he opened his eyes to sunshine peeking around the curtains of

Gerald's bedroom windows. A slight twinge or soreness caught his attention, but it wasn't too painful and tended to remind him of the loving he'd received the night before. Pushing back the covers, Dieter followed his nose through the house and into the kitchen.

"You're still naked," Gerald commented with a leer from the stove. "Not that I'm complaining." Gerald stepped closer, and Dieter found himself wrapped in strong arms with warm hands cupping his butt. "I like this." Their kiss tasted minty, and Dieter sighed as the kiss deepened and his body reacted, his cock sliding against the soft fabric of Gerald's sweats. "You should get dressed before I forget breakfast and just drag you back to bed."

Dieter thought going back to bed sounded like a marvelous idea, but his stomach growled, reminding him that he really needed to eat. Stepping away from Gerald's incredible hands, he padded back toward the bedroom. "There are sweats in the bottom drawer if you'd like to borrow a pair," Gerald said as Dieter walked down the hall.

Opening the bottom drawer, he found a pair of old gray sweats and stepped into them. They were clean, but they still carried a bit of Gerald's scent, which he found quite nice. Padding back to the kitchen, he saw Gerald placing breakfast on the small table. "What did you have planned for today?" Dieter asked after he sat down and Gerald had joined him.

"Other than spending most of the day in bed with you? I need to get some wine for dinner, and I thought we could visit your friends Mark and Tyler if you wanted. My mother practically commanded me to come to dinner tonight, but I told her that I had other plans."

Dieter swallowed a bite of his eggs. "I don't want to come between you and your family."

"You're not. It's just that I'd rather spend some time with you right now. Since we got back from Vienna, we haven't had a lot of time together, and I missed spending time with you."

Dieter smiled as he took another bite. "I was wondering…. What happens now? I mean, you filed suit, but what happens next?"

"We wait for the Austrians to respond. The court will notify them, and they will be given a certain amount of time to respond. I suspect that I'll be hearing from their legal representation fairly soon."

That's what he'd been afraid of. "You tried to warn me this could take time, but I just want it over with."

"Try not to think about it too much. Sometimes things can drag themselves out for a long time. We have to be patient. Sometimes, though, we get lucky and things move relatively quickly. We'll just have to see. If we were filing our suit in Los Angeles or New York, it could take years, but we filed in Milwaukee, where the bench has been fairly stable and full, so their docket isn't as backed up," Gerald told him, reaching across the table to take Dieter's hand. "I don't want you to worry about anything to do with the lawsuit right now. We've done all we can for now."

Dieter blew out the breath he'd been holding. "I guess you're right. You told me we were on a long road once."

"And this is just one of the early steps," Gerald finished, and they went back to eating, but Dieter still felt nervous and jumpy.

"What if we lose?" Dieter asked.

"No matter what happens, we'll know we did our best. If we didn't do something, you'd never have a chance to get the paintings back. So you're doing the only thing open to you." Gerald stood and moved behind Dieter, nuzzling behind one of his ears. "I know this is going to be hard and nerve-wracking. The other side is going to try to make it as difficult as possible, hoping you'll give up. That's what they do. Our job is to stand firm, and we'll need to fight the entire way. You may not always like the way I have to fight, but that's what I'll be doing." Dieter turned to look at Gerald. "I love you, Dieter, and I want this because you want this." Gerald kissed him lightly. "Now let's finish our breakfast and find something much more fun to take our minds off courts and lawsuits."

Dieter set his fork on the plate and turned toward Gerald, pulling him in for a kiss before standing up and moving them toward the bedroom. He'd had more than enough to eat, and it seemed Gerald had as well.

THE rest of their weekend was magical. They made love so many times, Dieter lost count. On Saturday afternoon, they visited Sean at the wine store. Gerald bought some wine while Dieter and Sean talked and caught up. They also walked to Tyler and Mark's, visiting with both of them for a while and agreeing to meet at Snugs for drinks and dancing later that evening. Then Gerald and Dieter returned to Gerald's, where they curled together on the sofa to watch a movie. The movie quickly became an accompaniment to kissing, petting, and another round of passionate lovemaking that left Dieter breathless.

"I think we can forget the movie," Gerald told him as he reached for the remote to turn off the television.

"Yeah," Dieter replied as he leaned against Gerald, soaking up his warmth and basking in his heady scent. "Were we meeting for dinner or just dancing?"

"I wasn't sure. They said they were meeting at the Kettle for dinner, and that we were welcome to join them. I wasn't sure what you'd like to do, so I left it open, but if you're up for it, we could clean up and join them."

Dieter held on to Gerald, not quite ready to move yet. "In a few minutes."

Gerald chuckled, deep and rich. "We have all the time in the world," he said as Dieter's arms pulled him tight. "But I think I'm starting to get a little hungry."

Dieter gave Gerald another hug. "Then I think we better get dressed." Dieter got up and walked with Gerald into the bedroom, where he dug some clothes out of his bag, and after dressing, they left the house, arriving at the restaurant as Mark and Tyler arrived as well.

"Hey, guys," Tyler called as he held the door, and they walked inside. Sean and Sam were waiting at a large table along with some of the customers Dieter knew from working at the wine store.

"Gerald," Sean said as he stood up to shake hands, "you remember Sam." They shook hands as well. "And these are our old friends, Tom and Bill, and this is Gary and his partner, Scott." Gerald shook hands with everyone, and Dieter shook hands with Gary and Scott, but got a warm hug from both Tom and Bill. They were both friends of Sean and Sam, and Dieter had met them many times at the wine store. Everyone sat down, and the conversation began in earnest. It was a great meal, and Gerald and Dieter told everyone about their trip.

After dinner, everyone walked over to the bar. Slow music drifted out when they opened the door. Dieter had been expecting hard beat, like at Dance All Night, but this was even better. Everyone made their way to the back of the bar, finding a few tables around the dance floor. After getting drinks, Tom and Bill began to dance, the two men holding each other close. Mark and Tyler joined them, and so did Sean and Sam. Gary and Scott sat at the tables with Gerald and Dieter, watching the others. Then Scott led Gary to the dance floor, and the two of them were left sitting alone. "You didn't bring me here to watch other people dance, did you?" Dieter asked.

"You know I have two left feet," Gerald retorted, and Dieter stood up and extended his hand.

"It's easy. All you do is hold me and sway to the music," Dieter said, rolling his eyes, and Gerald finally got up and demonstrated that even with two left feet, he was still great fun on the dance floor. Once Dieter got him to dance, Gerald didn't leave the floor all night. Songs played and ended, but Gerald held him and swayed to the music while Dieter spent most of the evening with his head resting against Gerald's shoulder. He had a difficult time remembering a more wonderful evening in his whole life. And once they made it back to Gerald's, they made love again, slowly and quietly, like they were still moving on the dance floor.

THE remainder of the weekend was calm and relaxed, and on Monday morning Dieter hated going back to work. He and Gerald talked every evening, but it was the call Dieter received on Wednesday afternoon that surprised him.

"Dieter, we received a call from the Austrian consulate, and they said that their attorney will be here at four today," Gerald told him, and Dieter felt a lurch of nervous excitement. "I don't know if that's normal, but I was calling to ask if you'd like to join us. You don't have to, and this meeting will probably be pretty boring, but I wanted you to know."

Dieter checked the clock on his desk. He had plenty of work he needed to get done. "I'll try to be there." Dieter hung up his phone before returning his attention to the program he was working on.

"Is everything okay?" Reed asked as he stepped around the partition.

"Yes," Dieter answered rather quickly, his nerves making him jumpy. "I need to meet with the lawyers after work, and I'm a little nervous. Thankfully I got in early this morning, but I need to figure out what's wrong with this code before I leave, and it's not cooperating."

Reed pulled up the chair next to his desk before peering at his screen. "What is it doing?" he asked.

Dieter told him as best he could. "There don't appear to be any issues with the data."

"This system is as old as the hills. Whenever I work on it, I have to ask what's happening now that's new, because these jobs have been running for fifteen years." Reed pointed to the screen and began looking through the code. Soon he said, "Do you see it now?"

"Yeah." Dieter turned toward him and smiled. "Thank you."

"No problem. These systems should probably be replaced...." He gave Dieter another smile and walked back to his desk while Dieter made the change and began completing the required documentation. Thankfully, the rest of the day was quiet, and Dieter had been able to move the fix into production without any issues, so after explaining the situation to his supervisor, Dieter left the office and managed to make it downtown and into the parking garage a few minutes before the meeting.

Pressing the button for the elevator in the lobby, Dieter looked around him as he waited and saw someone familiar approaching. He couldn't quite remember why he knew him, but the man had "attorney" written all over him. As the elevator doors slid open, Dieter remembered. It was Gerald's brother Angus. Dieter got inside and Angus got in as well, along with the two men with him. Angus glanced at Dieter briefly, but he didn't seem to recognize him. Dieter pressed the button for Gerald's floor, and he noticed that they seemed to be going there as well. Dieter got an unsettled feeling in his stomach and it wasn't from the elevator ride.

Reaching the floor, the doors parted and Dieter let the others exit first. Angus walked right up to the receptionist, explaining why he was here, and she asked them to have a seat. Dieter approached her once they had sat down, and she immediately recognized him. "He'll be right out," she explained, and Dieter took a seat, occasionally looking over at Angus, who still hadn't recognized him.

Dieter didn't have long to wait before the lobby door opened and Gerald walked up to him. "Come on back, we're ready for you." Dieter stood up and saw the exact moment Gerald realized his brother was sitting in the lobby.

"Good afternoon, little brother," Angus said, his voice dripping with superiority. "We're here for a meeting." Angus checked his watch before adding, "And it seems to be running a little late."

Dieter caught a hint of surprise in Gerald's eyes for a split second, and then it was gone. "It'll be just another minute," Gerald said stiffly before leading Dieter through the door and back to his office. He said nothing until the door closed behind them. "Their attorney is Angus," Gerald said softly. "This could be interesting."

"We rode up in the elevator together, and he didn't recognize me," Dieter said.

"That's Angus. He only remembers people who he thinks will be of use to him." Gerald paced for a few seconds, and Dieter watched and wondered what was going through Gerald's mind. "This really doesn't change much," Gerald said as he stopped walking and looked at Dieter. "In fact, this might be to our advantage. Let's go to the conference room, and I'll have them escorted back."

Dieter nodded, still a bit confused, before following Gerald to a large conference room with plush chairs. Since they'd met, Gerald had been the strong one in their relationship, or at least that was how Dieter saw it, and for the first time, Dieter was worried about his lover. Lawsuit be damned—he didn't want to come between Gerald and his brother. A pitcher of water and some glasses sat on a tray in the center of the table, and Dieter poured himself a glass, gulping the water as Gerald took the chair next to him. "Dieter, this is Brian, my managing partner. He'll be joining us if that's all right with you."

"Of course," Dieter stood up and shook Brian's hand. They'd met a few times, but Dieter hadn't remembered his name, and he was grateful Gerald had supplied the help.

"You know who the opposing attorney is?" Brian asked Gerald, and he nodded forcefully before standing up as Angus entered the conference room, followed by the two other men. Dieter saw no sign of surprise from Angus as he and his associates took seats across the table from them.

"Let's get this dispensed with, shall we? I've already filed a motion with the court to dismiss the case on the grounds of national sovereignty. The courts in this country have no jurisdiction, and you know it," Angus explained forcefully, speaking to Brian, and Dieter lowered his eyes to the table.

"The Austrian government made money on the property in question in the United States—that means the courts do have jurisdiction and national sovereignty doesn't apply," Gerald answered, and Angus's head snapped to his brother. "But before we go any further, I think introductions are in order. I'm Gerald Young, and this is Brian Watson, one of our partners." Brian stood and shook hands with the other man. "This is Dieter Krumpf, our client." Dieter shook hands with the other attorneys and saw the instant Angus recognized him.

"I'm Angus Young, and these are my associates, Steven Gillespie and Jonas Holt, and so there's no misunderstanding, Gerald Young is my brother," Angus added to his associates before taking his seat once again. "That still doesn't change the fact that your case is really reaching."

Gerald didn't rise to the bait. "Your client requested this meeting, so we're not going to debate the case here. That's for court." He spoke strongly and confidently, which Dieter found a little exciting. "So why don't you come to the point."

Dieter felt his eyes shift from Angus to Gerald and then back, like he was watching some sort of imaginary tennis match.

"I've also submitted a motion to have your 'evidence' gathered at the Belvedere suppressed. There's no way to know those copies are genuine, and without access to the original documents, they can't act as proof, and you know it." Angus glared across the table, and Dieter's eyes shifted back to Gerald.

Opening his case, Gerald pulled out one of the copies they'd obtained. "You mean the official seal on the document from the Belvedere itself isn't enough? You should have done your homework, Angus. All the copies were certified by the Belvedere and consequently the Austrian government, since they own the institution, so I tend to believe your motion to suppress will be denied, just like all the other frivolous motions you can come up with. Is there anything else? Or did you come here simply to throw your excess weight around. That may work with other people, but not with me," Gerald added, and Dieter swung his eyes to Angus, who looked almost murderous. "I have provided copies of all the documentation we're using to prove our case. It's quite voluminous and very thorough, so you'll need to be on the top of your game with this one. Is there anything else?"

"No." Angus stood up and walked toward the door of the conference room before turning around dramatically. "My client has authorized a return of the seven non-Pirktl paintings in return for dropping this baseless suit right now, but that offer terminates when I leave this room." Angus turned and took a step toward the door. Dieter's heart pounded in his chest, and his eyes turned to Gerald, wondering what he was going to do or say. He didn't know how he felt about just those paintings, but getting them back would be something. Gerald never looked at him, though; his eyes were glued on his brother. Angus took another step toward the door.

"About those particular works of art," Gerald started to say, and Angus turned with a smug look on his face. He looked as though he thought he'd won, and Dieter felt his heart sink slightly as he looked at Gerald. "I contacted a friend in the art-theft division of the FBI. He works closely with Interpol on a lot of cases, including a case last year that returned two Rubens stolen from a museum in Spain. It seems he's contacted his colleagues at Interpol, and they're quite interested in those seven paintings. They were fascinated to think that the Belvedere is in possession of stolen art." Gerald's voice seemed so confident and self-assured, but his brother's face fell and his eyes burned at Gerald. "So I suggest you inform your client that in order to avoid an investigation into their entire collection as well as international press and scrutiny, those seven paintings will be returned to my client immediately. And just so we're clear, the lawsuit will continue. We're not backing down," Gerald said firmly, and though he hadn't raised his voice much beyond a whisper, the power behind it was more than evident.

"Shouldn't you ask your boyfriend what he wants?" Angus asked with a raise of his eyebrows in his direction, and Dieter shifted in his seat. He actually opened his mouth to say something, but Gerald beat him to it.

"I know what he wants. Those paintings that hang in that gallery in Vienna are his family legacy. *The Woman in Blue* is a portrait of his great-grandmother. These aren't some nameless pieces of art being grabbed at by some greedy divorcee, like your usual clients. These are a link to his past, and they belong to him. They were stolen from his family first by the Nazis and then by the Austrian government. So take that back to your clients along with the fact that we will fight them with every weapon in our arsenal, and that includes the media. They'll eat this up, especially against a foreign government."

Angus moved back to the table and leaned over it, his face right in Gerald's. "You don't want to take me on, little brother," he hissed.

Gerald stood up, leaning back across the table. "No. You don't want to take me on, old man. I'm going to screw with you six ways from Sunday. I've seen you in court, and I know how you operate. So

I suggest you go back to your office and give your clients the bad news. Because we will drag them through so much mud, the Viennese tourist board is going to wonder why there are no Americans in town. Now, you have a lot of explaining to do, so I suggest you go to it." Gerald motioned his head toward the door. "I'll expect to hear from you soon regarding the tracking numbers for the shipment of seven paintings. My offer is limited, and then I let loose the hounds."

Gerald sat back down, and Dieter watched as he turned to him. "Just tell me when he's gone," he said very softly, and Dieter met Gerald's eyes before glancing up as the three opposing attorneys left the conference room. Dieter saw Brian get up and close the door behind them.

"They're gone, Gerald," Brian said before bursting into ecstatic laughter. "Jesus Christ, I thought he was going to shit a brick when you mentioned the FBI and Interpol. Remind me never to play poker with you."

Gerald turned his head toward the other attorney. "I wasn't bluffing. These officers on the art-recovery teams would love nothing more than to have reason to go into these museums and make them produce provenance for every item in their collections. Most museums have items in their collections that don't really belong to them. The Metropolitan in New York recently returned a number of items that were found to be looted art that had made its way into their collection over the years. The Austrians were among the worst in getting looted art that was turned over to them back to its owners," Gerald explained before turning back to Dieter. "Are you okay?"

Dieter nodded, still barely able to believe what he'd just seen. "I guess so."

"Brian," Gerald said, "would you give us a few minutes?"

"Of course." Dieter saw Brian leave the room, and he wanted to throw himself at Gerald to feel the other man's arms around him.

"What's bothering you? Don't say 'nothing' because I can tell by the way you're biting your lips that something has you shaken," Gerald said as he touched Dieter's arm, fingers brushing lightly over his skin.

"I don't want to come between you and your family." Dieter could no longer meet Gerald's eyes and looked toward the floor. He'd never had brothers and sisters, or much of a family, except Gram and Auntie Kate, and he didn't want to be the cause of Gerald losing his. "The way Angus looked, he's going to be mad at you forever."

"No, he won't, and so what if he is? I was doing my job, and he was doing his. That comes with the territory." Dieter felt Gerald's fingers under his chin and he lifted his head. "If you want me to step away from this case, I will. You are more important than any legal case, and you're also more important to me than my brother, who, in case you haven't guessed, is a bit of an ass, even on a good day. I don't want you to feel bad about anything."

"Is this one of those client/boyfriend separation things?"

"No. Not this time. This is one of those, 'I don't want my boyfriend to feel bad because I had to do my job' things. This is what I do, and I'm good at it. I know I looked angry with Angus, but that was just an act. The same as he was acting with me, at least partially. Part of the job is trying to intimidate your opponents. It's a bit of gamesmanship, and today I showed him we're not a team to be messed with."

"We?" Dieter asked.

"Yes, Dieter. We're a team."

"But I didn't do anything," Dieter said.

"Yes, you did. You were here, and I knew that and felt you here. In a way, it gave me strength and added that extra bit of conviction," Gerald said, and Dieter looked toward the glass door and saw a couple heads peering into the room. Ignoring them, he turned his attention back to Gerald. "I meant what I said. I'll turn this case over to Brian and become just your boyfriend if that's what you want. You are more important to me than anything. I waited a long time to find someone as caring and wonderful as you, and I'm not going to let you go over something as marginal as a legal case." Dieter felt Gerald smooth his hair away from his forehead, the touch soothingly kind and thoughtful.

"You'd really do that? I know you think this is your chance to make a name for yourself." Dieter didn't know what to think. "No," he added, making up his mind. "I want you fighting for me in the courtroom and loving me in the bedroom. You were amazing today." Dieter swallowed hard around the lump forming in his throat before putting his arms around Gerald's neck and tilting his head to kiss him.

A small knock on the door sounded through the room, but Dieter ignored it. He was the client, after all, and if he wanted to kiss his attorney in the conference room, he was going to damn well do it. "I think we have an audience," Gerald said, smiling against Dieter's lips.

"Don't care. Do you have more work to do or can we go?" Dieter asked quietly as he met Gerald's eyes. "I want to be alone with you right now. You were so strong, so confident earlier, and it was really"—Dieter swallowed, wondering what Gerald would think of him—"kind of super-hot."

Gerald smiled and then threw his head back in a deep rich laugh. "Sweetheart, you better believe I'm done for the day. And just for the record, you're always kind of super-hot." Gerald got up from his chair and tugged Dieter to his feet. "Let's go before we completely scandalize the straight people." Gerald walked toward the door, and Dieter followed him. Pulling it open, Gerald stepped out into the hallway, leading Dieter toward his office. Gerald seemed to be ignoring the looks he was getting from his coworkers, so Dieter did as well, until he saw Harold Prince standing in Gerald's doorway with his arms crossed. Gerald walked right up to him, staring him in the eyes.

"What was that in the conference room?"

"A meeting with my client," Gerald replied in a level voice. "I'd appreciate it in the future if everyone in the office would remember that client conferences are confidential."

Dieter suppressed a snicker as Harold stepped aside, looking slightly amused. "I heard that your meeting went very well. I'd like you to fill me in, but I think tomorrow morning is soon enough." Harold turned, and Dieter watched as he walked back to his office. Gerald gathered his papers, placing them in his case before saying good night to people as they walked toward the lobby.

A buzz of excitement thrummed through Dieter's body as he rode the elevator down with Gerald, standing close enough to feel the waves of energy rolling off Gerald from the confrontation with his brother. He seemed to glow with it, and Dieter felt himself drawn to him like a magnet.

"I'll meet you at my house," Gerald told him, holding his hand before letting go and hurrying to his car. Dieter watched Gerald go for a second before rushing to his car as well, and thankfully, traffic cooperated, and Dieter was parking in front of his lover's house as Gerald was getting out of his own car. Gerald waited for him, and they walked to the front door together.

Inside, the door closed behind them, and Dieter lunged, clutching Gerald as he pummeled his mouth with kisses. He felt Gerald's arms around him, and Dieter pressed him into the room until Gerald reached the sofa and they toppled onto the cushions. "Can we go to the bedroom?" Gerald asked, his voice cutting through the haze of desire that had clouded Dieter's mind.

Dieter nodded and got up from the sofa, breathing hard as he waited for Gerald to stand before taking his hand and pulling him toward the bedroom, unbuttoning his shirt as they moved. Within seconds of reaching the bedroom, Dieter had himself naked, cock standing tall and throbbing, and was already attacking Gerald's clothes. Once Gerald's pants hit the floor, Dieter flung himself at Gerald, and they fell onto the bed, bouncing slightly on the mattress as Dieter kissed Gerald hard, taking his lips and feasting on his mouth. He couldn't think straight. All he kept seeing was Gerald standing up to his menacing-looking brother, calm and collected, knowing he was doing that for him.

Dieter wasn't sure which was the bigger turn-on, Gerald being so forcefully strong or the fact that he was doing it for Dieter—maybe both. Not that it mattered or that he spent much time thinking about it, because as soon as he felt Gerald's skin against his and tasted his lips, his entire world narrowed to just him and Gerald.

Breaking their kiss, Dieter needed to taste and touch. So, hands roaming over Gerald's skin, Dieter licked and sucked his way across Gerald's chest. Warm, slightly salty, slightly sweet skin passed under his tongue, and it seemed the more he tasted, the more he wanted. Lifting Gerald's arms, Dieter ran his tongue under them where the heavy, pungent taste of his love was concentrated into a heady rich banquet. Then Dieter kissed his way down Gerald's side, teasing the divot just above his hip as Gerald moaned softly, hips rocking as Dieter tasted.

"Please…," Gerald said softly between clenched teeth, and Dieter knew what he wanted because he'd made that same sound and asked for the same thing from Gerald. Shifting slightly, Dieter ran his tongue along Gerald's length, and the room filled with a high-pitched, almost whimpering moan. Dieter felt a zing slide up his spine as he realized Gerald was making that sound because of him.

The intense taste of Gerald, his Gerald, burst onto Dieter's tongue as he sank his lips over the swollen head and down the silky hard shaft, his tongue teasing the underside of the head. Gerald whimpered again as Dieter took him as deep as he could before backing off and trying again. Gerald always blew his mind, and Dieter wanted to return the favor. Dieter ground his hips against the bedding as Gerald thrust lightly upward, groaning softly. Dieter sucked as hard and deep as he could, his hips thrusting his shaft against the soft cotton sheets. Then Gerald stopped moving, and Dieter peered into his eyes, clouded and half-lidded with unbridled, lustful desire.

"Love you, sweetheart," Gerald said, and Dieter let his lips slip away from Gerald as he was drawn up into a deep kiss. As they kissed, Dieter found himself rolled on the bed, Gerald pressing him deep into the mattress while Gerald's knees spread and Dieter lifted his legs. Dieter heard the snick of a bottle, and then a finger pressed into his opening, deep and rough. Dieter gasped and the finger slipped away. "Need you right now," Gerald told him, eyes locking on his, and Dieter nodded, not trusting his voice or his breath to answer. Dieter felt Gerald fumble for a second, putting on a condom, and then he felt his lover's cock at his entrance. "Can't be gentle," Gerald whimpered breathily before plunging deep into his body.

Dieter gasped and the breath whooshed from his lungs as he held onto Gerald's shoulders, crying out in sheer, mind-clouding pleasure that threatened to overwhelm him. Before Dieter could catch his breath, Gerald withdrew and drove into him again like a man possessed. "Gerald, don't stop…," Dieter managed to say through gasping breaths as he locked onto Gerald's blue eyes, and their bodies quickly came to a union of movement.

Pulling Gerald down, Dieter kissed him hard, and he heard Gerald grunt something that sounded like, "Mine." Dieter wasn't sure, and now was not the time to ask, but as Gerald's thrusts became more frantic, his voice became clearer, and Dieter did indeed hear a chanting of the word "mine."

"Yes, yours," Dieter cried, arching his back to meet each of Gerald's ragged thrusts.

"You! Mine!" Gerald cried before kissing him hard, nearly bruising his lips.

"Yours, all yours," Dieter reiterated, his voice losing its force as the pressure built within his body. Still holding onto Gerald's shoulder, Dieter brought his hand to his cock, only to have Gerald bat it away.

"Come with just me. Nothing else. Feel how I love you, how I'm playing your body," Gerald gasped to him as he drove deep inside him. "Show me how much you love me. Let me see it and let me feel it."

Dieter threw his head back as Gerald pegged the spot inside him. Lights flashed and his ears rang as he came hard between their sweaty bodies, feeling Gerald throb deep inside him. Dieter stared up at Gerald, meeting his wide, blue eyes as his lover's pleasure wrote itself on his face. Then he pulled him down into a kiss, holding him as they basked in their love's afterglow.

Dieter felt Gerald slip from his body and still he held him, listening to Gerald's deep breathing and letting his eyes drift closed. Dieter loved that happy, floating feeling he got after making love. "I love you," Dieter whispered before kissing Gerald's cheek as he held him close.

"I love you too," Gerald said as he lifted and turned his head for a kiss, and Dieter happily obliged. Dieter let his eyes slide closed, listening to the sound of Gerald's breathing, feeling his warmth as he stroked his hand along Dieter's back. "We should get something to eat," Gerald said, and Dieter made a sound of recognition, but had no intention of moving. He was too comfortable and way too happy to move a muscle.

"Eventually," Dieter replied, this time coherently, keeping his eyes closed as his mind wandered and he started to drift off to sleep. Movement jerked him awake, and he felt Gerald slipping out of his arms. With a small groan, Dieter followed him out of the bed and into the bathroom, his eyes still only half open. Gerald started the shower, and Dieter waited for the water to warm and Gerald to get in before allowing himself to be tugged in as well.

The hot water woke him fully, as did the slippery hands that worked their way over his skin. Sighing loudly, Dieter rested against Gerald and soaked up the attention like a cat soaks up the sunshine through a window. He couldn't remember being this contented and happy with most everything in his life. He felt like a kid again, with almost no worries and cares.

"Are you humming?" Gerald whispered in his ear, and Dieter nodded.

"I'm happy," he responded, and he heard Gerald chuckle as the slippery fingers washed his delicate bits.

"I am too," Gerald told him, and as the hands slid away from his skin, Dieter opened his eyes, reaching for the soap. It was now his turn. Lathering his hands, Dieter caressed and washed Gerald's chest and stomach, making him chuckle as he tickled lightly. Resoaping his hands, Dieter slipped them under Gerald's balls and then along his shaft, beginning to tease him back to life before pulling his hands away and motioning for Gerald to turn around. Getting more soap, he thoroughly washed Gerald's back and butt, slipping his fingers between his legs to tease the back of his balls before he'd finished the job. After squirting some shampoo into his palm, he washed Gerald's hair, listening to his small, contented moans.

Once they were done, Gerald turned off the water and stepped out of the shower, handing Dieter a big fluffy towel. "What happens next? With the case, I mean," Dieter asked.

Gerald motioned for him to turn around and gently dried his back, and Dieter laughed when Gerald teased his butt cheeks. "We wait," Gerald answered. "Angus has filed his motions, and there will be a hearing on them at some point."

"Do you really think they'll send me those seven other paintings?" Dieter asked as he turned around to face Gerald, his eyes traveling up and down his body as he feasted his eyes on his lover.

"If they were ready with an offer that quickly, they realize they don't have a leg to stand on, so I suspect getting them back isn't going to be much of a problem. But we'll have to see. I'm sure I'll hear from Angus fairly soon with his next salvo. I beat him up pretty good, so he's going to come back with his guns blazing. But whatever it is, we'll be ready for him."

"I know," Dieter answered as he hung his towel on one of the bars. "I was impressed with the way you handled him. I saw some of that when you were dealing with the guard in Vienna, but you had Angus wondering where the next shot was coming from." Dieter smiled and stepped close to his lover. "It was amazing."

"It was?" Gerald asked, and Dieter stepped closer, tugging away Gerald's towel.

"Uh-huh," Dieter responded, putting his arms around Gerald's neck.

"We just got cleaned up," Gerald told him, but he didn't back away.

"So we'll get messy and take another shower," Dieter cooed just before they kissed. Gerald's hands slid down Dieter's back and rested on his butt, squeezing his cheeks as he led him out of the bathroom and back toward the bed. Food could definitely wait.

CHAPTER 9

GERALD stepped into his car and started the engine before driving to the office. Checking his watch, he pressed the speed dial on his car's Bluetooth control and dialed Dieter's cell. "Hi," Dieter answered, in a soft but happy voice.

"Hi, yourself. I wanted you to know that I got a call from the court. There's a hearing on Angus's motions this afternoon at three. I'll be there early because I can't take the chance that the judge will be ready for us before that. It's just a hearing, so you don't need to rush over, but I wanted you to know."

"Will we hear something about those other paintings?" Dieter asked. They hadn't heard anything from Angus in the past few weeks, but Gerald suspected he was going to hear something today. He just had a feeling.

"I'm not sure, but I'll call you after the hearing to let you know how it goes." Gerald stopped at a light.

"Will I see you tonight?" Dieter asked.

"I was hoping you'd ask. After court, I'll need to clear up a few things at the office, but I can meet you at your house if that's all right."

"Okay. I hope you have your pajamas packed," Dieter teased. "I'll try to be at the hearing, but if I can't make it, I'll see you at the house. Love you."

"Love you too," Gerald said before disconnecting the call as the light turned green, continuing to work with a smile on his face.

Gerald worked busily all day. Early in the afternoon, he walked to Brian's office, and together they drove to the federal courthouse. "Are you nervous?" Brian asked as he drove his deep-blue BMW sedan.

"No. Well, maybe," Gerald admitted as he looked at Brian.

"This is only a motion hearing, and you know most of what is going to be argued," Brian told him. "But you know that there will be one motion that he'll spring on you."

Gerald turned to Brian, suddenly very nervous. While he'd done plenty of negotiations, he hadn't spent a great deal of time in court, and that inexperience made him wonder if he could really do this. "What kind of motion?"

"I really don't know. But he will have one. Just keep your head and think how you'll respond. You have great instincts. You showed that during the meeting with your brother last month. So whatever you do, don't let him throw you, and always remember, if you need me, I'll be in the chair next to you."

Gerald knew that Brian was trying to be reassuring, but all he felt now were butterflies in his stomach. "There isn't a person alive who knows more about this case than you do," Brian reassured him. "Not the opposing attorney and not the judge. You've studied everything to do with this case backward and forward. You know where the case is a little weak and you know its strengths, so play to the strengths and let them carry you through."

"I know. I just want to feel confident when I go in there."

"You should. But know that the case will not be won today, but it can be lost. So make good, logical arguments, and you'll be just fine." Brian looked over and smiled at him before turning into the parking garage and finding a spot. Gerald grabbed his case and followed Brian through the garage and into the courthouse. The judge was running behind, so Gerald and Brian found a place to sit. Brian made phone calls while Gerald worked on the outline for a brief until the judge's clerk informed them that they would be ready for them in ten minutes. Gerald thanked her and put away his papers, closing his case as he saw Angus approaching, his usual smug look on his face. As he approached the courtroom, Angus refused to acknowledge him in any way, and when the doors to the courtroom opened, Angus strode inside, the door closing after him. Gerald felt Brian's hand on his shoulder. Gerald smiled at him before pulling open the door and walking into the courtroom.

Brian walked to the front of the room and Gerald followed, taking the chair next to Brian at the plaintiff's table. Gerald opened his case and pulled out his notes, setting them in front of him before sitting down to wait. A door at the back of the room opened, and Gerald stood as Judge Ellis entered. "Be seated, please," he said and took his chair behind the bench. "This is simply a hearing on the various motions in this case." Judge Ellis looked toward the defendant's table. "Mr. Young, you've brought a number of motions, so we'll start with your motion on jurisdiction." Judge Ellis turned to Gerald, and he felt the man's gaze. "His motion has merit. The defendant is a sovereign nation."

"True," Gerald started, "but it's a sovereign nation that made money in this country on the assets in question. Therefore they are subject to US law, particularly on assets they've used as the basis to make the money here in this country." Gerald realized his nerves faded as soon as he began speaking, and he saw Judge Ellis turn his attention back to Angus.

"I believe I agree with you. Mr. Young, your motion for dismissal is denied. You also have a motion to suppress the documentation gathered by the plaintiffs at the Belvedere. I see no basis for suppression. The copies are officially sealed."

"They were obtained under false pretenses," Angus explained.

"How so?" The judge leaned forward.

"They did not properly identify themselves, Your Honor."

"Did they not use their real names?" The judge prompted.

"They did. But they falsely represented the reason they were there. On their research application, they said they were doing artistic research."

The judge smiled and turned his head to Gerald.

"We were. We were researching art. That's artistic research. When we entered, we gave our real names and showed our passports. We also paid for and received official copies, and each one has the official seal," Gerald explained.

"Mr. Young, you're wasting the court's time with these frivolous motions. However, I am going to ask for more information on this topic." He looked at Gerald, who nodded. "Do you have anything with merit?" The judge seemed to be getting impatient with Angus, and Gerald could feel hope building inside him.

"I have just one more motion. I'd like to request a delay," Angus said, and Gerald looked at Brian, who nodded at him. This must have been the surprise.

"On what grounds?" Judge Ellis asked, clearly becoming annoyed. Gerald heard the back door to the courtroom quietly open and close, and he felt eyes on his back that hadn't been there before. He shivered slightly but quickly regained his composure and concentrated on what Angus was saying.

"The Austrian government has set up a commission to research Mr. Krumpf's claims and determine the ownership of the five Pirktl paintings. So I request a delay so the commission can perform their work." Angus looked over at him with a slight smirk, and Gerald saw the judge sit quietly for a second before turning to him.

"I'm inclined to agree with the defense."

Gerald knew he needed to think fast, but his mind had suddenly gone blank. He knew he had to get his thoughts together, so he picked up the papers in front of him, pretending to fan through them. Turning his head slightly he saw Dieter sitting in one of the benches off to the side, looking at him with complete confidence.

"Your Honor," Gerald began, "the Austrian government can set up as many commissions as they wish." Gerald kept his voice measured as an idea began to form. "But I'd like to point out that this is the same government that denied my client's grandmother's request for a review of the ownership of the paintings on the basis of flimsy evidence that they then tried to bury in the archives of the Belvedere." Gerald felt a well of energy spring inside him. "So this motion should be granted only if you believe that the Austrian government would realistically agree on their own to return some of the most important paintings of the early twentieth century to my client." Gerald glanced at Angus very briefly before continuing. "That is, unless the defense feels my client's case is so strong that the Austrians will turn over my client's family legacy without a fight." Gerald saw a touch of amusement on Judge Ellis's face before he schooled it away and looked at Angus, who realized his motion was dead in the water.

"The motion to delay is denied, and I'm scheduling this case for the first week of November. I have an opening in my docket, and this case will work in nicely," Judge Ellis said, looking at both of them. "I'll send over the information request. Are we done? Good." The judge rose and left the courtroom. Gerald gathered his papers and shared a smile with Brian before turning to Angus.

"So, what about the seven paintings?" Gerald pressed, not ready to give up the momentum he'd built.

Angus swallowed before glaring at him with such malice that Gerald felt it all the way to his feet. "They're being packed for shipment, and I'll have my assistant call you with the information," Angus said, his words ground out between clenched teeth, and he turned and stalked out of the courtroom. Gerald turned toward Dieter and smiled, the tension immediately draining out of him. Motioning him over, he watched as Dieter came closer.

"I'd love to kiss you right now," Gerald whispered, "but I could get in big trouble." Dieter nodded his understanding. "But I have some good news. The seven non-Pirktl paintings are in the process of being shipped. I think Interpol appearing on their doorstep was great motivation. These museums rely on Interpol if they have a problem, and the last thing they want is them to not answer the phone when they're needed." Gerald arched his brows and watched a grin break out on Dieter's face. "It's not the end goal, but it's part of it."

"Thank you," Dieter said, his eyes shining with unshed tears. These paintings didn't include the portrait of his great-grandmother, but they were part of his great-grandparents' legacy, and Gerald knew this was an emotional experience for him. He wanted to hold him right now, but he was in court, and Gerald saw Angus standing in the doorway at the back of the courtroom glaring at both of them through the half-open door. "Are you going back to your office?" Dieter asked as they walked toward the back of the courtroom.

"Yes. The judge asked for some additional information regarding one of Angus's motions, and I want to get that done, but he set a court date for November. I'm surprised it's happening that fast, but I'm grateful for it." Gerald stopped himself from taking Dieter's hand as they approached the door, with Brian walking behind. Gerald saw Dieter look at Angus and Gerald followed his gaze. Gerald met Angus's eyes defiantly, almost daring him to say anything, and Gerald saw him actually step back. Then he turned to Dieter. "I'll see you at your house after I'm finished, and we can talk. There's something I'd like to discuss with you." Now that they were outside the courtroom, Gerald leaned close to Dieter, nuzzling his neck slightly. "Don't worry, it's not bad," Gerald whispered softly. "I'm glad you were here. I could tell the minute you walked into the room, and I liked it."

"You did?" Dieter sounded unconvinced.

"Yeah. It may sound funny, but even though I was busy, I could feel you looking at me. It made me feel good." Gerald smiled and sighed softly.

"Come on, Romeo," Brian said from behind him. "We need to get back to the office." Brian winked before looking at Dieter. "He did great today, but the judge asked for some more information on the motion to suppress some of our information, and we need to get it to him sooner rather than later."

"Okay, I'll see you at my house when you're done." Dieter gave him a quick smile before turning and walking toward the staircase down to the main floor, and Gerald stared at the tight little backside until he disappeared.

"You two are an inspiration," Brian told him, and Gerald squinted, more than a little confused. Brian had a stunningly beautiful wife and an eight-year-old daughter. "Come on. Let's get back to the office." Brian led the way through the hallways and down the stairs and into the parking garage.

"Do you want to tell me what that was all about in there?" Gerald asked once they were in the car. "You and your wife always seem happy."

"Barbara and I are good at projecting that image, but we haven't been happy in a long time, and we've decided to divorce. She complains that I don't spend enough time with her and…." Brian sighed and looked tired. "I could say it was the job, but it isn't—it's me. I met Barbara in college, and we were good friends. After a party where I got very drunk, one thing led to another, and I woke up in bed next to her. I honestly don't remember anything, but a month or so later Barbara said she was pregnant, and it took me a while to decide, but then I asked her to marry me. Looking back on it, she probably manipulated the whole situation. I was in law school by then, and she wanted to be Mrs. Lawyer." Brian paid the parking fee and turned into traffic. "I know I can tell you this because I'm confident you'll keep it to yourself."

"Of course, Brian," Gerald replied, wondering just where he was going with this. While Brian had been his managing partner since he joined the firm, they'd never really talked much about personal matters.

"The thing is, Barbara and I were friends, and I thought we could make things work. I never really loved her, but we had a daughter, and Zoe is the light of my life."

"So you stayed for her?" Gerald asked, as they rode through the busy city traffic, stopping at almost every traffic light.

"Yes, and because I made a commitment to Barbara. But the last few years since I made partner have been difficult. Barbara thought that once I made partner, our lives would be one big social event where she could rub elbows and show off her successful husband. I hate those events, and I told her that now that Zoe's in school, she needs to get a job. Not that we need the money, but all Barbara does is spend, spend, spend. I cut off her allowance and canceled her credit cards. So she got a job, which was good." Brian looked across the seat while they were stopped at a light, and Gerald knew this story wasn't going to end happily. "Last week I caught her in bed with her new boss."

"Oh God, I'm sorry," Gerald said sympathetically.

"I'm not. Not really. We haven't been happy in a while, and she told me she wants a divorce."

"What about Zoe?" Gerald asked, getting the feeling that was probably the issue.

"Barbara was never particularly maternal, and I've told Barbara that if she thinks of suing for custody, I'll dig up proof of every manipulative thing she's ever done." The lawyer Gerald usually saw came forward in Brian's tone. "She is the one who cheated, after all. We've worked most things out already, and I suspect that she'll move out within the next few weeks."

"Then what's the issue?"

"The thing is that I've buried myself under what I needed for my career or my marriage." Brian looked at him and seemed nervous. Gerald had never seen Brian nervous before. "Umm, I probably have more in common with you and Dieter than you might think."

Gerald was about to ask what he meant when it hit him, and Gerald gasped before snapping his mouth closed. "You're telling me you're gay?"

"Yeah. I set that part of myself aside years ago, and I never gave it any thought. But with Barbara leaving, and seeing how happy you and Dieter are together, I think it may be time for me to try to live my life again. I know I have to be careful for Zoe's sake, but I can't keep putting off my life. The thing is, I don't know how or where to start." Brian pulled into the parking garage near the office and parked in his reserved spot.

"It's funny, but in some ways, I'm a lot like you," Gerald said. "The job kept me busy enough that I never really had the time or the inclination to meet people, other than for a quick hookup. That is, until I met Dieter. He's an incredible man, and I'm lucky to have found him, and once you're ready, you'll be lucky too."

Brian turned off the car's engine and unhooked his seat belt. "Please don't say anything to anyone in the office."

"Brian," Gerald said pausing with his hand on the door handle, "this isn't my story to tell, and I know this isn't going to be easy, but I'll help you any way I can. When I first joined this firm, you were very supportive and helpful even when you didn't really have the time. Now it's my chance to return the favor." Gerald opened the door and got out of the car, waiting for Brian before walking toward the elevators, his head spinning just a little. Gerald had never gotten the slightest inkling that Brian might be gay. "I'll talk to you later," Gerald said as they entered the office, before hurrying to his desk. He had things he needed to get done, and Dieter was waiting for him.

It took him a while, but Gerald got the information ready and forwarded to Judge Ellis's clerk before shutting down his PC. Leaving the office, he got in his car and hurried through traffic to Dieter's house. It was still light, and he saw Dieter on his hands and knees, cleaning out debris from under the shrubs. "Hi, sweetheart," Gerald said as he approached, watching as Dieter stopped what he was doing before looking up at him, grinning to beat the band.

"Hello, yourself. I'm just finishing up here and then we can go inside," Dieter said before reaching under the shrubs and pulling out a handful of leaves and sticks, placing them in a leaf barrel. "I've wanted to get these shrubs cleaned out since spring, but never got the chance."

"Did you do all the work in the yard?" Gerald asked, noticing almost for the first time how colorful it was even in late summer.

"Yes. I started working on it when Gram was still alive, but she never liked me to take things out except when they died. So in the last few years, I've replaced many of the old, overgrown shrubs and bushes with fresh ones, and I've tried to put in plants that bloom. They may be green most of the year, but I like everything to flower. It's not a big yard, so I want it to be colorful." Dieter reached beneath the shrubs and cleaned out what Gerald hoped was the last of the debris.

"Can I ask you something? Would you be willing to leave this house? I mean, to live somewhere else?" Gerald shifted his weight from one foot to the other.

"This has always been my home. Why would I leave?" Dieter stood up and pulled off his gardening gloves before hefting the barrel and carrying it around the side of the house. Gerald followed and watched as Dieter pulled out the sticks before dumping the rest into a square wooden container behind the garage. He put the barrel and gloves in the garage before pulling the door closed. "What is it you're asking?"

"I was asking in a rather dumb way if you would move in with me. I'd like to spend all my time with you."

Dieter stopped what he was doing and stared at him, his mouth open in surprise. "You want me to move into your house? But what would I do with this one? I...." Dieter shook his head.

"You never thought that we might move in together someday?" Gerald asked, feeling his heart beating fast.

"Yeah, I did. But I guess I saw us living here." Dieter looked up at the house for a second before returning his gaze to him. Gerald could see the conflict on Dieter's face and a bit of disappointment. "This is my home, and I thought that maybe it could be our home. I like your house, and it's very nice," Dieter added hastily. "It's just that I've always lived here, but I guess I could live somewhere else. But what would I do with the house? I couldn't sell it. It wouldn't feel right selling the house where Gram lived, even though it's not really her house anymore." Dieter bit his lower lip. "I want to live with you. I really do. Maybe I just need to think about it." Dieter walked toward the back door, and Gerald followed him inside.

This had not been the reaction he'd hoped for. He'd thought Dieter would be excited, and they'd hurry upstairs to celebrate. Instead, Dieter had gotten quiet, and in the kitchen he moved slowly, without looking at him, acting like someone had just died. "Sweetheart, I didn't want you to feel bad." Gerald stepped to him, touching Dieter's shoulder. "I want to live with you and go to sleep with you every night and see you first thing every morning. It doesn't matter if we live at my place or if we live here. As long as we're together, that's what's important to me—the rest is just geography."

"Do you mean it?" Dieter asked, some of his energy returning. "But what about your house? It's really nice and you put a lot into it."

"It's a house. I bought it a few years ago, and while it's my first house, I guess what I want is a home, and that's with you. We could sell the house, or look into renting it, but I want to be with you."

"But you'll be giving up so much." Dieter stopped what he was doing and looked around the old-fashioned kitchen that probably still looked much the same as it did when his grandmother was alive.

"I won't be giving up anything that's important," Gerald replied wrapping his arms around Dieter's waist to tug him close. "That's just a building. I know you grew up here and have lived your entire life in this house. It has much more meaning for you, and I'd be more than happy to live here with you." Gerald leaned close, smelling the scent of Dieter's hair, and said, "And sleep upstairs in your bed with you, and make love to you for a very long time, in this house." There, he felt it, that little shudder that winged its way through Dieter's body. "That is, if you'll have me."

Dieter turned around in his arms and kissed him. "Yes, I'll have you," Dieter said with joyous laughter. "Do you want to celebrate now, or should we eat first?"

Gerald smiled at the playful look in Dieter's eyes. "We should eat first, because once I get you upstairs, I don't intend to let you go until morning." Gerald stepped back so Dieter could move. "But let's not take too long, okay?" Gerald expected Dieter to go back to work, but instead he set the dishes aside and took Gerald's hand, leading him out of the kitchen and into the dining room and then through the hallway to the living room.

"You probably think I'm holding on too tightly, and maybe I am, but in that corner is where Auntie Kate used to read me stories. I just can't sell this house—it's so full of memories." Dieter turned to look at him, eyes soft, almost pleading. "But I'd like to make some new memories here with you, and I'd really like it if you'd move in here with me." Dieter stepped close to him, placing his arms around his waist before resting his head on Gerald's shoulder, like it belonged there, and as far as Gerald was concerned, it did.

"Sweetheart, I'll be just as happy living with you here, or at my house, or in a tent, as long as I get to be with you," Gerald told him with a huge smile before gently using a finger to tilt Dieter's head up slightly. "I love you so much." Gerald kissed Dieter's lips ever so lightly.

"I love you too," Dieter said, and Gerald felt him bounce slightly in his arms. "I can't believe we're going to live together."

"And sleep together, every night," Gerald reminded him, tightening his grip, hugging Dieter tighter. He should have known how Dieter would feel about leaving this house. The man had lived here his entire life, and if Gerald were honest with himself, it really didn't matter where they lived as long as they were together. Yes, he knew it sounded like a cliché, but for him it was true.

"I should finish making dinner," Dieter said without making any effort to get away.

"You know, we could skip dinner and just go upstairs," Gerald offered, not feeling very hungry for food, but definitely ready to spend some quiet, alone time with his lover. Well, at least alone time, because if things worked out as he was expecting, they were rarely quiet.

Their stomachs answered for them, loudly. "We really should eat," Dieter said before giggling and rubbing Gerald's stomach. "I promise that after dinner we can have a nice, long dessert in our bed." Gerald liked the sound of that, he really did.

"Is there anything I can do to help?" Gerald asked, holding Dieter's hand as they walked back toward the kitchen.

"I have stuff for salad if you'd like one." Dieter got out the fixings, and Gerald made the salad while Dieter finished the rest of dinner. The food was simple but good, and they ate Dieter's burgers and salad with smiles on their faces. Afterward, they cleaned up, and then Dieter took Gerald by the hand and led him upstairs.

The bedroom door shut behind them with a quiet snick, closing out everything but Dieter's searing look and the shiver that shot down Gerald's spine. "I want to take care of you," Dieter murmured before taking his lips in a deep kiss. "Will you let me?" Dieter asked, and Gerald bobbed his head forward slightly. "You always take care of me and take the time to show me that you love me." Dieter's fingers began working the buttons on his shirt, and Gerald let his hands hang at his side. "You always tell me you love me," Dieter whispered, his voice, though soft, wrapping around Gerald like a thick blanket, "and then you make love to me and show me what your words really mean." Dieter slid Gerald's shirt off his arms and then Dieter's mouth sucked lightly at the base of his neck, and Gerald stretched without conscious thought to ask for more.

Warm hands trailed over Gerald's chest, stroking patterns that seemed to sear their way onto Gerald's skin as Dieter kissed along his shoulder. Dieter's hands moved slowly around to his back, stopping just above his butt, and Gerald arched backward, feeling Dieter support him, before molten lips clamped around a nipple. Gerald hissed and moaned softly, and Dieter sucked a little harder. Gerald spent much of his life thinking, and as Dieter's lips spread their heated magic over his skin, Gerald felt the thoughts that occupied his mind most of the time go silent, his racing mind quieting until only Dieter remained in his thoughts. This had happened before, but not like this, and Gerald began to realize just how deep his love for the man making his knees shake truly went.

Somehow, Gerald got his shoes off, a part of his clouded mind working to some extent, and he heard his belt tinkle and then the pressure around his waist fell away as his pants slid down his legs. Slowly, Dieter moved him until his legs hit the side of the mattress, and Dieter pressed him backward using only his lips. Dieter pulled Gerald's pants off his legs before tugging away his briefs, and Gerald lay naked, staring up into Dieter's love-filled eyes. Gerald had almost always taken control during sex. He hated feeling vulnerable, and he expected to feel that way now, but he didn't. He felt cared for, loved, and from the way Dieter looked at him, desired above everything and everyone else. He hoped Dieter would remove his clothes, but instead he felt fingers encircle him, and Gerald's eyes closed as the sensation of being held overtook him and his body relaxed into the feeling. Dieter loved him, and he could feel it in every single touch.

Slow strokes starting at the base worked their way along his entire length before ending with a light swipe across the head. "Sweetheart," Gerald mumbled as he bucked lightly into Dieter's grip. A light touch on the inside of his thighs caused Gerald to spread his legs, letting his lover take whatever he wanted.

"Dieter!" Gerald gasped, his eyes flying open when he felt his lover's lips slide down his length. Gerald's hips bucked forward, and he felt Dieter's hands on his chest, soothing him back onto the mattress. "You're gonna kill me."

Dieter shook his head slightly, and Gerald felt Dieter's fingers at his lips. Opening his mouth, he sucked in two of Dieter's fingers as though they were his cock, moaning slightly when they slipped away again. Then a warm, wet finger pressed to his entrance, and Gerald's first instinct was to balk. He'd only allowed one person to do that, and not in a very long time, but this was Dieter, his Dieter, his lover, and Gerald's protest died on his lips as the finger breached him, spreading warmth throughout his body. He felt Dieter's finger move around inside him, and he wasn't too sure he liked it, until Dieter touched the spot and took him deep at the same time. In that instant, Gerald wasn't sure which he wanted more, and he began flexing his hips in small movements, trying to figure out how to make both things happen at once, and he growled when Dieter's lips slipped away.

"Have you done this before?" Dieter asked, touching the spot once again, and Gerald felt the air rush from his lungs as he cried out.

"Not in a long time," Gerald answered, trying desperately to catch his breath.

"Oh," Dieter said softly, and Gerald felt the finger slip from his body. "I don't want to hurt you," Dieter said, "and I don't have any experience doing this."

Gerald realized he was being given a way out, and an easy one at that. But to his surprise, he found he wanted to feel Dieter inside him, and he wanted Dieter to make love to him. In fact, it was suddenly very important to him. His family was competitive and pretty dysfunctional, and Gerald had never really trusted many people in his life, but since he trusted Dieter with his heart, he knew he could trust him with his body. "You could never hurt me, sweetheart, at least not that way," Gerald said with a small sniffle as he brought Dieter's lips to his, pulling off his lover's shirt.

"Are you sure?" Dieter inquired, the concern in his voice evident even as he quickly shed his clothes in a flurry of excited activity.

"Yes, I'm sure," Gerald answered as he reached to the nightstand for the lube. When he looked back, a naked and very excited Dieter met his gaze. Taking the bottle, Dieter opened it, squirting some on his fingers before sliding first one finger and then a second into his lover's body. Gerald tensed at the invasion, but as soon as Dieter began sucking him again, his concerns floated away, and Gerald lost himself in the movement of Dieter's lips and the twist of his fingers. At some point, Gerald thought he felt Dieter add a third finger, but he was too far gone to register it until he felt the light stretch and then Dieter was pegging that spot while Gerald thrust into his mouth, the last of his control slipping. Gerald lost it, shouting God knew what as he came in a mind-blowing orgasm that left him as limp as a noodle, splayed on the mattress, gasping for breath as he tried to get his mind working again.

"Are you okay?" Dieter asked, and Gerald opened his eyes to find Dieter stroking his forehead, peering down at him, looking very concerned. "I didn't hurt you, did I?"

Gerald smiled, still trying to get enough air. "No, sweetheart. You blew my mind."

"Oh," Dieter said and looked pleased as Gerald pulled him into a kiss. "I guess that's okay, then."

"It's more than okay. It was amazing." Gerald had been able to take Dieter to a place like that a few times. He'd seen his lover a little dazed and confused after he'd come, but this was the first time anyone had ever done that to him, and Gerald realized that maybe it was because he'd never let anyone get that close before. "You were amazing and I love you so much." Gerald kissed Dieter hard, pulling him close so he could feel his lover's skin as they moved. The one thing he felt above all else was Dieter's length pressing insistently along his hip. "I think I'm ready for you," Gerald whispered into Dieter's ear before nibbling on it with his lips.

"Are you sure?" Dieter asked, biting his lower lip. "We don't have to."

Gerald repositioned himself on the bed so he was more comfortable. "I want you so much," Gerald said between kisses, surprising himself that what he was saying was very true. Gerald reached to the night table, and after finding what he wanted, he handed the silver foil pack to Dieter. "Maybe, since we're moving in together, we can get tested so we don't need these anymore," Gerald said hopefully, "because I only want to make love to you for the rest of my life."

Gerald saw Dieter's smile shine through the room, his eyes dancing as he slowly nodded his assent. "That's what I want too." Locking their gazes, Gerald watched as Dieter opened the packet and only looked away to roll on the condom. Positioning his legs on Dieter's shoulder, Gerald bent his knees and felt Dieter press at his opening, his body resisting at first, but then opening for his lover.

Gerald could feel every ridge and contour of Dieter as he filled his body, and every twitch sent ripples through his body. Hypersensitive to every movement, Gerald groaned long and low when he felt Dieter seat himself deep inside him. But what amazed him most was when Dieter slowly pulled away and Gerald moaned, loudly, surprised by the way it felt and by the sense of emptiness that engulfed him. He'd heard the sounds that Dieter made and he'd thought that was just him. It wasn't. Gerald gasped, feeling almost like he was balancing on the edge of a knife until Dieter slowly and deliberately pressed back into him. "Do you remember when you did this to me?" Dieter asked once he was fully seated again, leaning forward so their lips almost touched. "Fucked me so slowly, I thought I was going to die? Well, that's what I'm going to do to you."

"Oh God," Gerald managed to moan as Dieter withdrew slowly and deliberately. "Are you sure you've never done this before?" Gerald arched his back, trying to get Dieter to move faster or give him just that much more sensation.

"No," Dieter answered, pressing deep once again, then holding still, his hands stroking the skin of Gerald's chest, fingers tweaking his nipples. "But I had a masterful teacher."

"Masterful, huh?" Gerald's quip morphed onto a deep groan, and whatever else he was going to say flew from his head.

"Yeah," Dieter replied. "Now you know what you do to me every time we make love. Do you see how you make me feel? How good you love me?"

"Yes," Gerald hissed, breathing heavily because it was all he could do, and even though he'd experienced the climax of his life not fifteen minutes earlier, he could feel his excitement growing and his body reacting to Dieter's loving. Gerald wanted to swear and curse at the top of his lungs as Dieter refused to move any faster, but he gripped the bedding with one hand and stroked himself with the other as he slowly climbed the mountain of passion that Dieter built and then drove them steadily toward the peak. Gerald knew that no matter what he did, his pleasure was in Dieter's hands, and he loved it that way. Gerald had always done the driving, so to speak, and this was new and more pleasurable than he could ever have imagined. As they reached the peak, Gerald felt Dieter's control waver, his movements getting steadily more ragged, his lover's breathing coming in deep pants. A sheen of sweat covered both of them as Gerald's second release exploded from him, and he saw Dieter's eyes cross and his mouth hang open as he cried out like a wolf baying at the moon before throbbing inside him and collapsing onto Gerald's chest.

They lay together in a heap, breathing deeply, holding onto each other as though they both needed reassurance that they could find their way back. "Oh God," Dieter squeaked between breaths as their bodies separated.

"I know," Gerald responded through the fog that still clouded his mind. He didn't dare open his eyes or this amazingly ethereal feeling would evaporate like the morning fog, so he held his lover, listening to him breathe without moving or caring if they ever moved again.

"Love you," Dieter whispered, and Gerald made some sort of sound back, not having enough energy or ambition to actually form words. Instead, he simply held Dieter, and this time it was his turn to close his eyes and let his mind go. How long they lay together, Gerald didn't know, but eventually he felt Dieter shift and slip away. Then a warm cloth caressed his skin, followed by a soft towel, and then Dieter's warmth returned. "Can I ask you a question?" Dieter inquired, and Gerald smiled, snuggling close without opening his eyes.

"You can ask anything you want. Except maybe ask me to move."

"I saw you in court today, and it looked like we won." Gerald could hear the hope in Dieter's voice.

"All I did was stop the defendant's motions. We really didn't win anything." Gerald let his eyes slide open so he could see Dieter's face. "There's still a long way to go, but I think the judge is intrigued by our argument and wants to let it play out. It doesn't mean we'll win, but it's encouraging that our argument isn't being rejected out of hand. The good news is that the judge set an early court date, and the best news is that the non-Pirktl paintings are being prepared for shipment." Gerald rolled onto his side, running his hands over Dieter's chest. "Angus said he'd call the office when they were ready to be shipped." Gerald snickered softly. "I don't think the Belvedere knew what hit them when Interpol came calling."

"So what happens next?" Dieter asked, his eyes widening expectantly.

"Well, I decide what I want to do with my house, and we figure out when you want me to move in with you. We keep a lookout for your paintings, and I'll be ready for court. I've already sent the judge the information he asked for. So other than that, we wait and go on with our lives." Gerald shifted so Dieter was beneath him. "And we love each other and make each other happy." Damn, he could not get enough of this man. "From now on, things will happen in the court's time, and it's out of our hands, but we can make the most of the time," Gerald quipped lightly.

"I like the sound of that," Dieter told him and started wriggling under him. "I guess I can wait as long as I have you to wait with me."

"That you do." Gerald gathered Dieter into his arms, hugging him tightly as he smiled to beat the band.

"There is one thing, though," Dieter said seriously.

"What's that?" Gerald felt some of the ease slip away.

"In case you didn't see it in court, I know you think this is just a case for your brother, but it's not," Dieter said, and Gerald released his hug, looking into his lover's eyes. "I saw the way he was looking at you when you and Brian were talking. He hates you. It was as naked on his face as I am right now. He doesn't see this as a game, and it's not just another case for him. Your brother hates you with everything he has, and I feel guilty."

"Don't," Gerald countered. "My brother hating me is not your fault, and I'm not going to lose a case to make him like me. It's my job to do my best, and he's the one who's taking this personally." Gerald slid off the bed and began pacing the floor. "Angus was always a bully, and Dad sort of encouraged him because he thought it made Angus strong. And as a lawyer, he's still a bully. He intimidates opposing attorneys and their clients basically into giving up. You saw the way he acted in our first meeting. That wasn't for me—that little act was to try to intimidate you, but it didn't work. And like most bullies, he does not like it when people stand up to them."

"But he's your brother."

"Yes, he is. But I'll let you in on a secret. I've never liked him very much, even when we were kids, so if he hates me, he hates me. That's his problem. Not mine and certainly not yours." Gerald stopped pacing and looked at Dieter, who'd propped himself up on his elbows, watching him. "Angus is just another attorney as far as I'm concerned."

Dieter moved back onto the bed. "When I was a kid, I would have given anything to have had a brother." Dieter drew his knees close, wrapping his arms around them.

"I know," Gerald said, sitting on the edge of the bed. "And I had a great sister. I wish I could tell you that I had a great childhood, but I really didn't. My dad constantly pushed all of us to be better, faster, stronger than the other kids. It didn't matter what it was, we had to be the best, and since I was one of the youngest, I seemed to get it from my older brothers and sister as well. Thankfully I had Mary and Mom." Gerald shook his head. "Talk about dysfunctional." Gerald moved so he was sitting next to Dieter. "Not all families are what we'd like, and sometimes they're what you overcome, but they helped make me who I am."

Dieter smiled at him. "Then I guess I can't really complain, because I like who you are."

"Me too, and you know what? I like you." Gerald hugged Dieter close once again. "But I think we'd better get something to eat before my stomach thinks I forgot all about it."

"Yeah, I guess we'd better," Dieter said, getting up off the bed before rummaging in one of his drawers, that perfect little butt on perfect view. Finding what he was looking for, Dieter pulled on a pair of sweatpants and offered Gerald a pair before they headed downstairs to the kitchen to finish making dinner, with Gerald moving a little gingerly and Dieter snickering at him when he jumped a little before sitting on one of the wooden chairs. For him, it didn't get much better than this.

*C*HAPTER *10*

DIETER peered out the front window once again before returning to his work. Today was moving day, and he was waiting for the movers to deliver Gerald's things. Gerald had spent much of the morning at his place, directing the movers, while Dieter had spent the time making sure there was a place for the things Gerald was bringing. Gerald had decided to sell his house, and one of his neighbors who had been renting bought the house almost as soon as it went on the market. Gerald's closing was in a few days, and tonight they would officially spend their first night together in their home. Thankfully, Gerald wasn't a pack rat, and they had sat down and already planned where everything was going to go, so all they really had to do was direct the movers and then unpack the boxes. Dieter's phone chirped in his pocket, and he smiled when he heard Gerald's ringtone.

"Are you on your way over?" He was more than a little excited.

"The movers just left, but I got called into the office. Hopefully it won't take long, and I'll be home as soon as I can. I'm really sorry about this. I hate dumping all this work on you."

"I know. I'll be fine alone here with the hunky movers," Dieter teased, and Gerald scoffed before laughing.

"I'll see you as soon as I can. Love you," Gerald said before disconnecting the call, and Dieter went back to work, adjusting his game plan. A knock on the front door pulled him away from his work, and he opened it, expecting the movers, but smiled when he saw Mark with his small dog on a leash.

"I heard today was Gerald's moving day, and we stopped by to see if you needed any help," Mark said.

"Come on in. I could use all the help I can get," Dieter said, and Mark stepped inside, letting Jolie off her leash. She immediately began jumping around Dieter's legs, and he lifted her up, his chin immediately covered with doggie kisses. "Gerald got called into the office," Dieter explained as he heard the sound of brakes out front. Opening the doors, he saw the moving truck pull up in front of the house.

"You direct where you want things, and I'll help place the furniture and items, but first I'm going to take her home," Mark told him as he took Jolie from his arms before heading toward the house up the street.

Dieter met the movers and walked them through the house. By the time Mark returned, the men were already bringing things into the house. Peering into the truck, Dieter was surprised how little there was. Granted, a number of easily portable things had already been brought over. Dieter told the men where to place the furniture, and when Mark returned, they began opening boxes while the rest of the things were brought in. A little over an hour later, the men were done, and Dieter said good-bye after signing what they needed. As they pulled away, Gerald pulled up and parked in front of the house, followed almost immediately by another truck.

"What's all this?" Dieter asked as Gerald stepped out of his car.

"The reason I got called into the office. It seems that this particular truck contains fourteen crates. They sent them to my office."

"Fourteen crates?" Dieter asked, wondering just what was going on.

Gerald bounded toward him with a huge grin. "They're your paintings. They sent them to my office, and I redirected them here. They sent the paintings and the frames separately. There's also a letter with instructions for unpacking them, and it details which painting goes with which frame." Gerald handed him an envelope before hugging him tight, lifting him off the ground. "I know this isn't your great-grandmother's portrait, but it's a start, and I also found out today that your day in court begins on Monday." Gerald set his feet back on the ground before kissing him hard.

"Oh, hey, Mark," Gerald said with a smile as Mark joined them. "I think we may need your help. Some of Dieter's paintings arrived from Vienna, and even though they sent instructions...." Gerald looked at him and Dieter nodded. "We don't feel as though we know enough to unpack them."

"Let me make a phone call. I have a friend who knows everything about things like this."

"Where would you like them?" one of the delivery men from the truck asked in a deep voice.

"We can put them in the living room for now," Dieter replied before asking the man to follow him. After showing him where to place the crates and placing blankets on the floors to protect them, he got out of the way as the two men carried each of the wooden crates inside. Once they were done, Dieter signed what they needed and thanked them both before heading inside. To say the house was a mess was an understatement. There wasn't a single room that didn't have boxes packed against the walls or furniture waiting to be placed.

"Where do we start?" Gerald asked him, and Dieter shrugged his shoulders. "How about if I start in the dining room and you work on the kitchen? We can't do much with the living room until we figure out what to do with the paintings, and they're safest in their crates for now."

"Okay," Dieter agreed. "Did you see where Mark went?"

"Last I saw him, he was still outside talking on the phone." The front door opened and Mark stepped inside. "Speak of the devil. Would you like to join us for lunch?"

"I can't. I have an appointment at the studio in half an hour, but I wanted to tell you that I'll stop back about four and meet Peter. He's my agent as well as the owner of the Peter Barrett Gallery. He said he can help get the art unpacked. I told him about the works, and he's really intrigued."

"Perfect. We'll see you then, and plan on dinner. It's the least we can do for all your help," Gerald said as he shook Mark's hand, only to be pulled into a hug. Mark hugged Dieter as well and then hurried out the door.

"I'll make some lunch if you want to get started," Dieter told Gerald before walking into the kitchen. There wasn't a great deal to put away in here. Gerald had donated a lot of his kitchen things to charity, so there were only five or six boxes that needed to be put away—mostly small appliances and stuff like that. Dieter found the bread and began pulling things out of the refrigerator, making thick sandwiches. Carrying the plates into the dining room, he returned for cans of Coke before joining Gerald around their table. "It's looking better already," Dieter said after they'd sat down. Gerald had placed a lot of the furniture, even around the crates, and had emptied some of the boxes.

"It shouldn't take very long. I didn't move that much stuff, and I've already hauled a few of the boxes I don't need right now to the attic." Gerald took a bite of his sandwich, smiling.

"I can't believe you're here," Dieter said, and he felt Gerald take his hand.

"I am here, and I'm glad we decided to live here. This is a great house and now it's home." Gerald squeezed Dieter's hand. They finished eating, quietly looking at one another and then around their home. Dieter could barely sit still he was so excited. After finishing their lunch, they both went back to work, unpacking the boxes and getting their home in order. Together they'd already cleaned out the last things from Gram's and Auntie Kate's rooms. It had been hard for Dieter, but necessary. Dieter finished in the kitchen before climbing the stairs to get their bedroom in order. They had decided to set up one of the smaller bedrooms as an office, and the movers had set all of Gerald's things in that room. Closing the door, Dieter left it alone so Gerald could set it up the way he wanted.

Late in the afternoon, they'd accomplished a lot and were taking a break together on the sofa when the doorbell rang. Dieter got up to answer it and found Mark on the doorstep with an older-looking gentleman. "Dieter, this is Peter Barrett," Mark said, and Dieter stepped back so they could come inside. "He's probably one of the best people around to get your paintings unpacked and back in their frames.

"It's a pleasure to meet you both," Peter said, shaking hands with both Dieter and Gerald, who'd joined them, before looking around. "This is very nice." Dieter saw when his eyes fell on the crates. "Let's see what you have. Can we use the floor here in the hall? It looks like there's more room."

"I'll get some blankets," Dieter said, and he hurried upstairs. When he returned, he spread one of Gram's old cotton blankets on the floor, and Gerald and Mark hefted in the first crate. "The letter says that crates one and two go together. One has the painting and two contains the frame."

"Let's get the frame out first so we can insert the painting directly into it. I brought a cordless screwdriver. It's in my trunk. I also brought some basic framing tools I thought we might need." Peter handed his keys to Mark, who returned a few minutes later. There was so much excitement in the room Dieter thought his hair would stand on end as Peter began removing the screws from the first crate. There seemed like dozens of them, but finally he lifted off the lid before gently removing a large, flat bundle wrapped in bubble wrap. "Mark, carefully remove the wrapping and set the frame on the table facedown."

Gerald followed Mark, and Dieter could hear the two of them talking in the dining room as Peter began removing the screws in the next crate. "Does the letter say how they packed the paintings?"

"It's in German, but it says they are placed in some sort of cradle in the crate," Dieter explained, and Peter lifted off the lid and whistled.

"This is amazing. They constructed a system within the crate that holds the painting like a frame, only with shock absorbers around it so it couldn't get jostled. Leave it to the Germans." Dieter didn't correct Peter as he carefully reached inside, unfastening the framing system and withdrawing the painting and its protective cover. Pulling away the covering, Peter walked the painting into the dining room and set it carefully into the frame before fastening the painting in place. "We should find places to hang these for safety."

"Hang them in here and in the living room. It doesn't matter where right now," Dieter told him anxiously. "The hooks go into the studs," he added, wanting to see the painting so badly, he was nearly jumping out of his skin.

Peter carefully hung the painting, and Dieter stepped back, looking at the impressionistic landscape. The others looked as well, but then went back to work while Dieter simply stared. This was the first part of his family's legacy. After staring for a while, Dieter began hauling the empty crates to the garage, placing them carefully so they could be reused if they were needed. When he returned, Peter had the next painting in its frame and was hanging it on the wall.

Dieter kept himself busy while the others got each of the paintings in their frames and hung on the walls. Gerald helped him carry out six sets of crates. The last set of crates was smaller than the others, and Peter opened the crate with the frame. It was plainer than the others. Gerald took the crate to the garage while Dieter watched Peter open the last crate, taking out the painting. After unwrapping it, Peter placed it in the frame before turning it around so Dieter could see it.

"I have to tell you, these are amazing works, worthy of most any museum. They aren't masterpieces, but they are all very high-quality pieces. But I think I like this one the best," Peter explained.

The painting Peter held was the only portrait in the group, and Dieter stared at it and his mouth fell open. "Please hang that over the fireplace. I'll be right back." Dieter hurried upstairs to his room, grabbing Gram's photo album before hurrying back down, clutching it to his chest. "Look," Dieter said as he opened the album and carefully paged through until he found the picture of Anna, Joseph, and Gram. "Is that her?" Dieter looked to the painting and then at the photograph.

Peter studied the photograph and then looked at the painting. "They're definitely at different ages." Peter walked to the painting and carefully lifted it down from the wall. "Let's check the back."

Peter laid the painting on the dining-room table. "There seems to be some writing, but it's very faint."

Dieter looked at the back of the yellowed canvas, carefully peering where Peter indicated, seeing the faint, probably pencil markings. "G. Meinauer," Dieter said before checking again to make sure he wasn't seeing what he wanted to see before turning to Gerald with a smile on his face. "Gram was Gertrude Meinauer. It's her." Dieter clamped his eyes closed to keep the tears from spilling out. The document they'd found at the museum had listed a portrait of a child, but Dieter had never dreamed it would be a portrait of Gram as a girl.

Peter re-hung the portrait before looking at each of the paintings. "These are wonderful," he pronounced after he'd looked at them all. "If you want, I could take photographs of all of them, make a few notes, and I can provide you with written appraisals for insurance purposes."

"Thank you," Dieter said, shaking his hand. "I really appreciate you helping us. Tyler should be over soon, and we were going to dinner. Would you like to join us?"

Peter thought for a few seconds. "I think I'd like that. Will you tell me the story behind all this?"

"Sure," Dieter answered.

"You aren't going to believe it," Mark added as they headed for the door.

Peter looked from Mark to Dieter, who pointed at the portrait of his grandmother.

"Her mother is the Woman in Blue," Dieter explained.

"Meinauer," Peter muttered. "*That* Meinauer. No wonder the name was familiar. Your great-grandmother was Anna Meinauer?"

"Yes, and on Monday we go to court to try to get her back too," Dieter said, taking Gerald's hand. "I promise I'll tell you the whole story over dinner."

"I made reservations at Magellan's. I'll call and add one more. We'll meet you there at seven," Gerald said as he held the door for

Mark and Peter. "It looks like we have just enough time to get cleaned up."

"We have an hour before we have to leave," Dieter said, as Gerald began tugging him upstairs.

"Yeah, a whole hour, I wonder what we're going to do?" Gerald retorted, moving a little faster. "So what do you want to christen first, our bed or our shower?"

"Can we do both?" Dieter asked, laughing as they hurried up the stairs and down the hall.

"How about shower before dinner and bed after dinner?" Gerald asked as they reached the bathroom, pulling Dieter into a hug before kissing him, and the debate ended there.

THEY had a great dinner and an even better evening and night. Gerald spent much of Wednesday and Thursday at work, and Dieter continued unpacking when he wasn't at his office. On the weekend, they worked together to finish getting the house set up, and on Sunday evening, Gerald built a fire in the fireplace, and they sat together in the living room with Dieter held close to Gerald and loving every minute of it. "Are you nervous about tomorrow?" Dieter asked.

"A little, are you?"

"Yeah. You said I may need to testify." Dieter knew he sounded nervous.

"You may, yes. If Angus tries to make an issue of the copies we got in Austria, then you'll need to testify about how we obtained them. Most of the proceeding will be about things like proving you're the heir of Anna and Joseph and showing that you are the rightful owner of the paintings, stuff like that. I think the case is going to hinge on whether we can make the argument regarding the sovereignty issue. There isn't going to be a jury, just the judge. Angus and I present our facts and proof, anything we feel will boost our case, as long as we back it up based upon the law."

"When will we know if we've won? Will the judge tell us at the end?" Dieter asked, snuggling closer in the dark room, the firelight dancing on the walls. It should have felt romantic, but Dieter was too nervous and just wanted to be close, and thankfully, Gerald sensed that and held him.

"No, he'll decide and write his opinion. Judge Ellis knows that whatever he decides will probably be appealed, so he'll make sure he's got everything as solid as possible. So please don't be nervous. After we go to court, it could be weeks before we know," Gerald cautioned him lightly.

"I guess. It's just hard." Dieter rested his head against Gerald's shoulder.

Gerald turned his head toward the painting above the fireplace. "Whatever happens, I hope you know I've done my best."

"I do. No matter what," Dieter said as he looked at the portrait of his grandmother, "we've both done our best, and if nothing else, we brought Gram home, and I got back some of my family's heritage. I think Gram would be pleased." Dieter found himself looking at the portrait once again as he settled next to Gerald, listening to the sound of the crackling wood in the fireplace.

"I'll be right back," Gerald told him, and Dieter sat quietly looking around the room at the art that had once hung on his great-grandparents' walls. Gerald came back and handed him a glass of wine before sitting next to him once again. They didn't talk much for the rest of the evening. Having Gerald next to him was all he needed, and once the fire burned down and went out, Gerald took their glasses to the kitchen, and they went to bed.

Dieter didn't really sleep well, and at one point Gerald rolled over, rubbing his back lightly until he finally fell asleep. In the morning, they got ready for work. "Will you call me when they need me?"

"Of course. But you'll need to be ready on short notice," Gerald told him as he finished tying his tie.

"I'll do my best." Dieter had taken enough vacation time, and he really wanted to be able to take some time with Gerald over the holidays.

"I know you will," Gerald said before giving him a kiss. "I'll give you as much notice as I can." Gerald slipped on his jacket, and Dieter saw him check himself in the mirror before leaving the bedroom and heading downstairs. Dieter finished dressing and followed behind. Coffee was already on, and Gerald poured him a mug. Once they'd finished their coffee, the mugs were placed in the sink, and both of them headed to work.

At his office, Dieter went right to his desk and did his best to work, but his mind was on Gerald and what was happening downtown at the federal courthouse.

"Dieter, what are you doing here?" Carl, his boss, asked from behind him. "I thought you'd be in court today."

"Gerald said he'd call if they need me. I only have so much vacation time left."

"Go on," Carl told him. "You put in plenty of extra time, so call it comp time and go. I'll see you on Wednesday. You need to be at the courthouse, not here."

Dieter didn't have to be told twice. Shutting down his computer, Dieter hurried out to his car and drove downtown to the courthouse, considering himself lucky to find a parking space. Once inside, he walked to the same courtroom he'd been in before. Seeing the doors open, he walked in and saw one of the clerks up near the judge's bench. He told her who he was. "Gerald Young said I may be needed as a witness," he explained.

"Then come with me. We have a room for you to wait in because you can't hear anything in court until you testify."

"Okay." Dieter followed her to a room with chairs and a sofa.

"I'll let them know you're here," she said before walking to the door.

"Thank you," Dieter said before sitting down to wait. There was nothing in the room other than a few old magazines, and Dieter sat, letting his mind wander. He sort of lost track of time, but eventually the clerk returned.

"They've decided you don't need to testify, so you can go sit in the courtroom if you like." Dieter followed her out of the room and into the back of the courtroom. Gerald was reviewing Dieter's relationship to Anna and Joseph Meinauer, providing paperwork for each point he made. Angus looked bored, and the judge didn't seem particularly interested, but this must have been part of the business that had to be done. Brian sat next to him, watching Gerald as he spoke.

"Mr. Young," Judge Ellis said, turning to Angus, "do you wish to contest?"

"No, Your Honor, we are satisfied that Dieter Krumpf is the only great-grandchild of Joseph and Anna Meinauer," Angus said, and then Gerald began presenting evidence on the paintings themselves. Dieter noticed that Gerald did not talk about Anna's letter at all.

Angus and Gerald then got into it about the documentation, and the way they'd obtained the copies. They argued back and forth until the judge intervened. "Mr. Young, the copies were purchased under their own names in an archive that was open to them, so I'm ruling the copies admissible." Dieter nearly whooped, but kept quiet as the proceedings continued forward.

"The plaintiffs have not provided all the facts as to the ownership of the paintings in question," Angus said, stepping forward to hand the judge a piece of paper. "Anna Meinauer stated very clearly that she wished her portrait and the four Pirktl landscapes to go to the Belvedere upon her death. Regardless of how they got there, that is where they have resided and where they belong, according to her wishes." Angus looked smug as he took his place at his table once again. "I included a copy of the original document in the archives of the Belvedere along with a certified translation."

"Mr. Young," Judge Ellis said, looking at Gerald, "this statement of intent seems to discredit your entire case. Do you wish to challenge the translation?"

"No, Your Honor. However, I would like to present you with the rest of the document. It seems the defendants have only presented part of the facts, the way they did during the investigation requested by Gertrude Meinauer Wolfe." Gerald handed the judge a piece of paper. "This is the certified copy of the rest of the letter. What the defendants are saying is a will is actually a personal letter to her husband asking him to donate the paintings to the Belvedere. She did that because the paintings weren't hers. Her portrait was a birthday gift to her husband, as stated in that letter, and the four Pirktl landscapes were in fact the property of Joseph Meinauer at the time they were confiscated. Her actual will left everything to her husband." Gerald stepped forward, handing the judge another set of papers containing the will. "Courtesy of Interpol. I just received the copies this morning. Of course I'll make copies available to the defendant's counsel, but I believe they already know of their existence." Gerald looked pleased, but Dieter saw he stopped short of smug.

Angus was trying to keep his face schooled, but Dieter could see the color rising in his face, and to make matters worse, Angus denied nothing. "Is there anything else you'd like to enter into evidence, Mr. Young?" Judge Ellis asked Angus.

"Only the question of national sovereignty."

"Mr. Young?" The judge turned to Gerald.

"Not at this time."

"Very good. Then we'll break for lunch." Judge Ellis banged his gavel and stood up. The few people in the room stood as well, and the judge exited. As soon as he left, Gerald walked back to where Dieter was sitting.

"Pretty exciting, isn't it?"

Brian joined them on his way out. "We should get lunch and talk about strategy for this afternoon. Come on, I'll buy both of you lunch, and since we're going to talk business, we won't be eating here, so we need to move." Brian led them out of the building and down the street to a small restaurant, where they got a table in the back. Their server brought them water as they looked at the menus and placed their orders.

"That was a risky move," Brian said once the server was gone. "Presenting the document from Interpol and saying that the defendants already knew about it. What if Angus would have called you on it? He could have asked for a delay, and you know he's looking for a reason to request one."

"But the defendants did know about it. Interpol included an affidavit that they found the document in the archives of the Belvedere. It was the defendant's own document. They couldn't deny existence of it, and Angus knew it."

"But couldn't they take the fifth?" Dieter asked.

"Not really. This isn't a criminal trial," Brian explained, and Dieter sat back, half listening as Gerald and Brian talked shop. Most of the things they said went over his head, but it seemed to mean a great deal to both Gerald and Brian. By the time their food arrived, the conversation turned to more normal topics, and they had a very pleasant lunch before rushing back to the courthouse.

Outside the courtroom, Dieter stopped and watched as Brian and Gerald went inside. He wasn't quite ready to go inside yet. Walking down the hallway, Dieter peered into a few open courtrooms that appeared to be empty. "Can I help you?" an older man asked from behind him.

"I'm sorry. I'm just too nervous to go back inside right now." Dieter indicated the courtroom down the hall. "I'm probably being stupid. It isn't as though it's life and death, but it's important." Dieter wondered why he was rambling to a perfect stranger and looked back at the still open door to the court. "I'm sorry to have disturbed you," Dieter added.

"You weren't."

Dieter smiled and turned back toward the door, walking inside as the clerk was getting ready to close the doors. Sitting near the back, Dieter saw Brian sitting alone at the table with one of Angus's clerks sitting at the other table. Brian turned around and motioned for him to come forward. "The judge asked to speak to both of the attorneys in his chambers," Brian told him, and Dieter nodded, sitting back down to wait.

"Is that normal?"

"Every case is different," Brian told him before turning around again.

Dieter watched the doors at the front of the room, wondering what was happening, his nerves ramping up by the second. He used to think seeing how a court worked would be fascinating, but in truth it was nerve-wracking, and Dieter wasn't sure he wanted to come back tomorrow, but he knew he'd wonder what was happening all day if he didn't. Leaning forward, Dieter whispered to Brian, "Gerald isn't in trouble, is he?"

Brian turned around and for a second, Dieter tried to decipher the amazed and confused look on his face, but gave up. "I doubt it. The judge seemed miffed with Angus for some reason. We'll just have to wait and see what happens. That is very normal," Brian told him with a quirky smile and Dieter settled back to wait.

Finally, the door opened, and Angus entered the courtroom, followed by Gerald. Dieter couldn't read anything on either of their faces. Both attorneys went to their tables, and Gerald whispered something to Brian very quickly, and then turned to peek at him, smiling slightly, and Dieter smiled back. The judge entered and everyone stood. Once he was seated, everyone sat except Gerald, who laid out his arguments for being allowed to bring suit for the return of the Pirktl paintings here in the United States.

Then Angus began his summation. "Austria is a sovereign nation and is therefore not bound by US law, but by international law and treaty," Angus began when his turn came. "To sue another country here in the US would be precedent-setting and could change treaties and affect international relations for years to come." Angus went on to explain cases and other legal precedent that Dieter didn't really comprehend, but what he did understand was that Angus was making a very good case. All he'd wanted was to get his family paintings back. Dieter hadn't wanted to affect the entire country.

Gerald stood when his turn came. "Austria is bound by US law when they make money in this country based upon the property in question, and specifically property that has been proven in this courtroom does not belong to them, but to a citizen of the United States. That citizen should have recourse through the courts here in the United States." Gerald sounded forceful and passionate, his voice breaking slightly at one point. Dieter looked around the room and saw that no one else seemed to have noticed it, but Dieter had. Gerald went on to cite precedent as well as recent governmental and court actions that bolstered his case.

Judge Ellis asked questions of both attorneys, with one answering and the other providing a counterargument. At times, they seemed to be talking in circles, which Dieter found incredibly frustrating, and it only seemed to increase his nervousness. He kept expecting a knockout punch or some startling revelation, like on television, but that didn't happen. Instead, both attorneys stuck vigilantly to their positions, with neither giving any ground. It was exciting, exasperating, and eye-opening all at the same time. And Dieter wondered why anyone would want to be a lawyer. As the legal argument continued, Gerald and Angus argued over the meaning of simple phrases and terms.

Thankfully, sometime in the afternoon, the judge called a recess. "This is a good time to break for the day. Court will reconvene tomorrow at nine o'clock." The gavel banged, and even the judge seemed to breathe a sigh of relief. Gerald gathered his papers, and he and Brian stood up and left the courtroom. Dieter looked at Angus as he watched his brother leave the room. Dieter expected to see the same hateful look he'd seen in the past, but he didn't. He wasn't sure what it was, but something had definitely changed.

Trying not to look like he was watching Angus, Dieter looked away before getting up and following Gerald and Brian out into the hallway. "Do you have to go back to the office?" Dieter asked Gerald.

"No," Brian answered for him. "Go get some rest. You've been through a lot today, and you'll be better prepared for tomorrow by resting and getting a good night's sleep."

Dieter moved closer to his boyfriend. Gerald looked exhausted, and Dieter wanted to take him home and take care of him. "Did you come with Brian?"

"No. My car is next door in the garage," Gerald answered as they began moving down the hallway. Dieter saw Angus exit the courtroom, and he appeared to be heading their way.

"You did good today, little brother," Angus said, and Dieter felt Gerald tense next to him. Gerald was clearly expecting more, maybe even an insult, but Angus walked on without saying any more. As a group, they walked toward the stairs. At the bottom, Dieter saw Angus talking to another man who he recognized as Gerald's father.

They continued talking, and then Angus moved toward the exit, and Gerald's father walked in their direction. "Can I speak with you?" Gerald's father looked at his son, and Brian nodded and moved away. Dieter had no such plans and remained standing next to Gerald.

"It's okay," Gerald said softly.

"No, it's not," Dieter replied defiantly, moving slightly closer to his lover, and Gerald nodded slightly before turning to his father, who seemed to get the idea.

"Dad, if this has anything to do with the case, I won't discuss it."

"I wanted to talk to you about Angus. He's a pit bull of a lawyer. I send him in whenever I want to intimidate the other side, and I thought he could intimidate you. He didn't. You've built a good case and you've argued it incredibly well. Those are your brother's words, not mine, though I agree." He looked at Dieter before his attention returned to Gerald. "I'm not here to influence you in any way. I just wanted to say that no matter how this case goes, I'm proud of you. If what I saw today was any indication, you're one hell of an attorney. And if the protective looks Dieter here keeps giving me are any indication, one hell of man, as well. I should have seen that before." Other people walked by, and Gerald's father gave his son a small nod before joining the other people on their way out of the courthouse.

Gerald didn't move at first, and Dieter saw the stunned look on his face. "That's the first time I can ever remember my father telling me that."

"Then he's a fool," Dieter retorted spitefully before walking, actually more like stomping, toward the exit. Gerald caught up to him, and they left the building together. "If he couldn't see who you were before now, then your father is a complete ass as well as one of the biggest morons on the planet," Dieter mumbled loud enough that he knew Gerald could hear.

"I know. He sees everything through the lens of an attorney, rather than a father. But it was still nice to hear," Gerald added as they walked through the parking garage toward their cars. "I know what Brian said, but I have a few things I need to get done at the office. I'll meet you at home in an hour or so." Dieter wondered if he'd hurt Gerald, but Gerald's kiss told him he hadn't.

"Don't be long, or I'll come looking for you," Dieter responded with a wink.

"I promise," Gerald told him softly, and Dieter hurried to his car and went home.

Gerald arrived home less than an hour after he did. Dieter made dinner, and they went to bed early. He was still nervous, but less so now that he knew how things went. "You don't have to sit in court all day tomorrow," Gerald told him once they were in bed together.

Dieter curled close in the cool room, a hand lightly caressing Gerald's chest. "I know that, but I want to be there for you and for the case. I know it sounds kind of dumb and doesn't make a difference, but I also want the judge to see that I'm there and know that this is important. It isn't just two attorneys arguing over a point of law. It's something that affects someone's life, and he needs to see that."

Gerald gave him one of his deep, sexy chuckles before tugging Dieter closer. "My main fear is that I'll forget something or state something wrong and blow the whole case."

"You won't," Dieter said. "You know this case better than anyone, and I can tell that you're passionate about it. Everyone can see that. It comes through in the way you talk. It's compelling. To Angus it's just a case, but to you it's more, and that comes through."

"That's part of what I'm afraid of. What if my feelings cloud my judgment somehow?" Gerald was clearly worried, and Dieter could hear it in his voice.

"Being passionate about something is never bad. Gram told me that once," Dieter said, resting his head on Gerald's shoulder. "And I know your judgment is clear, so don't even think about it. You haven't steered me wrong yet, and you aren't about to start." Dieter knew Gerald was exhausted and let their conversation lapse, and soon he heard Gerald's soft snores. Rolling onto his side, Dieter closed his eyes and felt Gerald roll over as well before spooning up behind him.

In the morning, they both dressed for court, and Dieter rode to the courthouse with Gerald, walking up to the courtroom with him. They met Brian outside the courtroom and walked inside together. Dieter sat where he had the day before and waited for the hearing to continue.

Judge Ellis entered, and the day's entertainment commenced, with Gerald and Angus picking up almost exactly where they'd left off. Angus tried another tack, and Gerald shot it down. Gerald put a new spin on his argument, and Angus redirected back to the original argument.

"Gentlemen, I believe we've already thoroughly covered this ground again and again," Judge Ellis broke in. "Is there anything new that either of you wish to add?"

"No, Your Honor," Angus answered, and Gerald echoed it.

"Then we'll recess for fifteen minutes, and I'll hear final summations. Brevity is appreciated." The gavel banged and Judge Ellis left the courtroom.

Dieter breathed a sigh of relief. It appeared to him as though Angus had made no headway over the past few hours, while Gerald had been able to make some very clear points, but Dieter had no idea if it was enough or if they had any realistic chance.

"Are you ready?" Dieter heard Brian ask Gerald softly.

"Yes," Gerald answered Brian, before looking at Dieter. "I think I know exactly what I'm going to say," Gerald told both of them before looking at Brian. "Have you ever had a case where you've had your summation in your head for months?"

"Yes," Brian answered with a laugh, "but it always changed as the case went on. Why?"

"Because mine hasn't," Gerald said before standing up and walking to the water cooler to get a drink. Dieter looked at Angus, who was conferring confidently with his clerks.

The low chatter continued until Judge Ellis was announced, and then everyone stood. "Mr. Young," he said as he looked at Angus, who began his summation. "This case revolves around the simple issue of national sovereignty...."

Dieter listened, but he'd already heard Angus explain the same thing in almost the same words a number of times over the last two days. Thankfully, like the judge asked, Angus was brief. When he'd concluded his remarks, he thanked the judge and sat down.

"Mr. Young." Judge Ellis turned to Gerald, who looked at Dieter briefly before facing the judge.

"Your Honor, the national sovereignty argument is a legal red herring. The question before this court is simple: can a United States citizen be wronged by a foreign government doing business on United States soil, and have no legal recourse in the courts of the United States? The Austrian government, doing business under the guise of the Belvedere Museum, is doing just that to my client by withholding property that belongs to him and by profiting from the sale of books and posters in the United States. Furthermore, under these circumstances, United States citizens should not be denied access to the fair and impartial United States judicial system. Thank you." Gerald sat down quietly.

"Thank you, gentlemen, you will both be notified when I have rendered my decision. This court is adjourned." The gavel banged for the final time, and the judge left the court. To Dieter's surprise, Angus and Gerald shook hands before gathering their papers. Dieter joined Gerald and Brian as they exited the courtroom.

"I need to go back to the office," Gerald explained. "Harold asked me to tell him how it went, and he asked you to stop by as well if you could."

"I'll see you there," Brian said as he headed for the exit.

"Are you okay?" Gerald asked.

Dieter smiled at his lover. "I was going to ask you the same thing."

Gerald shook his head and sighed. "We're quite a pair."

"Yes, we are. Now let's go see what Harold wants and then maybe we can go home." Dieter didn't really want to go back to Gerald's office, and he wasn't in much of a mood to talk to anyone. All he really wanted was to go home… and maybe up to bed with his lover.

They rode the short distance to Gerald's office in near silence, but Dieter rested his hand on Gerald's leg the entire time. "I thought your summation was brilliant," Dieter commented softly, as they turned into the parking garage at Gerald's office.

"I was afraid I hadn't said enough." Gerald sounded tired.

"I think this was one of those times when less is more. You made your point, so don't worry about it and don't second-guess yourself. It's over, and now we have to wait for the judge. This is a man who's seen multiple trials and isn't going to be swayed by theatrics or a summation. He's going to weigh the facts and the law carefully."

"How do you know that?" Gerald asked, turning off the engine.

"For someone who prides himself on reading people, didn't you take the time to read the judge? He seemed thoughtful and deliberate. What more could we ask for?" Dieter said before opening his door, getting out of the car, and following Gerald to the elevators. After pressing the button, Dieter waited for the doors to slide open. Then he and Gerald stepped inside.

"What if we lose? And what if it's my fault?" Gerald looked kind of miserable.

"If we lose, it'll be because we didn't have a strong enough case. Not because of anything you did. There wouldn't have been a case at all if it weren't for you. And I wouldn't have gotten the paintings I did, especially the portrait of Gram. So stop beating yourself up and worrying. If we lose, we lose. I'll still love you just as much." Dieter stepped closer to Gerald, tugging him into a kiss.

The doors slid open, but Dieter ignored them, kissing Gerald harder until they closed again. It wasn't until he realized the car wasn't moving that he broke the kiss and pressed the door open button. Half the ladies from Gerald's office were waiting for them and watching. Gerald looked as though he was going to try to explain, but Dieter just took his hand, leading him into the office before Gerald could open his mouth.

"What was that?" Gerald asked, as they approached Harold's office.

"I'm the client, and they don't deserve an explanation."

Gerald stopped moving, and Dieter turned around questioningly. "When did you get all forceful?" Gerald leaned closer. "I really like it."

"Oh, there you are," Harold said from behind them, and Gerald stepped away, maintaining a reasonable distance. "Come into my office," Harold added. Gerald led him through the hallway to Harold's large corner office, closing the door behind them. "Brian tells me you were, to use his words, amazing in court today." Dieter could feel Gerald relax slightly next to him. "But I want to caution both of you not to get your hopes up. National sovereignty is a huge issue that many courts have refused to take on, but if any case has a chance, it's this one."

"Mr. Prince, I wanted to thank you for everything you and the firm have done, and I wanted to tell both you and Gerald that if we lose, I'm not going to appeal. I know if we win, the other side will, but I've given this a lot of thought, and I've done what's right by Gram and even by Anna and Joseph. I don't think dragging this out needlessly if we lose is in anyone's best interest." Dieter turned to

Gerald. "I hope you aren't angry, but if we lose, I want us to be able to move on with our lives."

"I want that too," Gerald told him, touching Dieter's arm.

"Thank you for telling us, Dieter. I appreciate a client who is up front with his wishes. And now, Gerald, go home. We'll see you in the morning." Harold walked behind his desk. Dieter stood up and left the office with Gerald right behind him.

"Let's go before he changes his mind," Dieter said, already tugging Gerald toward the elevators.

"I need to get some things from my office. You wait out front and I'll be right there." Gerald touched his cheek and then hurried away. Dieter walked to the reception area and sat down. Gerald joined him about ten minutes later.

Gerald drove them home, and thankfully, didn't get a ticket. Once they were in the house, he led Dieter to the living room. Dieter had been expecting the bedroom, and couldn't keep the surprise off his face. "There's something I want to speak to you about, and I wanted to tell you first. If we win in court, it will most certainly be appealed, and I plan to turn the case over to Brian." Dieter opened his mouth to object, but Gerald calmed him with a gentle touch on his arm. "Today when I was in court, all I could think about was you and what winning or losing would mean to you. The thing is, I couldn't be objective, and that's not good." Gerald took Dieter's hand in his, intertwining their fingers. "I'd rather be your boyfriend than your lawyer. You mean so much more than any case." Gerald leaned forward and kissed him. "When we first met, I thought I could do both, but I can't, and it's you I want more than anything else. Is that okay?"

"Of course it's okay." Dieter threw his arms around Gerald's neck. "Whatever you want is okay as long as it involves you, me, and preferably a bed. I love you more than life itself, and I want you to be happy."

"Then I am happy because you make me happy."

"How about you show me just how happy you are." Dieter slipped his hand beneath Gerald's shirt, caressing his skin.

Dieter giggled as Gerald ticked his stomach before pressing him back against the cushions. "Oh, I'll show you how happy I am and how happy I'm going to make you," Gerald teased before lifting Dieter's shirt and licking across a nipple. "I love you so much, sweetheart."

"I love you too," Dieter croaked as Gerald licked his nipple again. "But could you show me upstairs in bed?"

"Cute, sweet, and forceful—I'm a lucky man," Gerald said.

"Yes, you are." Dieter giggled as fingers slid along his ribs. Once the tickling stopped, Dieter locked his arms around Gerald's neck. "Now take me to bed, because until the judge issues his ruling, I'm still the client." Dieter heard Gerald laugh, and then he was practically carried up the stairs.

*E*PILOGUE

A fire crackled in the fireplace and Christmas carols rang through the house as Gerald climbed to the top of the ladder. "Why did you have to get the biggest tree on the lot?" Gerald groused, with a smile lurking just below the surface.

"What's the use of having high ceilings if you can't have a tall Christmas tree?" Dieter rolled his eyes, conveying the "duh" at the end of his comment. "Besides, you're almost done, and the tree looks amazing." Dieter broke into a huge smile when he stepped back. "The gingerbread men look great with all the other ornaments."

Gerald placed the final trimmings in his hand before climbing down the ladder. Folding it up, Gerald set it aside and stood next to Dieter. "It does look very nice, except it's making me hungry." He and Dieter had spent one Saturday afternoon making and decorating non-edible gingerbread men. Where Dieter found the recipe Gerald had been afraid to ask—it was hard to imagine making inedible cookies on purpose—but they were colorful and really cute, especially the ones Dieter had done from the back, their little gingerbread butts mooning from the tree. "I just have one question. What would your Gram say?" Gerald looked at the portrait hanging above the fireplace.

Dieter laughed and slipped an arm around his waist. "I have no idea what Gram would say about anything. But I'd like to think she'd want me to be happy." Dieter leaned in for a kiss. "I was wondering. We've got almost everything ready for the party tomorrow night— after dinner, could we go dancing?"

"Whatever you want," Gerald answered, pulling Dieter in for a deeper kiss that tasted sweet, and Dieter moaned softly, putting his arms around Gerald's neck as the kiss continued, the tingles Gerald got reaching to his toes. Then the kiss softened, and Dieter rested his head on his lover's shoulder, and Gerald lightly stroked his soft hair, sighing contentedly.

"God, I don't want to move, but I need to finish cleaning up my mess in the kitchen." Dieter held him tighter, and Gerald smiled, happy to be with his lover and looking forward to the rest of his three-day weekend. Dancing tonight, their Christmas party tomorrow, life was good.

"I should put the ladder away and clean up in here."

Dieter lifted his head. "Why? You're not done yet." Dieter slipped out of his arms, walking into the kitchen, returning with a stack of candy-cane boxes. "These need to go on the tree too."

"All of them?"

"I only bought twelve boxes," Dieter said with a chuckle as he handed then to Gerald. "They go with the candy theme, and some of the people I invited have children. It won't take long, and by the time you're done, I'll be finished, and I'll help you clean everything up." Dieter gave him another kiss, and then Gerald watched him bound away. Gerald loved Dieter's energy and excitement. He threw himself wholeheartedly into everything they did together. Setting down the stack of candy canes, Gerald unfolded the ladder before opening the first box and beginning to place them on the tree.

Candy canes in place and the boxes flattened, Gerald folded up the ladder for the final time before carrying it to the basement. "Gerald," he heard Dieter's voice calling from the top of the stairs. "It's your office."

Gerald hung the ladder on its hooks before hurrying back up the stairs, and Dieter handed him the phone. "This is Gerald."

"It's Brian. Harold just left my office and asked me to call and see if you could come into the office. He asked if Dieter could come as well. He said it affects him too."

"Then Judge Ellis has issued his decision." Gerald's heart began to race with excitement and hope.

"It looks that way," Brian responded.

"How did Harold seem?" Gerald asked almost afraid of the answer.

"Somber," was Brian's one-word answer, and Gerald knew what that meant. Hanging up the phone, he looked at his lover and saw the smile that had lit his face all day slide away.

"It seems that Judge Ellis has issued his opinion. Harold wants me to come into the office, and he asked if you'd come as well." Gerald saw the hope spring into Dieter's eyes. "Before you get excited, Brian described Harold as being somber when he told him, which isn't good news." Gerald placed his phone in his pocket before pulling Dieter into a hug. "I'm sorry."

Dieter squeezed him in return. "There's nothing to be sorry about. You did your best. I know that, and you have nothing to be ashamed of or regret." Dieter lifted his head off Gerald's shoulders, meeting his eyes. "I mean that. I doubt anyone else could have done what you did. So hold your head high and let's get ready to go." Dieter kissed him before stepping away.

They doused the fire and turned off the lights and music before grabbing their coats. Dieter was already outside when Gerald realized he'd forgotten his keys. Hurrying into the kitchen, he grabbed them off the counter, walking back through the dark and quiet house, stopping to peer at Dieter's grandmother's portrait. "I really tried," he said softly before leaving the house.

They rode in silence from the house to the office. Gerald parked in his spot, and they rode the elevator up. In the lobby, Gerald waved to the receptionist, who was talking on the phone. She waved back and Gerald continued into the office. Dropping their coats in his office, they walked back up front to find Harold.

As he approached Harold's office, Gerald saw a crowd gathered, and then someone began to applaud and then that person was joined by the others, along with a few cheers. Gerald turned to Dieter and then looked back at the crowd. Harold and Brian now stood in front, both men walking toward them. "Congratulations," Harold said with a huge smile, literally patting Gerald on the back. "You did it."

"We won?" Gerald asked, looking at Dieter and then at Brian.

"You won. Judge Ellis issued an extremely strong opinion, and he ordered the Belvedere Museum to turn over all five paintings to Dieter. Of course, he had to stay his ruling because it's already being appealed, but we expected that. The thing is that you've already set a precedent," Harold told him with a grin on his face. The sound of popping bottles filled the room, and Gerald felt a glass being pressed into his hand as Dieter vibrated with excitement next to him.

"So drink up and celebrate, because on Monday you start the appeal."

"Well," Gerald said after sipping from his glass. "Dieter and I have talked it over, and we've agreed that we'd like you to handle the appeals," Gerald told Brian, and he saw his eyes widen.

"Kid," Brian said, doing his best John Wayne impression, and Dieter snickered. "Then we'll handle the appeal together, because I have a feeling there's going to be enough work to keep you busy for a long time." Brian hoisted his glass, and Gerald glanced at Harold.

"The story has already been picked up by the local paper and even a few of the newswires," Harold explained. "We're already getting calls from prospective clients who want help getting art returned. I got off a call ten minutes ago with a lady from New York whose family had a Tiffany window stolen from their mausoleum, and they want help getting it back from a collector in Japan. And they are specifically asking for you. So I'd say you are going to be a very busy man." If Harold were grinning any more, he'd have looked like the Cheshire cat. "We'll talk over the details of your promotion to full associate on Monday," Harold added softly before turning back to the group and raising his glass. Everyone followed suit and drank a toast of congratulations.

Once glasses were emptied, everyone trickled back to their work areas. "I can't believe he's turning over the appeal to Brian," someone said, and Gerald smiled, confident in the knowledge that he was doing the right thing.

"I'm looking forward to your party tomorrow," Brian said as he placed his empty glass on the tray with the others. "Is it okay if I bring Zoe?"

"Of course," Dieter answered from next to him. "I take it you didn't actually read the invitation." From the look on his face, Brian hadn't. "I addressed it to both you and Zoe." Dieter smiled and drank the last champagne from his glass before setting it with the others. "We need to get home so we can finish getting ready for tomorrow," Dieter explained, and Gerald set down his glass.

"I'll get our coats."

When Gerald returned, he handed Dieter his coat, and after a few final good-byes, they left the office and headed home. "So what would you like to do to celebrate?" Gerald asked as they drove.

"We have to finish getting ready for the party, and then you promised to take me dancing," Dieter reminded him. "We can celebrate on the dance floor, and afterward, we can do a little horizontal celebrating up in our bedroom."

"Can we do the bedroom celebrating first?" Gerald asked with a wink before pulling up in front of the house, and Dieter didn't answer him, which seemed very strange. Getting out of the car, Gerald watched Dieter closely as they entered the house and took off their coats. Dieter immediately began climbing the stairs.

"I thought we were celebrating," Dieter called before running up the stairs. Gerald dropped his coat, leaving the closet door open as he took off in hot pursuit, catching Dieter just as he bounced on the bed. "Love you," Dieter said as he squirmed in Gerald's arms, not completely realizing that Gerald was using the movement to divest Dieter of his clothes.

"Love you too, beautiful," Gerald said, and Dieter stopped squirming, his pants pooled at his ankles, shirt up around his shoulders. "You know, we may have found out we won the case today, but I've felt like I won the real prize months ago," Gerald said before licking a swipe up Dieter's chest. "You are the best thing that has ever happened in my life, Dieter Krumpf, and I thank God for whatever twist of fate brought you into my life."

"Thank *The Woman in Blue*," Dieter hissed through clenched teeth as Gerald sucked on a perfect, pink nipple.

Gerald slid down Dieter's body, his lips poised just above Dieter's cock. "I'd rather thank her great-grandson in the best way I know how," Gerald said with a grin before sliding his lips down Dieter's length.

"You're welcome!"

ANDREW GREY grew up in western Michigan with a father who loved to tell stories and a mother who loved to read them. Since then he has lived throughout the country and traveled throughout the world. He has a master's degree from the University of Wisconsin-Milwaukee and works in information systems for a large corporation. Andrew's hobbies include collecting antiques, gardening, and leaving his dirty dishes anywhere but in the sink (particularly when writing). He considers himself blessed with an accepting family, fantastic friends, and the world's most supportive and loving partner. Andrew currently lives in beautiful historic Carlisle, Pennsylvania.

Visit Andrew's web site at http://www.andrewgreybooks.com and blog at http://andrewgreybooks.livejournal.com/. E-mail him at andrewgrey @comcast.net.

Contemporary Romance by ANDREW GREY

http://www.dreamspinnerpress.com

Also by ANDREW GREY

http://www.dreamspinnerpress.com

Contemporary Romance by ANDREW GREY

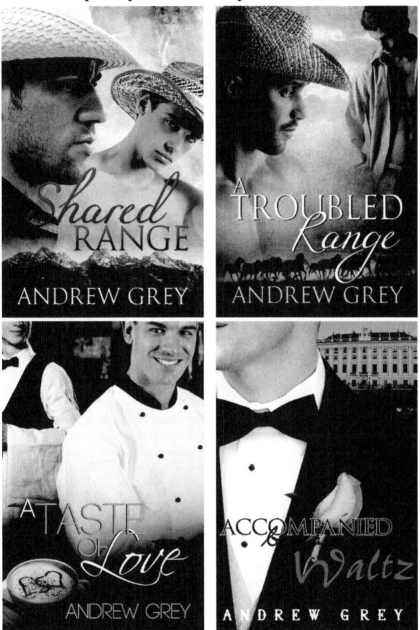

http://www.dreamspinnerpress.com

CPSIA information can be obtained
at www.ICGtesting.com
Printed in the USA
LVOW04s0411030116

468750LV00024B/504/P